A Fowl Murder

by

Joanna Sheen & Julia Wherrell

Victoria Farm Press Ltd.

This edition published 2016 by Victoria Farm Press Ltd,
Stokeinteignhead, Devon TQ12 4QH
www.victoriafarmpress.co.uk
ISBN 978-0-9926844-4-0

Printed and bound in Great Britain by:
Maslands Printers Ltd of Tiverton, Devon.

Set in Minion Pro.

To my little granddaughter Grace who loves chickens
but is far too young to enjoy detective stories yet!
Joanna

For my very good friends
Linda, Maureen, Judy and Jeanne
for their endless patience, support and encouragement.
Julia

About the Authors

Joanna Sheen has published over 40 non-fiction books and 'A Fowl Murder' is her fourth novel.

Joanna is better known for her presence in the craft world and regularly appears on Create and Craft TV demonstrating cardmaking and more. Having run her multi award-winning company for 36 years she now feels able to follow her dream and focus on writing as well.

Joanna lives in Devon with her husband, and has two lovely daughters who have perfected the art of rolling their eyes at their impossible mother.

Julia Wherrell is a professional writer, designer and photographer. 'A Fowl Murder' is her third novel. When she is not writing fiction, she writes copy for websites, blogs and magazine articles. She has attended numerous creative writing courses (usually with Joanna) and has written many thousands of words of fiction – all of them good, but not necessarily in the right order.

She lives on Dartmoor with her dog and chickens. She grows her own vegetables, makes things out of willow and goes to tango classes. She has also been known to go rock climbing.

The Swaddlecombe Mysteries:
A Sticky End
A Violet Death
A Fowl Murder

All the novels are available on Kindle and in paperback.

If you'd like to find out more about Victoria and Albert and the residents of Swaddlecombe, go to: www.swaddlecombe.co.uk or follow Swaddlecombe on Facebook

Acknowledgements

Joanna and Julia would like to thank Pippa, Emily,
Judy and Linda for their input and suggestions.

Chapter 1

"So which is it going to be?" asked Victoria. "You can come to mine and have tuna salad or an omelette if the hens have been laying today, or we can eat at yours and have something like a huge beef steak that you probably have handy in the fridge?"

Albert looked crestfallen for a moment. "I'm not sure if there's anything much in the fridge, I'd have to check, but it seems a shame to end such a lovely day on just an omelette but if that's the only option..." He gave her a hangdog look and she smiled at him indulgently.

In the back seat the thud-thud-thud of Moss the puppy's tail confirmed that he was listening to the conversation and suspected food was involved. He quite fancied the off-cuts from a steak.

Victoria was sure that Albert's larder and freezer would be stuffed with all sorts of wonderful food, so this must be his way of saying it was her turn to cook. They had spent the most amazing day walking over Dartmoor and enjoyed a fabulous picnic that Albert had prepared, so it really was her turn. As much as she loved food she was still finding it hard to adapt to the country way of life. In London she had been surrounded by shops, cafes and takeaways open virtually twenty-four hours a day. Here in Devon the shops closed at a sensible time and many of the villages still had half-day closing and she could never remember which closed on what day. While she appreciated the slower pace of life she hadn't yet got the hang of planning ahead! The local pub, the Swaddle Arms, was great, but she felt she knew the menu off by heart.

Swaddlecombe had been a complete culture shock for her six months ago – but a lovely one. She'd moved into Aunt Edith's cottage not knowing what lay ahead, not even if she would stay or sell up and move back to London. But it had been a fast and furious induction and she loved her country life more than she could have believed.

Luckily for her, everything had fallen into place: her contacts in the magazine world meant she now earned just about enough writing a monthly 'Country Business' feature and running an 'all things country'-related blog for the biggest country magazine in print. True, she wouldn't be able to afford designer shoes these days, but as wellingtons were the footwear of choice that wasn't really an issue. So with the rent from her London flat and inheritance she managed just fine. Best of all had been the gift from Albert a few months back of a young black and white collie cross pup that she had called Moss. And it had been love ever since.

Then, of course, there was Albert. She could never have foreseen their romance in a million years. He was a rugged farmer with completely different interests to hers, but strangely they just seemed to fit together perfectly. She had grown to love his smile and his strength. There had been several incidents even in the short time she had lived in Devon where awful things had happened, several murders in fact, and Albert had been a stalwart companion and support when things had turned very nasty. Whoever would have guessed she would have come across more deaths in the last six months than most inner city dwellers do in a lifetime?

Albert took the left turn into the driveway a little too sharply and Victoria bumped against the door of the Land Rover. "Ow, slow down! That hurt!"

Moss yipped as he slid about in the back.

"Sorry, maid, wasn't thinking." Albert seemed to be concentrating more on the driver's side window than the windscreen.

Then Victoria saw the feathers; for a moment she thought it was snow, but no, definitely feathers.

"I think maybe I was wrong. I do have some steaks in the fridge," said Albert hurriedly. "Why don't you go and get things started over in my kitchen? I just have to check something."

"What's the matter?" He seemed strangely agitated.

"No, really, you go across into my house. I've just got a few things to sort out here first."

"Sort what out?" Victoria felt as though she was missing something … and then light dawned. Feathers should not be floating around the farm and over her hedge in enough quantity for her to think it was snow for a moment. Her hens: something must be very wrong.

"I'm coming, too." She started climbing out of the Land Rover.

Albert shook his head. "No, I'd rather you didn't. It might not be a pretty sight."

"It can't be that bad,"

'Famous last words' was the thought that went through Victoria's head as they reached the chickens, or rather, what was left of the chickens. Moss was growling and barking furiously; too little too late, she thought. The chickens had been ripped apart, their frail bodies unrecognisable with blood and feathers trodden into the ground.

"Mr Fox may look a handsome chap, but he's vicious." Albert put his arm round Victoria and brought her in to him for a hug. "I'm sorry, maid, it's just nature red in tooth and claw. Foxes have to eat, just like we do."

3

Victoria, with tears pouring down her cheeks, wasn't very coherent. "But that's the worst of it, they've just been ripped to pieces and NOT eaten. I always rather admired foxes, but how can they be so vicious? Are you sure this is the work of a fox? Should we call the police?" She turned away, not wanting to look at the carnage for a moment longer.

Albert smiled sadly and hugged her tighter to him. "No, my lover, not a job for the local bobby. Fox is only doing what is natural to him. They enjoy the thrill of it, the chase – much like cats do." He let out a long sigh. "There's people like it, too, sadly, but we don't get too many of them round these parts, I'm pleased to say."

Victoria fished in the pocket of her jacket for a tissue and blew her nose loudly. "I never realised quite how fond I was of the hens until now. It was such a lovely 'new home' present from Gray and Sebastian."

Albert pursed his lips. Victoria knew he thought the whole thing ridiculous, the twee coop, the colour co-ordinated hens, but he was kind enough to say nothing. He'd liked the hens well enough, and the eggs had been wonderful in his cakes.

Victoria gave a start and looked up at Albert in horror. "Oh no! September! Gray and Sebastian! No hens!"

Albert understandably looked a little confused. "Sorry, you've lost me there, maid."

Blowing her nose again, Victoria looked up at him. "I did tell you – Gray and Sebastian said they were coming down at the end of the month to see Gray's mother in Cornwall and wanted to drop in and see their hens. What do I say, what do I do?"

"Well, there's always new hens about. I'm sure we can find some. Maybe Newton market next week? It'll make a nice outing." He patted her shoulder.

"No, no!" Victoria said, horrified, "We can't just get any old hens. They have to be the same or Gray and Sebastian will notice."

"So these London types that bought you some hens six months ago – very probably by mail order – are going to come down here and notice they are different?"

"Well, of course! I bet they chose them really carefully, well…" Victoria tailed off and then added, "They'd know if the colour was wrong, I'm sure."

Albert laughed and shook his head as he moved forward to check the wire fencing. Sure enough, there in the back corner near the hedge were the signs of digging. The fox had taken his chance while they were out and tunnelled under the wire. Victoria still stood with her back to it all, like a child.

"Ah, the beggars, that's where they got in. It's my fault, maid, I should have dug down and put the netting in deeper to deter the damned fox and I'm sorry, it'll be better before we gets any new girls, I promise."

"But where do we get new ones?" asked Victoria "I feel clueless. I'm guessing I don't ring a pet shop?" She noticed the look of amusement on Albert's face as he walked round to face her. "OK, I do realise we can look up breeders on the internet. I was just teasing."

"There's no need, maid. I got contacts." Albert tapped the side of his nose wisely. "I knows a couple of hen breeders round these parts. We'll get it sorted. Now, why don't you leave me to sort this mess out and you get on up to my place and work on some supper?"

"I'm sorry, Albert, I couldn't face anything, but I will take you up on your offer to leave you to clear up. I am feeling quite sick even from this distance and…" Victoria's tears started welling up again.

"Go on now, go on, back to my place and at least get the kettle on. Cup of tea or coffee will see you right. I'll be up directly."

Victoria wandered off to Albert's house, feeling sad and bereft. She turned to make sure Moss was following, but working with dead hens was obviously far more exciting and he was with Albert, running round in circles.

Victoria had finished two cups of coffee before Albert finally came up to the house.

"Thank you, Albert, I am really grateful. I think that would have upset me for weeks."

"You'll need to toughen up a bit if you're going to survive this rough old country life, you know, but 'tis all in a day's work to me. I will just go and have a shower, though, if you could put the kettle on." Victoria noticed he looked somewhat grim and had taken his jacket and shoes off outside.

Ten minutes later he returned to the kitchen and Victoria made him a mug of tea just as he liked it, good and strong, and looked around for the cake tin where she knew something delicious would be stowed.

"Left-hand cupboard," said Albert. "Chocolate ginger."

Sure enough, there was a large chocolate cake in the slightly battered 'Charles and Diana' wedding cake tin that Albert, a staunch royalist, had kept despite the subsequent royal traumas.

Settling down at the table with a large slab of cake in front of him and the mug of tea in his hand, Albert sighed.

"Sorry, rough end to the day. I blame myself, should have found time to dig the fence in deeper. I meant to do it at the time, but it got left a bit temporary, like."

"Please, don't be silly, you always do more than I have a right to expect. Maybe we'll make it more like Fort Knox when we get new chickens. But I tell you what – I am never smiling at a fox and saying 'ah how sweet' ever again!"

Albert smiled affectionately at her. "Well, I'm sure that's put the fear of God in him and he'll change his ways overnight!"

Victoria glared at him. "You rotter! I mean it, it's changed how I feel totally." Noting Moss's pleading eyes upon her, she found some puppy food in a cupboard and poured it into a cereal dish and set it in front of the little dog. He seemed to happily live in either house.

"Well, it's just nature's way. Animals do what they're programmed to do. We'll just tighten up security a bit."

Leaning back and stretching in his chair, Albert said, "Now, what shall we do for a meal? I know you're upset, but I'm still hungry. Shall we go down to the pub, then no one has to cook and you can just skip eating if you don't want anything?" Albert held both her hands and smiled at her encouragingly. How could she resist?

* * * * *

Settled down in the pub, Albert predictably chose the steak and kidney pudding, but Victoria still felt too miserable to eat much and chose a small salad.

"So who are these contacts of yours then, Albert? I'd really like to get some new chickens as soon as possible. Apart from anything else, I will miss them. I found their clucking so soothing. It always seemed to help clear my brain when I got an attack of writer's block on an article. I'm not sure how, but it did."

"Well, I'll have to get checking, but I remember Pat Podger – nice girl, lovely hair – " he went off into a reverie. "Anyway, her mum was into breeding all sorts and some fancy chicken breeds, too. Lives over the other end of the village on the road to Bovey Tracey. Burntwood Farm it's called. She always cared more for her hens than her children from memory. Let me find my old black book with all me contacts in it." Albert grinned at Victoria and she felt an unnecessary twinge of jealousy, annoyed that he might still have a girlfriend's phone number and wondering how long ago they went out.

"I am sure it can wait till tomorrow," said Victoria primly, aware that she was being petty and hoping this Pat person wasn't a stunning beauty who would steal Albert's heart back again when they went to look at the chickens. Burntwood Farm, rather a forbidding name, she thought, but knowing the locality, it was probably very pretty.

* * * * *

The following morning Victoria walked over to the chicken coop, knowing they were gone, but half hoping it had all been a ghastly mistake and that it had never happened. But there were still telltale signs, forlorn feathers caught in the rose bush and one or two others up against the coop doorway, but that was all. Albert had worked hard to clear the murder scene.

Moss was barking loudly again, obviously still agitated by the smells and signs of death. Victoria idly wondered whether he would attack a fox and then, realising that he was still somewhat smaller than a full-grown fox, thought it was highly unlikely.

Albert came down towards the hen coop waving his mobile phone at her.

"Sorted. Said we'd be over directly."

Victoria told herself to stop worrying about this old flame and to trust Albert and concentrate on getting new hens. "So she was at home?" she asked brightly.

"Nah, seems I had an old number. She moved away years ago, but they gave me her mum's number and I rang her. She's the one with the hens anyway."

Victoria smiled warmly, feeling suddenly generous towards the woman who, with any luck, might be old and past it by now.

"Martha Podger, that's Pat's mum, she keeps various fancy breeds.Might even enter them in shows, I'm not sure, but she definitely breeds and sells. Sounds like fancy fluffy things you want. So, no time like the present. You coming then? Moss, come on boy, in your bed."

Victoria opened the door of the Land Rover when they arrived at Burntwood Farm. She looked down at the ground where she had to stand and was glad she had chosen to wear her wellies. The recent rain had left a slurry of mud across much of the farmyard. Her feet squelched as she climbed out. Ah, the country life, she thought.

A stout, elderly woman marched across the yard. Her white hair was thinning and was very poorly cut into what passed for a bob, although pudding basin came to Victoria's mind. Her fleece jacket was patched in places and she seemed unaware that she had chicken droppings over one wellington and half way up one trouser leg. Victoria assumed her fondness for chickens didn't include too much cleanliness and wondered if they should actually be buying from her, but they'd arrived now, so it had to be worth at least looking.

"You Albert?" she said sharply, fixing him with a fierce stare.

"That I am, Mrs Podger. Don't you remember me?"

"Well, it's been a while and you've got old and my eyes aren't what they were, but yes, now you mention it, I do remember a very hungry young man that ate me out of house and home on every visit and then upped and offed and never married my Patricia after all that feeding anyway."

Victoria bit her lip to suppress the urge to laugh. It made a change to see Albert's charm fail to hit the mark so spectacularly.

He was human after all!

"Well now, I'm sorry about that, Mrs Podger, but 'twas a long time ago and I'd like to think I've matured a bit since then." Albert seemed slightly abashed, but amused too.

"Well, I knows it's just my birds you've come to see this time, eh? Good job, too. Patricia's spoken for. She lives over in Westerley. No chance there, my boy, too late."

"This is Victoria," introduced Albert. "She's the one wanting some pretty birds. I'm more of a good layer type of man."

Albert looked across at Victoria and his eyes challenged her to laugh, but she kept her lips firmly locked together and held out her hand to Martha, hoping the woman's hand was cleaner than her boots. But it didn't matter as Martha just glared at Victoria and stomped off towards a field with various small sheds dotted around it and lots of chickens strolling about, with a "Follow me" thrown in their direction.

As they followed her across the yard a tall, well-built man cannoned out of the back door of the farmhouse into their path shouting, "You'll do it and you'll damn well like it!"

A slight, dark-haired woman appeared in the doorway wringing her hands in a theatrical manner. "You know I will always do my best, Morris. I was just saying it's a long way…" She stopped suddenly as she realised they had company.

Martha pointed a grubby finger towards the man. "Son, Morris. You might remember him, even if he was only a kid when you came here. Difficult one to forget is my Morris. Girlfriend, Sonia, Sylvia, or something."

Morris spoke up in Sylvia's defence, hands on hips, all indignation. "It's Sylvia, Mother, and you know full well what her name is. You're just being a besom." Victoria thought it was like watching a rustic version of East Enders, everything was so melodramatic. Did they keep this up all the time? Morris poked his head forward and squinted. "Albert Moreton, isn't it? I remember you, flash bugger with lots of old cars. You broke our Pat's heart."

Victoria wondered if Albert was now regretting using an old contact to get her new hens, but he didn't seem too worried and stood, hands in pockets, regarding Morris in a nonchalant way.

Morris looked at Victoria, his eyes taking her in from top to toe, and she felt distinctly unsettled by his gaze. He exuded a sort of animal magnetism, dark, brooding and almost ape-like. Even though he was so far from being her type, she knew men like that could be hugely attractive to some women. The waif-like Sylvia was obviously one such woman and she had crept up to stand next to her man.

"So who's the little lady then?" Morris smiled, almost a leer, ignoring Sylvia and looking at Victoria with a directness that was downright rude.

Albert stepped a little closer to Victoria and introduced her. "This is Victoria. She is after some of your mum's fancy birds."

"Fancy bird, indeed!" Morris grinned.

Martha pushed her way between Albert and Morris and seemed keen to get on with proceedings. "Come on, no time to be standing around all day. You pair." She gestured to Albert and Victoria. "You come and look in the chicken coops with me and we'll talk about birds. And you," she said turning back abruptly in front of Morris, "you sling your ruddy hook!"

Albert led the way across the yard and, as Victoria followed, Sylvia brushed past her and hissed, "You keep your hands off my Morris or you'll be sorry." She glared at Victoria with narrowed eyes and it was hard for Victoria to know whether to be honest and say, 'My God, I wouldn't touch him with a barge pole,' or to just smile and move on. She chose the latter and bolted after Albert's receding back.

"Right then," said Martha, opening a gate into the field and shooing them through it like a pair of dawdling sheep. "What is it you're after 'zactly?" She stood, legs planted well apart, arms folded.

"Well," said Victoria, feeling stupid, "I need to find some nice cream-coloured chickens, or maybe even apricot ones, if possible."

Mrs Podger narrowed her gimlet eyes and looked at Victoria as if she were a simpleton. "You goin' to eat their eggs or arrange them round your lounge, maid?"

Victoria hid a smile. "Yes I know, ridiculous and very townie, isn't it? But I had three really pretty hens as a gift and the fox killed them, and now I need to get some more that look very similar, do you see?" She smiled brightly at the woman and hoped playing up her ignorance might win her some sympathy.

Martha Podger made a sort of harrumphing noise and turned to Albert. "Do you know what sort she wants?"

"I'd reckon maybe a Buff Orpington might do the trick and a Cream Legbar, at a push," said Albert. Victoria goggled at him.

Martha gave a curt nod. "Aye, got a few of them just coming up to point of lay." She trotted off to a large coop, or was it a shed? When was a shed a coop? Victoria felt she ought to know but didn't. To her, they looked more like quaint gypsy caravans, as most of the coops were on wheels.

"Mind the wire!" barked Mrs Podger, but just a fraction too late as Victoria yelped and shot into the air like a frightened deer.

"Ow!" She looked at Albert in horror and clutched her right hand. "I got a shock!"

"That's 'cos it's an electric fence," said Albert calmly. "Won't kill you, maid, but might make your hair curl, though!" He couldn't suppress a grin as she looked so put out. "You need to put your hand on this plastic cover bit here, see, that protects you from the shock, and step over it carefully. Sorry, I should've explained."

"Well, yes, I think you should! That was quite a, well a shock!" She had to admit her hand no longer hurt and it had been momentary, but yes, a complete shock. "Doesn't it hurt the hens?"

"Nah, they're a bit quicker on the uptake than most humans. They get one belt from it and they don't go near it again. We use electric fences all over the place, for sheep, cattle – and hens."

Mrs Podger was waiting, not very patiently, next to the coop. "This what you'm wanting?" She waved her arm about and Victoria looked at the various hens contentedly pecking about on the grass. "More in here," she said and opened the shed door to reveal about another twenty birds, hopping on and off perches and pecking at corn from a feeder. Some were perched high up on branches cut especially for them and piled up in a corner. A cabbage on a string hung from a hook in the roof and a couple of hens were pecking at it and chattering away to each other.

"Oh, they're wonderful!' said Victoria. "I love the fluffy ones. Ooh, I'll have two of those!"

"They're the Buff Orpingtons," said Martha Podger. She tipped her head towards Victoria and asked Albert, "Has 'er got a proper coop and everything, young Albert? I don't want my hens going to some place where they won't get looked after proper."

Albert laughed. "The poshest coop you've ever seen and, don't worry, they'll get spoiled to death."

"I always used to give my girls brown bread every morning – two slices," said Victoria deciding she may as well keep up the appearance of being a complete and utter townie airhead.

"They will be very well-cared for, don't you worry. I didn't do a thorough enough job with the netting last time. I hold my hand up to that."

Martha nodded. "You need to dig it in at least a foot into the ground. Chain link's best if you really want to keep the wily fox out, much better than chicken wire."

"Ooh, and what's that one that looks like it's wearing a little hat?" said Victoria, bending down near a pretty cream and brown flecked bird.

Mrs Podger gave Albert a look that said 'Is she right in the head?' and barked "Cream Legbar."

"Two of those as well then, please."

"Hang on, Victoria, you only had three before."

Victoria grinned at him. "I know, but there's no reason why I can't have added more to my original flock, is there? I just can't have less."

"Is the coop big enough?" growled Martha, who didn't seem at all interested in selling more hens which, Victoria knew, was a good thing; she was more concerned about their welfare. They were certainly well kept. Everywhere was spotless, with lots of wood shavings on the floor of the coop. It all looked very cosy.

"I reckon the coop would hold six or eight birds, but – " Albert realised too late what he had said.

"Oh, that's good. I think six would be a nice number," said Victoria. "Half a dozen!"

Albert sighed. "Well, it's up to you, Victoria. You'll be the one cleaning them out."

"I know, but their old bedding is all good for the compost."

"D'you want to see some of my fancy fowl?" Martha was addressing Albert again as if he was the responsible adult in the set-up.

"Oh yes, please!" trilled Victoria, even clapping her hands in mock excitement. Albert shot her a look that clearly said she was overdoing the dumb blonde act.

Martha trudged off towards a larger shed in the far corner of the field.

"Victoria! Mind the – " yelled Albert, but too late, as with another yelp, Victoria shot over the fence, clutching her leg this time.

"Ow, ow, ow! Damn! We are definitely not having an electric fence at home!"

Albert was laughing and shaking his head. "I don't know what's got into you this afternoon, really I don't."

As they followed Martha Podger's stout figure across the field, Victoria stopped and said, "Oh, look at that one – isn't it gorgeous! Those amazing tail feathers! How about having one of those?"

Albert sighed and gave her shoulder a quick squeeze. "That, my lover, is a cockerel. And I, for one, am not having him strutting around the farm and waking us up at all hours crowing his bleddy head off. And no, before you say it, they don't only crow in the morning, they crow all hours of the night and day and are a damned nuisance."

"All right then." Victoria gave in meekly. She knew she didn't want a cockerel either, and carefully picked her way over the next electric fence to where Mrs Podger stood, with a protective hand on the shed door.

"Now these," she said, "are my prize winning Frizzle Polands." She opened the door and Victoria gasped.

The shed was warm, bathed in golden light from some sort of heating lamp. "Oh, they're too gorgeous!" She was confronted by what, at first glance, looked like children's toys, exquisite powder puffs of birds carefully posed on branches and perches, their plumage too extreme in design to be real. But they flapped and squawked and strutted just like any poultry, but in miniature and wearing the most extraordinary costume. Ranging from cream to black, some had gold-edged feathers, while others were spangled.

All had extravagant pompoms on their heads, some so huge all you could see was a beak sticking out with no eyes visible at all. Victoria thought they looked as if they had been violently blow-dried, or frizzled by an electric shock from one of those damned fences. A particularly blonde one reminded her of Rod Stewart in his early days.

"Hell's teeth!" said Albert. "Have you ever seen the like?" He seemed more appalled than entranced. "I mean to say, what's the point?"

Martha snorted. "They're mostly show birds, but a lot of people do keep them. They're like Bantams, small and quite feisty. Real characters, too."

A small bright gold bird was framing up to Albert's right boot and gave a very high pitched 'cock-a-doodle-do' and fluffed itself up aggressively. "Now then, young man, no need for that!" Albert took a step back, laughing.

"They are absolutely beautiful," said Victoria squatting down to look at the birds more closely. "But so tiny I'd be frightened of stepping on them."

"No, they're not what you want," said Martha decisively and led them back outside, closing the door carefully behind her. "They're my pride and joy and people likes to see 'em. Now then, what about a couple of Goldlines to make up the half-dozen? That way you're sure of getting a good lot of eggs. That's what they're bred for. A cross between a Rhode Island Red and a Light Sussex."

Victoria, fascinated by all the names, felt the stirrings of an article forming in her mind. "Yes, that sounds good. But what – "

But before she could finish her question Martha pointed at some small rusty-coloured hens. "Colour all right, is it?" she asked. "Goes well with the others."

Victoria felt herself start to blush and Albert covered for her.

"That looks ideal, Mrs Podger. I reckon she'll be happy with that selection."

"They'll be ready by the end of the week. I'll get them off growers' pellets so when you come back to collect them they'll be onto layers' pellets and you can just go on from there. They should be laying by then, too."

"Sounds champion," said Albert "How much?" He and Martha wandered off toward the house and Victoria stood and watched the various hens as they ambled about making 'pock pock' noises and singing happily to themselves. Such contented sounds. She didn't want to think about the noise there must have been when the fox struck. She hoped Albert would have enough time to get the fencing sorted out for her new flock.

Martha and Albert waited for her in the farmyard. "Come in and I'll write you out a receipt."

They walked into the hallway. Victoria paused to take off her boots – but soon realised there was no need. The old stone floor was encrusted with mud and worse and there was a distinctly strange aroma in the air. Old copies of farming magazines were stacked in perilous piles along the wall. A large ginger cat sat on top of one leaning tower at eye level and gave Victoria the benefit of a languid green-eyed gaze as she crept past.

Albert had stopped in the kitchen doorway and Victoria could only see glimpses of the chaos within. A radio was blaring out a local radio station and Martha was talking over it. There was an exchange of laughter and Albert pocketed a receipt and turned to shoo Victoria back down the hallway. "Come on, maid, time to get out of here," he said in an undertone.

Back out in the fresh air, he and Victoria took deep breaths, appreciating the mild September weather. They looked about them, feigning interest as they tried to expel the ghastly smells from their throats and noses.

"Is that barn conversion new?" Victoria asked Martha, pointing to a large expensive- looking pile on the other side of the Podger's barn, partly hidden by a hedge and few trees.

"Been working on it a year or so and moved in now. Right carry-on! All that building work and knocking things down and then building them back up, putting in ponds and decking and nonsense, if you please – looks ridiculous. I dunno why they comes and lives out here. All they ever do is moan about the lack of lighting and the noises of the countryside," said Martha, almost with relish.

"It is certainly very grand," said Victoria, thinking it was lovely but did look rather out of place in such a rural setting, especially set so close to the chaos of Burntwood Farm.

"And they thinks they're grand, too, swanning around like Lord and Lady Muck." She tutted and folded her arms. "Course, I can't prove anything, but I've lost a few hens lately and only last week I found Henry with his throat cut. Blood everywhere!"

Victoria clutched at Albert's arm. "What? Who…?"

"My prize Orpington cockerel. A magnificent bird, he was, fine voice on him and there he was, slaughtered."

"That's a bit much," said Albert, secretly thinking the cockerel had probably earned its despatch.

"Oh, 'tis no worry to me. I just moved three of my coops up against their hedge and they can get the full benefit of half a dozen cockerels then. Far noisier than poor old Henry." She cackled wickedly and Victoria knew this wily old woman would not be defeated by a couple of soppy townie neighbours. She imagined them watching through their expensive blinds in disbelief as another load of crowing birds was wheeled into battle.

"What a shame. It can't be nice having hostility between

neighbours," she said, remembering some horrible people she'd had to endure in her London flat who had made her life hell until, thankfully, they moved on.

"They're hostile all right!" Martha shook her head. "He's a bit doolally, if you ask me. Always red in the face and shouting and carrying on, making threats and all sorts. I leave my Morris to sort it out. He likes a good row."

"Oh dear." This was completely ruining Victoria's hopes for a lovely article on a dear old farmer peacefully rearing her beautiful birds in a rural idyll.

"Well, I reckon we'd best be making tracks," said Albert who had been hopping from one foot to the other while Martha had been talking. "I need to check my cows and Victoria's dog needs walking."

"Righto, see you at the end of the week then, Albert." She fixed Victoria with a look, and gave a curt nod.

Pulling out of the farm's drive, Albert braked suddenly and swore, narrowly missing a speeding white Range Rover that shot past and turned into the driveway to the posh barn conversion, gravel flying in all directions. "Idiot," said Albert. "I've a good mind to – no, maybe not, I don't think I want to know any more about the set-up in this neighbourhood!" They set off down the narrow lane.

"Well, it certainly all seems to happen around Burntwood, doesn't it? What a peculiar bunch of people! That Morris is very odd, as is Sylvia."

"Best keep out of it, maid. I rather wish I hadn't gone there in the first place, but we'll go and fetch the hens and that'll be that."

"You didn't tell me what they cost? Can I have the receipt and then I'll give you the cash."

"No need: my treat. I sort of feel responsible for the last lot."

"Oh Albert, that is kind, but you really shouldn't."

"Done now."

Victoria sat back and admired the passing scenery. "I'm always surprised at what goes on in the countryside, I still have this sort of naïve view that it's all idyllic and gentle and everyone loves their neighbours."

Albert gave a bark of laughter. "You are daft! 'Tis the same the world over. Wherever you go, whether Exeter or Timbuktu, you'll find the same set-up – the cruel, the kind, the criminal, the wise, the pig-ignorant, the selfish, the cheat… they're all there, whether it's a tiny village or a big city."

"You're sounding very philosophical."

"Don't worry, it'll pass!"

Victoria frowned. "I was thinking of writing my next article about chicken breeding, especially those peculiar frizzled ones, but I'm not sure if it's a good idea."

"Now don't you go poking your nose in at Burntwood, Victoria. Go and find something nice and gentle."

"It wouldn't just be about Burntwood Farm and the Podgers. I'd talk to the Reverend Ruminant as well, and other people who keep hens, whether for eggs or for showing."

Albert sighed. "Well, maid, it's up to you, but it's not what I'd choose!"

Chapter 2

Albert parked the car outside the village shop, turned off the engine, and folded his arms. "I'm staying put. I know they three will start nudging and giggling about us. They means well, but 'tis embarrassing. You go on in and I'll just wait here."

Victoria laughed, Albert could be so bashful sometimes, yet extrovert and amusing when he felt in the mood. The triplets in the village store, Dahlia, Iris and Lavender, were a local institution and their shop, full of random items, rife with gossip and always welcoming, was one of the parts of her new country life that she loved.

The strange cow-bell-like clanging of the shop door bell announced her arrival and Iris, the middle triplet, looked up from her careful arrangement of local cheeses.

"Hello, my lover," she welcomed Victoria, "we haven't seen you for a day or two. Albert keeping you snug in your love nest, is he?" She smiled and the other two customers in the shop tittered.

"Thank you, Iris. Poor Albert is outside hiding in the car as he gets so embarrassed by your teasing!"

"Oh, she means no harm, do you, dear?" said Dahlia as she joined her sister behind the counter. "Just enjoying our own little village romance, that's all. Now, what can we get for you?"

"Main thing I need is foil and cling film," said Victoria. "I keep forgetting and it's so annoying when you've got leftovers and want to put them in the fridge."

"Put them in the fridge and then throw them out later in the week. I know that's what I tend to do." Dahlia shook her head sorrowfully. "I keep hoping that one morning I will wake up and be that Dahlia off the telly."

"No, it's Delia, Dahlia, she's Delia and anyway she wouldn't use up old leftovers, would she? She'd make some posh dish none of us would want to eat. There's nothing wrong with your hotpot, dear, we all likes that!"

Dahlia seemed cheered by this vote of confidence and produced a large wholesale- sized roll of kitchen foil.

"Goodness! Haven't you got anything smaller? There's enough foil on that roll to last me a lifetime!" said Victoria, peering to read how many metres were on the roll.

"Sorry, dear, Lavender went with us to the wholesalers just after Christmas and I think they were selling off foil for turkeys cheap and she put these in the trolley. Didn't have the heart to put them back."

"Oh well, how much is…" Victoria stopped as the door bell jangled with such force it sounded as if it would fly off the door. A man pushed into the shop and seemed unaware of her presence or indeed the idea that anyone might be in front of him.

Addressing Dahlia loudly, as if she were deaf or stupid, or possibly both, he said, "I say, my good woman, can you get me a couple of bottles of Dom? Quick as you like!"

Victoria wondered if he realised his manner and ridiculous turns of phrase might reduce the quality and speed of the response he got.

Dahlia looked at him over her spectacles. "Dom?" There was a pause. "Dom?" Then a frown and some thought. "Isn't there some kind of pasta sauce called Dom something? Well, we've got ragu, plain tomato, but not the one with garlic." She looked at Victoria and added, "Made our Iris smell for a week. Awful!"

A blank look crossed the man's face and he shifted uncomfortably. "Well, any brand then, whatever you have. I'm talking about champagne! Champagne, not pasta sauce!"

"Well no, there's no champagne." She leant forward and explained, as if to a slow child, "You see, there's not a lot of call for that sort of thing around here. We do have some of Harold Flitcross's potato and burdock wine, though. I've heard it said that has much the same effect. Would you like to try a bottle of that, my lover?"

"Look." He clutched his head and took a breath. "Just forget the booze, and give me a couple of packs of Camels, could you?" He turned away, sighing loudly, to look at a text on his phone and missed the pitying look that passed between the sisters and Victoria.

"I'm sorry, but we don't have no camels. I don't think many folks around here would have a use for them. We tend to go in for horses more. Maybe you should try a bigger town, dear?"

Victoria bit her lip hard and fought the urge to laugh out loud.

The young man raked his fingers through his black hair and shifted his weight, almost jigging with frustration. "Look, it's urgent – just give me some fags – any brand of cigarette – OK?"

Frustrated and itching to get out of the shop, the man had now dropped all pretence at politeness.

"Cigarettes are bad for you," said a new voice as Lavender joined her sisters behind the counter, only hearing the last part of the conversation. "Cigarettes kill people and turn your lungs black. And I don't like the smell."

"I'm so sorry, sir, we don't sell cigarettes. None of us approves, you see." Iris nodded primly and all three sisters were now standing behind the counter in a row, their similarity making the effect quite surreal.

"Christ!" The young man's eyes darted from one triplet to the other and back again. "You're all completely barking!" With that he turned and flew out of the shop with as little good grace as he had entered, the door bell almost clanging itself to pieces as he slammed the door. The sisters meanwhile were unflustered and Dahlia turned to Victoria.

"Now then, dear, you wanted cling film as well?" And with that she produced an equally king-sized roll of film.

Victoria sighed. "On offer as well when you went to the wholesalers?"

"They're the same size, see? They'll sit on top of one another in the kitchen, saves space." Lavender was nodding earnestly. "A very good buy. It makes economic sense."

"Well, who am I to argue?" said Victoria, smiling. "I'm sure they will do fine and if all else fails I can start a rental company for all your foil and cling film needs…" The sisters were frowning and Victoria knew her attempt at wit was completely wasted on them.

"I'll just have a bar of milk chocolate, too, then, something nice."

"I like Turkish Delight," replied Lavender, "then you can blow the icing sugar off the top. Or toffee, if you need to pull a tooth out."

"I'm keen to keep the teeth I've got, thanks, Lavender, but a normal bar of milk chocolate, yes that one's fine, many thanks." Victoria handed over a twenty-pound note and wondered if there would be any change, given the industrial quantities of foil and wrap that she had bought.

"I've seen them do strange things with cling film on that internet," said Iris, looking intently at Victoria "Is that why you wanted such a large roll?"

"But I didn't… " Victoria bit back her answer – she didn't want to think what Iris had seen on the internet – and the last thing she wanted was to get caught up in one of the sisters' convoluted conversations which ended up with you feeling as though you were trapped like Alice in Wonderland and trying to work out why a raven was like a writing desk.

So she simply adopted a huge grateful smile and said brightly, "I'll be off then. Bye for now!" Victoria grabbed her purchases and left the shop hastily.

Opening the driver's door of her little hatchback, she pushed the rolls of foil and film towards Albert, who was sitting in the passenger seat peering intently at a car parked further down the road.

"Albert, grab these, would you? They're pretty heavy."

Albert absent-mindedly held out his hands to take the rolls, not taking his eyes off the car he had been watching and then nearly dropped them as the weight registered.

"Well, strike me down! For a woman who rarely cooks this is a bit of a major purchase, isn't it?"

"Mmm, I did try and ask for smaller rolls, but apparently these were a great deal in the cash and carry."

"Well, never mind, looks like you got a bargain anyway."

"So what were you looking at so intently?" Victoria settled into her seat and thought again what a nice little car her Golf was. True, it wasn't as glamorous as Albert's MGB, the elegant Gloria with the open top, but it was a lot more practical, especially with winter not far away.

"Beautiful bits of machinery they was in their day,"

Victoria scanned the other cars parked and assumed he couldn't be talking about the Japanese hatchback or the Ford estate parked in front of them, so assumed it was the white car on the other side of the road. "What is it then?"

"Triumph Stag. Lovely girls they were back then, always wanted one, never got around to it. That's a mighty fine one, too. Wonder if he wants to sell it."

"Who does it belong to?" asked Victoria

"Dunno. Some tall, skinny bloke, dark hair, in a hurry, just came out of the shop before you did."

"Oh him! That was funny, he must be a visitor – wasn't at all happy that the girls don't stock champagne or Camel cigarettes! They ran rings around him, of course." Victoria could see Albert's puzzled look. "Oh never mind, you had to be there, as they say." Albert shrugged as they drove towards home past the beautiful Triumph Stag.

"What's for dinner tonight?" asked Albert. Victoria guessed that this casual question signified that he was hungry.

"Nothing planned at the moment," she answered truthfully, "but with all this cooking foil I could do fish in a parcel or perhaps some nice vegetable crepes?"

Albert brows dipped and he looked for all the world like a small boy that had been offered a spinach leaf when he thought it was going to be a sweet.

"Not sure we should put you to all that trouble of cooking. Bet you could do with a night off." He smiled generously.

Hiding her amusement, Victoria replied, "Well, yes, that would be lovely of course," wondering when she had last produced a full meal for him.

"Right, pub it is then," said Albert, for some reason looking almost relieved.

* * * * *

Heavy rain during the night had kept Victoria awake and she was feeling distinctly dopey and under the weather – nothing to do with her four glasses of wine in the pub the night before. The first coffee of the day was always her favourite and this morning the first coffee tasted particularly good.

"Morning, Miss West!" said Albert as he breezed into the kitchen, full of beans as usual. "Kettle on?"

"Yes, it's just boiled. Can I make you tea?"

"That'd be grand. My cows are looking relaxed and happy, which means I am, too, and young Moss came with me and had a good long run around the farm."

Victoria looked up to see a pleasantly exhausted pup flaked out near the back door.

"So, we off to collect your daft birds today then, eh?" said Albert as he washed his hands at the sink and then wiped them on his trousers, which Victoria felt negated the whole act of washing them, but never mind.

"Yes, we are. I'm so relieved we have got replacements. I got a text first thing from Gray saying they had postponed their trip to his mother's by a week or so and that they would be dropping in the first week of October. Gives the birds a chance to settle in and grow a bit more."

Albert snorted. "And you think your hen experts from London would even notice if they'd been stuffed and nailed to the perch?"

"Oh, you are rotten! No, I suppose they won't, but at least they will have time to settle in and look like they belong. Sort of thing."

He smiled. "They'll be just fine; you stop fussing. They've got their smart new reinforced run waiting for them, so all will be well."

"I think we agreed we'd go and collect them at about eleven o'clock, didn't we?"

"Well it's ten already, so tea, a few rounds of toast, perhaps a slice of that banana bread in the tin and then it's skates on, we'll get going." Albert was already poking around in his collection of cake trying to find his current passion, coconut and banana cake.

Victoria wished she had half Albert's get up and go in the mornings. Hers had definitely got up and gone. Since they were only visiting an aged chicken breeder, Victoria went for the natural look and gave her hair a brush and ignored her make-up bag. She felt quite pleased with her laid-back attitude. She would never have gone out 'naked' up in London.

The winding lane leading to Burntwood Farm was virtually free of traffic and they arrived ten minutes early. Victoria knew to her cost that, despite the farm being only a mile or so the other side of the village, a slow tractor, a flock of sheep or a visitor who couldn't reverse could turn a quick trip into a slow trek. Albert slowed down as the farm came into view and at least the last few potholes felt less painful than all the previous ones had done. His Land Rover was very useful but comfortable or luxurious it was not.

Just up ahead of them was a passing place so cars could shuffle past each other should they meet in the single track, high-banked lane. Parked slap in the middle of the passing space was a glossy BMW convertible. It didn't appear to be in any trouble and then Victoria noticed the driver was, in fact, chatting on her mobile phone. She looked up furtively as Albert's Land Rover squeezed past.

"Oh – stop, Albert!"

Albert slammed on the brakes, which were one of the few parts of the Land Rover that worked perfectly, and the elderly vehicle shuddered to a halt. Despite being strapped in, Victoria still banged her knee on what passed for a dashboard. She opened her mouth to complain and then thought better of it. She had asked him to stop, after all.

"What's the matter?" said Albert, looking worried.

"Oh, nothing's wrong. I just thought I recognised the woman in the car back there and thought I'd say hello."

Albert sighed and pulled on the handbrake. "Get on then, maid, but don't be all day. We're completely blocking the lane."

Victoria opened the door and climbed out, almost falling into the hedge. She went over to the BMW and yes, she was right! She knocked on the window and the driver turned and jumped, managing to look both furtive and yet defensive.

"Caroline? Caroline Johnston?" said Victoria, smiling.

The electric window lowered an inch and the woman peered suspiciously up at Victoria. "Yes," she said hesitantly as if she was unsure of her own name.

"Victoria, Victoria West. Don't you remember? We worked on 'Country Idyll' together."

"Oh my God, you're right," replied Caroline, now looking far less worried and opening the window wide. "But it's Caroline Peacock now, darling!" She reached out to Victoria in an elaborate gesture of welcome and the two women air-kissed through the window.

"Wow, how wonderful! Well, it was what – five or six years ago, I suppose?"

"Closer to six years, I think, Tori. But tell me," Caroline put her mobile phone in her bag and fished out a pack of cigarettes, "what brings you to these backwoods? I hope your excuse is better than mine!"

"We're just on our way to a place called Burntwood Farm, collecting some new chickens. Mine got eaten by a fox. It was terribly upsetting." Victoria paused and saw that Caroline was completely bemused by this speech.

"Burntwood Farm?" said Caroline, "Oh wow! That's an

amazing coincidence. I live next door at Upper Burntwood – the big barn conversion. You must have seen it, darling?"

"No, really?" said Victoria. "Well, that is a coincidence isn't it?" She realised how stupid Caroline sounded with her exclamations and terms of endearment when it was all so utterly meaningless. "I live out on the other side of the village."

"But why would a sane person like you be going anywhere near that nuthouse? I mean, the old girl is senile and her son – well, I think he's a psychopath. Seriously. I really feel our solicitors should have done their homework before we bought the place, or it could at least have been mentioned in the survey."

Victoria felt anger rising and, despite thinking that the Podgers were indeed rather strange, she didn't feel Caroline should be being quite so rude about them. She was the incomer, after all. Victoria had found the country life exactly what she had always wanted, although she hadn't known that when she arrived, but if Caroline thought it was so grim, why didn't she clear off back to London and leave them all in peace?

Albert hooted the horn a couple of times and Victoria realised they should get a move on.

"Well, it's been fun to meet again," she said to Caroline, wishing she hadn't been so nosey and had just driven past.

"Oh but darling, now we've re-connected and you're a local, you might just be my sanity's saving grace. Don't desert me now!" She laughed affectedly and laid a beautifully manicured hand on Victoria's arm. "I insist you come in for a coffee later, assuming, of course, you get out of the farm alive!" She gave another false laugh.. "And do bring your driver in, too. We have all sorts round to the house, no standing on ceremony during the day." Victoria wondered what on earth Albert would say if she agreed. But then again, it would be interesting to hear what had happened to her friend over the last few years.

"Well, I guess we might be half an hour or so. I can't think it will take too long to collect some hens."

"Fabulous! I'm only, er, nipping out for something. I won't be long. See you – ciao!" The window slid soundlessly back up and Victoria assumed her audience was over and waved as she returned to the Land Rover.

"What on earth was that all about?" asked Albert, tetchy after being stuck in the middle of the road for so long and wrestling with the gears to show his annoyance.

Victoria paused, wondering how to ask him to put up with Caroline. "Well, it was an old colleague I worked with about five or six, well, I can't remember exactly how many years ago. Anyway, oddly, she has bought Upper Burntwood next to the Podgers and she has invited us in for coffee once we have the hens on board."

"Great," replied Albert looking as though it was anything but great.

"Please, just for a short while? She might have nice cakes." As she said it Victoria realised it was a forlorn hope. Caroline had always been on a diet and still looked rail-thin so it was unlikely she would have any carbohydrates at all in the house, let alone cake. However, she had a husband and with luck he just might eat cake.

Victoria wasn't completely sure why she had agreed to go. Partly it was the polite knee-jerk reaction to accept an invitation. And partly it was her need to connect with some gossip and news from her old life. As glad as she was to be out of it, there was an almost morbid curiosity to hear how their moneyed, shallow lives were continuing without her.

Collecting the hens took all of five minutes as Martha had them all boxed up and ready to go, in old cardboard boxes previously used for packs of crisps, with crude holes punched in the sides for air. But the straw inside was clean and the hens all seemed quite calm and happy when Victoria peered at them through the flaps. "They're fine," said Martha, seeing Victoria's anguished expression. "Happy as sand boys. They're always quiet and content in the dark. Simple beasts. If it's dark, it's time to sleep. So they'm happy." She handed a box to Victoria and shoved her towards the Land Rover.

"Know what you're doing? Got feed and stuff?" she asked Albert, ignoring Victoria again. She wondered whether to start her dumb blonde act, but a warning look from Albert brought her up short.

"All in order, Mrs P. New fence all dug in proper, coop cleaned and full of fresh straw. All we need now are some eggs."

"Well, I reckon they'll start in a day or two if you treat 'em right." And she turned on her heel and toddled off toward the shed where the fancy fowl lived.

"There you are then," said Albert carefully stowing the boxes in the back of the Land Rover. "Sorted."

They slammed the ill-fitting doors and Victoria smiled brightly. "Right, so let's just drive round next door then, shall we, and see how the other half live?" Albert sighed, but she detected a certain curiosity as well as resignation in his expression as they bumped their way out of the farm and onto the smooth crunching gravel sweep of Upper Burntwood.

Albert parked behind the BMW that was sitting snugly inside a huge open-fronted and gabled garage, looking like a romanticised idea of a hay barn. Victoria frowned and wondered how such a thing had got planning permission. As if reading her mind. Albert squinted up at the beamed roof and muttered, "Amazing what a few quid can do in the right places."

They walked across the immaculate gravel, past a rather grand circular pond, complete with stone fountain at its centre, and up some granite steps onto decking that ran the length of the barn. The side of the barn overlooking the gardens was almost entirely glass. The view was wonderful. The garden sloped gently down to a stream and beyond the vista looked out across rolling farmland and woodland with a glimpse of Swaddlecombe church spire in the distance – idyllic as long as you didn't let your gaze stray too far to the right and the Podgers' chicken sheds and tatty old barn. Just then a cockerel gave a deafening crow and both she and Albert couldn't help but laugh.

"Blimey, 'tis a hell of a size," said Albert, letting his eyes run the length of the glass façade. "No bleddy privacy, mind. I don't reckon I'd want Morris Podger ogling me in the altogether, thank you very much!"

A swishing sound announced Caroline sliding back a huge glass panel behind them. "Darling!" she cried and, in kitten heels, wobbled across the ridged decking to greet Victoria with air kisses and a hug for the second time in less than half an hour.

"Caro, this is my friend, Albert," said Victoria. She saw an expression of surprise, then confusion, then coquettish delight cross Caroline's face.

"Oh how lovely!" she trilled, clasping her hands girlishly, but, Victoria noticed, making no attempt to kiss or embrace him. She felt quite hurt.

"Albert is my partner. I live next door to him," she said, and then felt cross as she really didn't need to justify herself.

"Lovely!' Caroline gushed again and, this time extended a limp hand which Albert took and shook vigorously. She was pleased when Caroline winced slightly. "Shall we?" Caroline gestured to the open doorway and they moved inside.

Just as she'd known it would be, Victoria saw it was like a magazine feature – everything arranged to perfection, huge glass vases full of flowers, pale wood floors and cream sofas – utterly impractical and utterly Caroline. "Wow!" she said, as she knew she must. "This is simply stunning, Caro, and so 'you.'"

"Really, do you think so? How kind. Let's go into the kitchen," she said, eyeing their clothes anxiously.

"Don't you worry, maid," said Albert, even more rustic than usual. "I'll just take me boots off there. Don't want to make a mess of your lovely polished floors, does I?" Victoria hid a smile and slipped her boots off as well, and put them neatly by the doorway. "I don't have much in the way of carpet at home," he added. "Too much cow muck, see?" Oh God, thought Victoria, there I was playing the dizzy town blonde to the Podgers and here's Albert playing the stupid rustic to Caroline – what are we like?

"Tea, coffee?" asked Caroline, wafting into the vast kitchen, all stainless steel and polished granite. Victoria thought of her dear old wooden dresser and the chipped enamelled utensils of her aunt's that she had proudly on display and knew which she preferred.

"Coffee would be great," said Victoria. She glowered at Albert, seeing he was about to 'ooh ahh' his way towards a cup of PG Tips and added, "For both of us, thanks."

They perched themselves on chrome and white leather stools that would have looked more at home in a cocktail bar and sat, looking lost, at the huge granite island that dominated the centre of the kitchen. Albert made faces at her and indicated the weirdness of anyone wanting two sinks – the inset sink and fancy chrome tap in the island, as well as the more conventional sink by the window where Caroline was daintily filling some bit of plastic with water which she then slotted into a vast coffee machine. "Latte? Cappuccino? Espresso?" She waved at them vaguely.

"Two cappuccinos would be great," said Victoria, kicking Albert before he could say something facetious.

Caroline served their coffees, small and elegant, and gone in one sip. Victoria waited for Albert to ask for another and a piece of cake, but he seemed to be making an effort. Caroline herself had a glass of something pale green and steaming and Victoria tried to work out what it was. "Nettle," said Caroline catching her gaze. "Very cleansing."

Albert covered a snigger with a polite cough, "Well now," he said, "how long have you been living in this neck of the woods?"

"Let me see, we bought the barn – a complete wreck, of course – about two years ago and began extensive works. I think we actually moved in about four months ago, but we are still snagging even now – such a bore!" She sipped her nettle tea. "Of course, we're not here all the time," she added, as if the very idea was insane.

"No, no, of course not," agreed Albert, nodding seriously.

"We still have a place up in Chelsea. I'd go mad if we didn't still have a bolt-hole in London."

"Oh yes, we know what you mean. Victoria is glad she still has her flat up there, aren't you, my lover?"

Victoria looked at him as if he was mad. "Oh yes, absolutely, but, to be honest, Caro, I'm very happy here. I enjoy the slower pace of life."

Caroline was gazing at her, shaking her head incredulously. "I take my hat off to you, really I do, Tori. I've seen your pieces in the magazine and the way you've thrown yourself into it, really doing your research and going native. I think it's terrific! And chickens, too – heavens! It will be a dog next!"

Victoria laughed and made a show of touching Albert's arm. "Actually, I already have a dog. Albert gave him to me, he's called Moss and –"

There was a roar of a powerful engine and then a deafening crash as metal hit rock. Gravel was flung against the glass windows and a car horn blared. Caroline started screaming and Albert jumped up, staring out of the open doorway. "Hell's teeth! There's a Range Rover in the bleddy pond!" He pulled on his boots and strode outside. A male voice could be heard shouting and swearing impressively in the distance.

Caroline was repeating over and over, "Oh my God! Oh my God!" and shaking and whimpering like a cornered animal. Victoria was sorely tempted to slap her, but made do with a firm shake of the shoulders.

"Caroline! Get a grip! Let's go and see what's happened." But before they could get outside a large man, of Albert's height but heavier had roared into the kitchen, red in the face and furious. Victoria winced at the outpouring of what her mother would have called 'language' and waited for him to subside. After downing a large whisky, which he'd poured himself while questioning the parentage of Morris Podger, the ability of the builder and the competence of car manufacturers, he suddenly fell silent and looked from Caroline to Victoria.

"Giles Peacock," he said thrusting a meaty hand in her direction. "I'm terribly sorry, I didn't realise we had guests. I saw that Land Rover, and matey out there in his gum boots, and thought some bugger was trying to sell us logs or something." There was a silence and then he said,, "And you are –?"

"Me? Oh, I'm Victoria West. I used to work with Caroline on 'Country Idyll'. I live the other side of Swaddlecombe – we bumped into each other in the lane this afternoon."

"Not literally, I hope? One trashed car is quite enough for one day!" He glared at Caroline. "What's wrong with you? It's not your bloody car in the pond, is it?"

He marched outside again and the two women followed in his wake, Victoria struggling into her wellingtons as she went.

"Well?" demanded Giles, hands on hips, chin thrust out, as he glared at Albert who was peering underneath the Range Rover. Victoria half expected him to add "my good man," but luckily he didn't.

The sleek white Range Rover was nose-first into the pond, its bonnet creased up against the fountain, which remained impressively unmoved by the experience. The rear end of the vehicle was stuck up in the air at a jaunty angle, the rear wheels on the granite edge of the pond. Although the stonework was intact, the liner must have been damaged and the pond itself was now dry and the water had flowed away down the incline to a natural stream at the bottom of the garden where it no doubt felt a great deal happier.

Albert stood back and folded his arms. "Your verdict?" asked Giles gruffly.

"To use a technical term, it's knackered," said Albert.

"Sod it," said Giles, but he didn't look that upset and Victoria assumed everything was well insured. Giles pulled a mobile phone from his pocket, squinted at it and then swore again. "Of course! No signal! How could I possibly expect such a thing in this godforsaken part of the world?"

"Come and have a drink!" said Giles as he strode back into the house. Albert and Victoria exchanged amused glances and followed him back inside. Caroline seemed to have regained her composure and was lolling against the huge fridge. Victoria noticed the vile-looking nettle concoction seemed to have given way to a large glass of white wine.

"Giles Peacock," he barked and took Albert's hand.

"Albert Moreton."

"And you are with…" He waved vaguely in Victoria's direction.

"… Victoria, yes. We live over at Upper Swaddle Farm, the

other side of the village."

Giles was nodding while fiddling with the buttons on a cordless phone. He glanced at Caroline, who made a sort of 'I don't know' face at him. "You're local then?"

"That I am," said Albert in as broad an accent as he could manage, beaming, and sitting back down on the cocktail bar stool. He patted the one next to him to encourage Victoria to join him.

"Hmmm," said Giles and then, "Yes? Westerley Garage? Hello. Giles Peacock here. Peacock – like the bird. Yes. Got a problem. Can you send out someone to extract my Range Rover from a tricky situation?" He turned away and walked slowly into the lounge area as he spoke into the phone.

"Should call Tufty," said Albert. "He'd sort it out in no time." Tufty was the local garage owner and car enthusiast with whom Albert and the Reverend Ruminant regularly knocked around.

Caroline wrinkled her nose. "Tufty?"

"Great chap, owns the garage in Swaddlecombe," said Albert. "Us calls him Tufty on account of him looking a bit like a squirrel. Isn't that so, Victoria?" Victoria nodded and grinned. She was enjoying watching Albert playing this snobby couple so well.

"What?" roared Giles from the lounge. "But that's the day after tomorrow! Don't be ridiculous. Surely you can get out here before then?" He huffed and puffed, tapping his foot and somehow getting even redder in the face. "Put me onto the manager. What? Oh, you are the manager. Well, this won't do. I shall be taking my business elsewhere, I can assure you." He marched back into the kitchen and picked up his whisky glass again and drained it.

"I was just saying to your missus," Albert jerked his head towards Caroline who shuddered visibly, "that you oughta ring Tufty who runs the garage in the village."

Peacock glanced at Albert as if he'd forgotten he was still there.

"What? Oh, I don't think so, old man. I'll get onto the dealership in Exeter, what the hell are they called? Caro, can you remember?"

She blinked at him. "Me? I haven't the faintest idea, darling. Why should I?"

"I don't reckon they'll be keen to come out this far and their big recovery vehicle will have a hell of a job getting down the lane. Tufty's got a small but powerful old truck, got me out of many a scrape. Why, he towed the Jag out of Bramley's field a few months back when we got bogged down after the Show, didn't he, Victoria?"

Victoria had no idea what he was talking about, but nodded enthusiastically.

"You have a Jaguar?" asked Giles, tearing his eyes away from his phone.

"That I do, and a Merc, among others, and a very nice little MGB that Victoria is very fond of, aren't you, my beauty?" Victoria smiled idiotically again and nodded, finally realising what game he was playing.

Giles was staring at him now. "Really? So you're a bit of a collector then?"

"Oh yes, always been keen on cars. Got plenty of space on the farm, so no problem storing them under cover. Used to have a Lamborghini, but the damned thing used to get stuck in the potholes, no ground clearance, so it had to go." He gave them his idiot farmer grin and sat back.

"I see, hmmm, that's interesting. Wouldn't mind coming and having a look some time."

"Be my guest!" Albert opened his arms expansively.

"Meanwhile, could you, er, give me this Tufty's number?"

"I tell you what, gimme the phone and I'll call him myself. Probably get here quicker if he knows it's me." He took the phone out of Giles's hand and strolled outside.

"Versatile chap," said Giles. "How did you meet?" Victoria was amazed to find herself part of the conversation.

"I inherited a cottage from my aunt and Albert lives next door, literally, and the rest, as they say, is history." She smiled sweetly. "He is rather wonderful. Knows everyone locally, a very useful chap to know."

Giles smiled, lizard-like. "So it seems. Jolly handy. Caroline, can't we offer these poor people a drink?"

Albert wandered back in looking smug and handed Giles the phone. "He'll be here in ten minutes."

"Well, that is impressive! Whisky?"

"Too early for me, thanks. We'll have to get back before long. Got to check on my livestock."

"Livestock?"

"Yes, I runs a mix of cattle and sheep on the farm, more of a hobby these days."

"So you have quite a bit of land then?" asked Caroline, suddenly seeming to take an interest.

"Oh yes, quite a bit." Albert looked bashful.

"Albert, we must get back – those poor hens are still in the back of your Land Rover!" exclaimed Victoria who, in the excitement, had completely forgotten about them and now felt guilty.

"They'm fine. Don't you worry, maid." He patted her knee and she glared at him.

"Are you sure you don't want a glass of wine? Anything?" asked Giles refilling his own tumbler.

"We're just fine as we are, thanks."

Caroline suddenly gave a gasp. "Oh God, Giles, we've got the bloody housewarming next weekend and you've gone and trashed the pond! That's going to look a complete mess. How did you manage to run into it anyway?"

"I wondered when you'd take an interest in my predicament, sweetie. I came down the lane, past that retard's place next door and swung into the drive – no brakes! Went straight on – bang! Gave me a bit of a shock actually." He turned to Albert. "Only nipped up the road for some tonic water from that god-awful shop in the village – are those three old maids for real? – and when I got back – no brakes!"

Albert was nodding as if he already knew what had happened. "I reckon Tufty'll have a look once he's hauled it out and he'll let you know what the problem is."

"Excellent. Tell you what, if you're free next Saturday lunchtime, come on over. It's the housewarming bash. I'm sure my chaps will be thrilled to hear about your vintage cars."

Caroline snorted. "But I was going to cancel it, Giles. The pond is a main feature, one of the first things people will see. I don't want it looking like a bomb site!"

"Nonsense! We'll get that man back in, what's his name – Dawson – stone mason chappy, check it's all OK and then those pond people, they'll sort it out in no time. Don't you worry your pretty little head!"

Caroline shrugged. "OK, if you think you can get it all sorted – but I won't have time to deal with it, Giles. On your head be it." She smiled at Victoria. "But do say you'll come, Tori! A perfect excuse for a drink and lots of gossip! I expect you'll know some of my London friends from the 'Idyll' days – what fun!"

"That is kind, thank you," Victoria simpered, thinking she couldn't think of anything she'd rather less do, but then if Albert was going to keep up this pretence, maybe it would be quite a laugh.

Just then, a loud toot-toot was heard and Albert stood up. "That'll be young Tufty, here to save the day!"

They went outside and there was Tufty, ginger hair sticking

41

up like a brush as usual. "Morning!" He beamed at them and shook everyone's hands. "Blimey, you done a good job on this, Mr Peacock, if you don't mind me saying! Anyway, we'll soon have her out of there. I got a powerful winch on my old truck here and I'll get her back to my garage. Then I'm guessing you'll want me to arrange for it to go the dealers in Westerley?"

Giles looked sulky. "Well, I'm not too sure. They haven't exactly covered themselves in glory so far. I was wondering about using that lot in Exeter?"

"Exeter?" Tufty looked as shocked as if Giles had said Paris or Milan. "Nah, you don't want to use them. Funny lot, they are, I knows someone who works at the Westerley garage. You leave it with me, Mr Peacock, I'll get it sorted for you." He almost touched his forelock and Victoria could tell he had spotted Giles was a fat cat worth snuggling up to.

Giles looked much happier knowing that he had a good chap on the case. "Excellent. Well done. You carry on then."

Albert winked at Tufty. "You got the boy with you?"

"That I have, me and Eddy, we'll get this sorted out in no time. Eddy?" he called and a slightly smaller replica of himself hopped out of the cab. "Come on, son, let's get on."

With much handshaking from Giles and air kissing from Caroline – which Victoria was amused to see now included Albert – they made their escape.

* * * * *

Back at the farm, they carefully unloaded the new hens and put them into the run, now with six-foot-high sturdy chain link fencing strong enough to keep out everything and everyone. After a bit of flapping and resettling of feathers, the chickens began exploring

42

their new home and seemed quite content. "Oh, it is nice to hear the sound of hens again," said Victoria. "It's so very restful."

"What, better than the sound of London traffic droning away in the background?"

"Much better, and stop teasing." She slapped Albert's arm playfully. "You were on form today with the ghastly Giles and Caroline. I've never seen you like that before!"

Albert smirked and picked up Moss for a cuddle and to stop him from chewing his shoelaces. "Well, I'm sorry, I was probably a bit over the top, but I couldn't help myself. I mean to say, they're like characters off some TV programme – The Townie Twits or something! And what a pair of snobs! I just felt it was time to have some fun and play the stupid rustic." He nudged her. "Anyway, 'tis no different to you playing the dumb blonde like you do with Martha Podger."

Victoria laughed. "That is perfectly true. What are you and I turning into?"

They laughed and then heard a polite cough and a familiar voice said, "Yoo-hoo!"

"Oh, Edwin – how lovely to see you, and what great timing!" Victoria turned to greet the local vicar who was today attired quite sensibly in dog collar, patterned cardigan, fawn slacks and sandals – complete with socks. "We have just introduced the new hens."

"Ah yes, I was sorry to hear about the loss of the last flock. Mine is definitely dwindling, but has yet to be wiped out in one fell swoop!" He gave his funny high-pitched giggle, which set Victoria off.

Albert rolled his eyes. "Here, take hold of this puppy, Reverend and I'll go and put the kettle on while you two talk chickens."

"The fox is a beautiful beast, but a ruthless one." Edwin paused. 'Always reminds me of the bishop's wife, actually..." They smirked companionably. "They look like fine birds, Victoria. I think you chose well."

"Thank you, I do hope so. The people who gave me the original hens are visiting in a few weeks and I do so want them not to notice anything has gone awry."

"I shouldn't worry. To most people, one hen looks much like another. Shall we?" He took Victoria's arm and steered her toward the cottage and the awaiting tea and cake.

When they entered the kitchen, Albert was just finishing a phone call. He replaced the handset and poured the tea and cut thick slices from the banana cake, moist and lightly scented. "That was young Tufty on the phone," he said.

"So he's got the Range Rover back OK?"

"Oh yes, no problem."

"And?" said Victoria. The reverend was looking from one to the other, cake poised.

"And as I thought, the brakes had been tampered with." Albert took a swig of tea.

"No!" said Victoria. "You didn't say anything to me earlier."

"Well, I wasn't a hundred per cent sure, but even an idiot like Giles, who drives way too fast, wouldn't crash into his own pond without due cause."

Edwin's eyebrows had just about disappeared into his hair. "I don't wish to pry, but…"

"Sorry, Reverend." Albert sat forward. "Toffee-nosed friends of Victoria's out at Burntwood. The male of the household drove his Range Rover into his hideous monstrosity of a pond, wrecking both in the process."

"Oh dear, what rotten luck," said the vicar, looking concerned for the poor driver.

"As we now know, luck had nothing to do with it. But I imagine that man could put anyone's back up enough for someone to tamper with his car."

"Would they be the Peacocks, the people who live next door to Martha Podger?"

"It would. You come across them then?"

The vicar sighed. "Well, not exactly. But I've ended up in the hedge a couple of times trying to avoid them both in their flashy vehicles and really, you know, it's not fair on Gertrude. At her age her paintwork just doesn't like it." Edwin's Morris Traveller, Gertrude, was the love of his life. "I never understand why such people choose to come and live here. It really is most odd. They very plainly don't like it, so one wonders... why?" He chewed a piece of cake. "I do apologise, that isn't very Christian of me but, really, one does want to say why don't they go back to where they came from?"

Chapter 3

"May I park your car, sir?"

A uniformed valet spoke to Albert through the driver's window.

"May you what? I've been parking me own cars for more years than you've had hot dinners, my lad." Albert was a little red in the face. "Bleddy stupid idea."

Victoria suppressed a smile. "Albert, just let him park it, hand over the keys and let's get inside. It's probably because Giles and Caroline are short of space and want to cram as many cars in as they can."

Albert looked at her and raised both eyebrows. "Well, unless they're having several hundred to this damn housewarming, I reckon most of us could manage to arrange our own cars in that darn great field." He gestured to a large field behind the barn where five lonely cars were sitting next to each other, perfectly aligned, having clearly been parked by the valet.

Victoria cleared her throat and fussed with her handbag to hide her giggles. "Albert, shhh, just hand over the keys and get it over with! The poor chap is only doing his job."

Huffing loudly, Albert stepped out of the Land Rover and handed the keys to the young and clearly embarrassed lad who was waiting patiently by the side of the car.

Pointing a large farmery finger in the lad's face, he said, "No joyriding now, mind."

"Albert… do you think… in the Land Rover? I mean, is it likely?"

"Well, 'tis all stuff and nonsense."

At that point, Caroline stepped out of the front door and waved frantically at them.

"Coo–ee! Tori, Albert come on in!"

They walked towards the front entrance and the moment they crossed the threshold Caroline pushed a small maid towards them, gesturing for them to hand over their coats.

"Just give Doris your coats, darlings, and join me in the cocktail bar. Well, it's normally the study, but the caterers have made a wonderful job of repurposing it."

Doris took their jackets, but with great difficulty as she seemed to be trying to hold up her skirt at the same time. "Blast it!" she muttered as she dropped Albert's jacket and clutched at her skirt. "Sorry." She retrieved the jacket and backed towards the doorway. "I usually does washing-up. This is Ada's skirt and there's a lot more of 'er than me."

"Don't you trouble," said Albert cheerily and rubbed his hands in a proprietorial manner. "Poor little thing," he muttered. "Needs a good square meal." Victoria caught Caroline looking at Albert with a restrained mixture of horror and disbelief on her face.

"So, what are you drinking, young Tori, or is it Victoria now? Sorry, I forget. You girls, always changing your hair or your names or something!" A very jovial Giles greeted them, his face blotchy and his manner just a little over-familiar. He kissed Victoria very firmly on both cheeks and shook Albert vigorously by the hand while slapping his shoulder with the other hand. For a terrible moment, Victoria thought a man hug might be on the way, and wondered if Albert would shy away like a frightened calf or flatten him like his prize bull. Luckily, Giles restrained himself and all went well.

"Just a glass of wine for me, please," Victoria said, smiling.

"Nonsense! Champagne, I insist." Giles leered a little at her and Victoria felt glad she had chosen a smart trouser suit to wear rather than a skirt.

"Albert, old man, champagne for you, too, or are you a Scotch man? I have a damn fine single malt if you fancy a dram."

"Well, I'm driving, so just the one glass of champagne, thanks. It'll get mopped up by the food, I'm sure." Albert peered around hopefully as he said this.

Clutching the long and delicate champagne flute, Victoria looked around at the barn and, wandering over to the huge glass window, she gazed at the panoramic view and marvelled yet again what a lovely part of the country Devon was. The interior reeked of money, from the strange and contemporary sculptures to the expensive cushions. As she was currently researching new sitting room furniture, it was obvious to Victoria that the sofas had cost an arm and a leg and that the cushions were silk, not quite what she had in mind for her little cottage. Moss would destroy them in minutes.

"My God! Is that you Victoria?" A tall glamorous woman walked directly up to Victoria. She had a very handsome young man on her arm, possibly younger than her, Victoria thought, and then chastised herself for being uncharitable.

"Mandy? Mandy Parkin? Well, it's been a while since, well, since…" Victoria tailed off as she didn't know quite how to describe the circumstances under which they had last met.

"Oh just say it, sweetheart! It's been months since those ghastly murders and tangling with that complete fruitcake that almost got you, too! But hey, strange how things work out, isn't it? Now, here I am running both Janner's and Primrose Cottage Jams and doing very well, thank you very much!"

Victoria felt rather awkward, but she knew Mandy had never been one to mince her words, or not grasp an opportunity when she saw one. The tall statuesque redhead was now eyeing Albert and giving him a slow-burning smile. "Hey, Farmer Moreton, hero of the hour, how's life been treating you?"

Albert almost blushed, but instead gave her a self-deprecating smile and said, "Can't complain, Mandy, and you seem to have got yourself a nice new friend, I see."

"Touché, Albert! Let me introduce Kyle, my fiancé. Kyle, this is Victoria West and Albert Moreton – Swaddlecombe's very own Holmes and Watson!" Kyle looked blank and Mandy laughed, rather unkindly, Victoria thought. "Oh, you are such a baby, but even you must have heard of Sherlock Holmes!"

"Oh yeah, right," said Kyle, sounding as if he neither knew nor cared.

"So what are you working on at the moment, Victoria?" Mandy turned her intense gaze in her direction.

"Oh, you know, this and that, any country-related issues that catch my eye. I think my next monthly article will be on keeping hens and in particular breeding fancy hens. I think they're so pretty and I hope the readers will be interested." Mandy's answering smile managed to convey exactly what she thought of Victoria's readers and the utter pointlessness of fancy hens. No words were needed. "How do you know Caroline?" Victoria added hastily.

"Caro and I are at the same yoga class on a Wednesday, vain attempt to keep the old figure." She looked across at Kyle who was meant to lob in a suitable compliment at that point, but he said nothing and his single brain cell seemed to have got stuck in 'smile' mode and couldn't switch to 'speak'.

"Well, fancy chickens, what fun!" said Mandy. "Anyway, must

circulate, talk later, Victoria, or perhaps we'll bump into you in the pub?"

"Absolutely." Victoria forced herself to maintain her smile. "How embarrassing was that?" she hissed at Albert once Mandy and the vacuous Kyle had moved on.

Ignoring her, Albert was scanning the room anxiously and she wondered if he was looking for someone he knew. More couples had arrived and the place was starting to fill up. "No food out yet then?" he said, sounding desolate. "It's usually the saving grace of a do like this."

"Come on, Albert, there's bound to be loads of food. Caroline won't skimp on the catering. She'll want to be seen as Lady Bountiful. Let's move into the next room."

In the cavernous barn, minimalistically bare of carpet and curtains, the noise was increasing rapidly, just like in all those trendy restaurants where you couldn't even hold a conversation with your nearest neighbour, Victoria thought grumpily. And then felt even grumpier for realising how rustic she was becoming. She'd loved the noise and bustle and excitement of London wine bars, and yet here she was, a country girl for all of six months, and she preferred the carpeted hush and soft Devon accents of the lounge bar in the Swaddle Arms.

Victoria took Albert's hand and pulled him towards what appeared to be another living room or maybe a dining room – yes, it was a dining room. The table had been pushed to one end and was laden with some amazing-looking food – from caviar and huge prawns to devilled eggs and intricate mini bundles of asparagus wrapped in prosciutto ham.

"There you are, Albert, told you it would be a good spread!" Victoria let his hand go and hoped the array of food would keep him happy for a while. She realised this kind of party was probably his idea of hell.

"That's not what I'd call it, maid. No proper food at all. Where's the sausage rolls, pork pies, that sort of thing? 'Tis all fiddly twee stuff." Albert wore a particularly petulant expression and Victoria thought how dear he was to her, even the quite irritating bits of him.

Black-and-white-uniformed waitresses flitted to and fro, passing plates of canapés, topping up drinks. Many of the waitresses were young and pretty, students on holiday, Victoria thought. Giles was clearly loving being the alpha male and behaving quite inappropriately with an arm where it shouldn't have been, a hand resting too long and gazes being held. Victoria looked away; it was really quite unpleasant.

"Tori? Tori West? Oh my God! Darling! It's been forever." A tall, very camp man swooped down on Victoria and kissed the hand that was not holding her champagne.

"Colin? Good heavens, I remember! You were in advertising on 'Country Idyll', always persuading hotels and small companies they couldn't survive without our classified section!"

She turned to introduce Albert, but saw that he had made a move on the dessert table as the selection included chocolate brownies and an elaborate pink structure that she assumed might be a strawberry something or other.

"So what brings a girl-about-town like you down to this neck of the woods? Hilarious, isn't it, that Caro has decamped down here! I can't think it will last long, ghastly hole, if you ask me."

"Actually I live here, too. I moved down last Easter, I love it down here. I have a beautiful farm cottage, chickens, the whole green thing going on."

"Oops, Mr Big Foot strikes again. Sorry, darling, never dreamed you had been hoodwinked, too. Just wait till the winter!"

"You sound as though you know," said Victoria.

"Darling, know? I am your complete and utter expert! My parents still live up on Dartmoor. I was brought up, or should I say dragged up, round here. Hated every moment and school, well, just the cruellest place. Best day of my life was moving up to the smoke. The absolute best!" He waved his hand about flamboyantly to make the point, and Victoria reflected that you never saw such things in the Swaddle Arms, not even when the darts team were playing Muchampton.

"Oh, I'm sorry, Colin, I didn't know you hailed from round here. You know Westerley then?"

"Absolutely. Went to sixth form college there before I escaped. Anyway, onto things more fun: what are you doing despite being closeted away down here in Nowhereland?"

"Still working away in the trade, writing a column for 'Country Days' and a blog and anything else that comes my way." At that point Albert materialised at her side, plate piled high with cake and brownies.

"Ah, Colin, this is my friend, Albert. He lives next door to me."

Colin looked Albert up and down and smiled. "Well, now I see why Devon has its appeal." He held out a limp hand to Albert, who took it politely with his free, non–plate-holding hand.

Victoria peered at the crowd to see if she knew anyone she could use as an excuse to engineer an escape. The waitresses still hovered and Victoria put her arm out to stop one.

"Excuse me, could I have another glass of champagne?"

The waitress was older than the others, in her thirties with her hair roughly pulled back and looking very poker-faced. Glaring at Victoria as she clutched a tray of canapés that seemed to consist of celery stuffed with various things, she replied, "P'rhaps if one of them others brings some round." And with that she walked off and Victoria, speechless, noticed she had a hole in her tights. Such a shame when all the other waitresses looked so well groomed. She frowned, feeling that somehow the waitress was familiar, but she couldn't place her.

"Albert! Victoria!" A voice hailed them and, to their very great relief, the Reverend Edwin Ruminant sailed into view.

"Do excuse us," said Victoria to Colin and turned to the reverend.

"How marvellous to see you both," he sighed, kissing Victoria, and patting Albert in a paternal way. "I always feel so dreadfully awkward at these social gatherings and at least we can talk about chickens now!" He seemed inordinately pleased to have found some friends.

Behind them came a whinnying sound. They all turned as one, half expecting to see a horse, but instead saw a heavily made-up lady with a bouffant hairstyle who laughed again to leave no doubt that the laugh was human rather than equine. But it was a close call.

Caroline whisked past them and whispered, "Ex-girlfriend of Giles' who we found lived nearby – ghastly luck – hates us both with a passion, but her husband is a local councillor, so needs must!" She waltzed over to the horsey laugh and made equally ridiculous sounds herself and made small talk, very small talk.

Looking across the breadth of the room, Victoria realised all she could see were people engaged in a ludicrous show of false bonhomie and utter insincerity, with no genuine interest in what anyone else was saying. A shower of "darling this" and "darling that" rained down and Victoria reflected on how wonderful it was that she no longer had to endure this sort of nonsense on a regular basis.

Albert and Edwin were in deep discussion about his Morris Minor, so Victoria decided to explore the luxurious spread of food.

There were so many pretty morsels that she suddenly felt quite hungry. Anything with asparagus or smoked salmon got her vote. As she selected a few choice items and put them on her plate, the background chatter rose and fell like a gaggle of geese all gabbling away, with odd words and phrases drifting across to her.

"Quite ghastly, these London types."

"My God, we had to come just for politics' sake! One never knows when some dratted 'blow in' will decide to stand and we have to be in the know. The committee depend on my input."

"Quite so, Clarissa. I really don't know what the local Conservatives would do without you."

"Oh my dear, don't forget your marvellous Bring and Buys! Without those the Party would be on its knees, complete life savers…"

The conversation droned on, but Victoria's hearing selectively filtered out any more of the political stuff. Politics had never interested her. She always voted, but apart from that, her immediate life had always held so much more appeal.

"Hello," said a soft, seductively low male voice, so close to her ear that Victoria jumped. She turned expecting to see Giles playing the fool, but instead it was a dark, skinny, rakish and rather attractive man. Victoria was sure she'd seen him somewhere before, but couldn't place him. He turned on a blindingly white smile of megawatt proportions and offered his hand. "Freddie Montague – I don't think I've had the pleasure, yet?"

Victoria gave a tight smile and briefly held his hand, amazed that such a corny chat up line could still be in circulation. His eyes crinkled attractively at the corners, but the eyes themselves were cold and almost black. 'Dangerous' seemed to flash above his head in neon lights and Victoria shivered involuntarily.

"My dear, are you cold?"

"Oh, no, really, I'm fine. Really." Victoria felt her lips sticking to her teeth in a ridiculously forced grin.

"So, friend of Caro's, I assume? You don't look like a local, that's for sure." He laughed at his own attempt at humour and took a huge gulp of his champagne. He wore the cuffs of his shirt unbuttoned, and they flopped over his wrists in a foppish manner that Victoria found unaccountably irritating.

"Yes, and no," she said brightly, sipping her own drink. "Friend of Caroline's, but now classed as a local yokel and enjoying every minute of it." Before he could think of a witty riposte, she went on, "By the way, did you manage to track down any camels, or did you have to make do with something else?" His brow furrowed and she could almost see the cogs turning as he tried to make sense of her comment. "I think we're probably all a bit 'barking' in this neck of the woods, but we get by quite well on it."

She smiled sweetly and wandered away, leaving the young man, the one who'd made such a fool of himself in the shop the week before, to find someone else to letch at. She was glad she'd been able to place him. What a nasty piece of work. Victoria was surprised if he was a friend of the Peacocks. He looked rather too racy for their circle of friends.

She stopped to look out through the huge glass expanse at the front of the barn and marvelled again at the view. Giles and Caroline had known what they were doing when they bought this property. It really was a case of location, location, location. She sighed and then spied Giles making a complete idiot of himself. He was laughing with two of the waitresses, a hand on each of their bottoms. The girls looked unhappily at each other. Giles had clearly drunk a lot more since they had seen him on arrival, and he'd been quite tipsy even then.

A third waitress arrived, slimmer and prettier than the others, and wordlessly dispatched them. She curled her arm around Giles and poured him another glass of champagne. Thrilled by this approach, Giles was soon nuzzling her neck in a first-class impression of a dirty old man and Victoria felt unable to look.

"We thought we ought to come and look for you, Victoria, dear," said the reverend.

"Well 'twas also an excuse to go past that food again really," confessed Albert.

"Absolutely, old chap, some first-class nosh on show!" The reverend beamed and patted his stomach appreciatively.

They looked down at the piled-high plates they were both clutching.

"Here, you share some of ours," said Albert. "Think I might have taken more than I need."

"I knew you'd find something you liked. But it is rather good, though. Brilliant caterers," said Victoria. "Knowing Caroline, she flew them down from London or Paris or some such."

"No, actually they are a local firm of go-getting youngsters, hence why there are so many lovely young things milling around serving and doing such an excellent job," said Edwin, as he tucked into one of the five mini quiches he had on his plate and with his mouth full gestured to Victoria to help herself. She did and relished the blue cheese and pear flavour she selected.

"Have you seen that amazing wall of glass looking onto the garden?" asked Victoria. "Quite stunning. You have to hand it to them, such a beautiful house."

"Nope," said Albert. "Haven't had a chance really, between talking to people and sampling this food, not at all bad for a do like this." He was inspecting a tartlet closely, obviously trying to work out the ingredients. The three of them wandered over to the windows to admire the landscaped gardens as they fell away to the rolling countryside beyond.

Unfortunately, Giles was still playing up to the waitress and seemed unfazed by the glares he received from both the reverend and Albert. He was now leaning forward and feeding small morsels off his plate to the pretty young waitress, who was giggling and encouraging him. He picked up one of the stuffed celery sticks and, very suggestively, put one end in his mouth and offered the other end to the girl, who, still giggling, bit the other end and they nibbled their way closer towards each other.

"I say that really isn't on," said the reverend quietly. "Shouldn't one step in, I wonder? Not age appropriate or, come to that, marriage appropriate."

"He's making a bleddy fool of himself, which I don't care a damn about, but that poor young maid needs rescuing. I'll have a word." Albert stepped forward. Victoria glanced at Edwin and they exchanged pained glances, both hoping Albert would employ tact.

Pushing past some other guests, Albert stopped beside Giles and raised his hand to start speaking when, to everyone's horror, Giles appeared to throw himself onto a nearby glass-topped table. It broke spectacularly under his weight and crashed into one of the huge panes of glass – double-glazed and probably toughened, it didn't break, but made a loud booming noise before cracking into an impressive pattern, not unlike one of Caroline's modern pieces of artwork. There was a shocked silence and then a few screams as people realised something was wrong. Victoria went quickly to Albert's side.

"What happened? Is he all right?"

Giles was lying completely still, covered in bits of food, glass shards, and spots of blood where the glass had cut him.

"I didn't even get close, I …"

There was a high-pitched scream and then a long drawn

out moan of pain and the young waitress who had been flirting with Giles crumpled into Albert's arms. He held her, but almost stumbled under her weight.

Victoria felt a scream rise in her throat, but pressed her hands to her mouth to stifle it. "What's happening? My God, is she all right?"

"I don't know. Keep calm now, and don't touch anything," said Albert as he gently laid the young waitress on the floor. "Someone call an ambulance!" he shouted.

There was much commotion and pushing to see what had happened. The reverend had already grabbed Caroline's phone and was summoning help. Albert seemed to be one of the few people keeping his cool. Several women were squawking like hens, others talked hysterically, while one or two had sat down hurriedly, as if about to faint. Husbands patted hands and fanned flushed faces.

Suddenly, Mandy Parkin pushed her way roughly through the gawping onlookers. "I'm a trained first-aider. Can I help?"

Albert glanced up at her. "You're welcome to try, maid, but I don't think there's any point."

He caught Victoria's gaze as Mandy knelt and felt Giles's neck for a pulse, then bent to put her ear close to his lips and shook her head. "Nope."

Mandy turned and felt for a pulse on the girl, listened for a heartbeat and then put her ear very close to her mouth, too, to check for the slightest flicker of breath. The girl's eyes were open and already Victoria was distraught to see the light was fading out of them. "She's dead."

"Shouldn't we try CPR, or something?" whispered Victoria, but Mandy shook her head.

Albert's face was ashen and he took a couple of deep breaths, clearly not as calm as he appeared. He bent down, picked up a linen napkin and laid it gently over the girl's face. The eyes had been open and staring blindly at the ceiling. Victoria squeezed his hand. "Dear God," muttered Albert, "that beautiful young maid." Victoria felt tears prick her eyes.

Albert offered his hand to help Mandy to her feet. "Well done, maid," he said quietly. "But you'm bleeding."

Mandy looked at her knees, her expensive stockings ripped into holes and ladders and a trickle of blood running down her shin. "I'll live," she said, "unlike some." And she took Kyle's hand and walked towards the kitchen, head bowed.

Two of the other young waitresses stood holding each other and sobbing. "Jessica can't be dead, she can't be," keened one of them, over and over.

There was a great flurry and suddenly Caroline was in front of them, her eyes glittering, face flushed – surprise turning to anger as she saw Giles lying on the floor. "Oh, for God's sake! Has he overdone it again? The man is virtually an alcoholic! I'll get someone to help him up to bed. Freddie? Freddie – where are you?" She whirled round, staring wildly about.

"I don't think so, Caroline." Victoria gently took her arm and sat down with her on one of the sofas. "They can't find a pulse. We have called for an ambulance, but I'm afraid he's dead."

Caroline gasped and seemed to deflate visibly. "What?" she sobbed. "What do you mean? Don't be ridiculous. He can't be dead! My father died of a heart attack, not Giles, too! I never dreamed I'd be left a widow. I mean," she gave a great despairing gesture, "I am even younger than my mother was. This cannot be true." Pink spots of anger and indignation had formed high on her cheeks.

Ironic, thought Victoria, that even at this stage Caroline was already thinking of herself rather than Giles, or indeed the beautiful young woman, Jessica, who had barely even started on life's journey.

Freddie, looking distinctly shifty and perspiring slightly, appeared and pulled Caroline to her feet. "Darling, how awful!" He held her and she instantly began to howl extravagantly, before going limp in his arms, so limp that he almost dropped her back down on the sofa with a thud as Victoria moved quickly out of the way.

The party guests were milling about like lost souls, telling each other what they had seen, going over and over it as if, by repeating it, the whole drama might turn out to have all been a very bad practical joke.

But it hadn't. Victoria held Albert's hand tightly as they watched the reverend thread his way carefully through the stupefied people, a bundle of tablecloths, like tattered sails, in his arms, to drape them softly, and with much care, over the two lifeless bodies.

Patting Victoria's hand, Albert let it go and went into a huddle with Edwin. They broke apart, and the reverend cleared his throat and, in his ringing tones well-practised at filling half-empty churches and village halls, asked everyone to leave the area and stand outside on the decking while they waited for the police to arrive. A few of the older men made blustering noises and coughed, obviously piqued that they hadn't seized the moment to take command of the floundering ship. People began to move slowly outside, some fussing to collect coats or handbags, the waiting staff bustling to pick up trays and collect glasses. "No, no, leave all that, my dear," said Edwin, shepherding them out of the building in a kindly but very firm manner.

Albert headed off to the kitchen and disappeared through a door. "The caterers, Brock's, have their van and a sort of service tent at the rear of the barn," explained Edwin, as he and Victoria made their way outside. "Albert has gone to roust them out."

He reappeared moments later at the side of the building with a gaggle of people in aprons and overalls, some drying their hands, and marshalled them onto the decking with the others.

"This is all so shocking. What on earth could have happened? I thought Giles was drunk, or had a stroke or something, but that young girl…" Victoria looked up into Edwin's troubled face, just as Albert arrived next to her.

"Nasty business," he said. "Dreadful. Never seen nothing like it and never hope to again." He had colour back in his face now and seemed more himself. Victoria gave him a hug. "I'm all right, maid," he said and patted her back.

"But what do you think happened?" Victoria asked again.

He shrugged. "God knows – excuse me, Reverend, but I can't think of a sensible explanation. Well, I can think of a few crazy ones, but..."

Edwin was frowning. "Two people struck down like that." He scratched his ear. "Hmmm, we shouldn't speculate."

"No," agreed Victoria, "but – ."

Albert shushed her as a young couple approached them. Both slim and very fair, they looked like twins.

"Tom, Katie, terrible business," said Edwin, gently taking both their hands in turn. "Victoria, this is Tom and Katie Brock, the young geniuses responsible for the excellent catering we were enjoying before this dreadful turn of events. Albert, I think you already know." The Brocks nodded, almost in unison.

"Did you see what happened?" Tom, his pale blue eyes, round with fear, stared at Albert intently. "One of the waitresses said you were right there when – " He stopped. "Me and Katie, well, we were wondering, erm, I mean…"

Katie cut in. "Was it the food? Did they choke or something? We're worried sick people will say it was our fault!"

"We really don't know what happened," said Albert.

"But you were right there, weren't you?" insisted Katie, hands on hips, demanding answers.

"Well yes, but who can say why they collapsed like that? Giles just seemed to keel over sideways. I think we all thought he'd had a heart attack or something," said Victoria, hoping to calm the situation.

Tom folded his arms. "Giles was as tight as a tick from the start, so I was assuming something like that, but Jessica…" There was a silence as they all thought of the beautiful young woman lying dead.

"She gave a cry and then she just fell. I managed to catch her," Albert said. "'Twas pretty instant."

Tom put his head in his hands and gave a quick, anguished sob, and then pulled himself together. "I can't believe it, I just can't." He shook his head. "She was brilliant, beautiful, had everything going for her, about to start her final year at uni. She'd waitressed for us for the past couple of years, great at her job, the punters loved her." He paused. "Well, the male punters loved her."

Katie snorted. "That's one way of putting it. She was an appalling flirt. We'd had more than one complaint from an angry wife, Tom, don't fool yourself." Tom turned his back on his sister and an uncomfortable silence descended.

In the distance, a faint wail began and grew gradually louder. People's heads went up like dogs catching a scent and the word 'police' spread softly from group to group. Victoria looked around the unhappy band. Mandy and Kyle sat together on a swing seat while Freddie and Caroline stood, heads together, smoking and gesticulating over by the recently rebuilt fountain. The waiting staff stood like bedraggled magpies in their black and white plumage, shoulders hunched, some crying. The reverend was quietly circulating with consoling words and kindly smiles to the other bemused guests.

The crunch of gravel and squealing brakes heralded the arrival of three police vehicles. The leading one, a black Range Rover, had slithered to a halt inches from the very spot where Giles had demolished the fountain with his own Range Rover only a week or so before. "That would have been a bit embarrassing!" said Albert under his breath and he and Victoria exchanged brief conspiratorial smiles, before turning serious faces toward the various police officers making their way towards the huddled guests.

The police took charge and soon had everything organised, taking names and addresses from everyone and sending the majority on their way. Those that were close to the dreadful happening – Albert, Victoria, Edwin and Mandy – were asked to remain and give brief statements. The waiting staff were herded into a separate room to be interviewed, and the house guests, which now consisted of Caroline, Freddie and Colin, were put into another room, rather like a series of holding pens for sheep, Victoria thought. Quite sensible really.

As they waited to give their statements, Victoria said quietly to Albert, "Did you see what was going on between Giles and Jessica?" Albert gave a contemptuous laugh. "No, I didn't mean the cringeworthy flirting by Giles. I meant with their food?"

Albert frowned. "What d'you mean, maid?"

"They were being all soppy and lovey-dovey and he was feeding her food from his plate. You know, he'd eat a bit, then he'd feed her the other half, sort of thing."

Albert nodded. "OK, right, so..."

"Well, I don't want to sound like a complete idiot here, but, well –"

"Come on – out with it!"

"It seems to be the only reason two people might collapse like that was if they'd been, erm, poisoned." She waited for him to laugh, but instead he nodded slowly.

"Yep, reckon I had the same thought."

"Really?" she squeaked, and one of the policewomen stared at her. "Sorry, sorry, just can't believe something so bizarre."

"I reckon it has to be something like that. I mean Giles was a prize-one pillock that I could imagine plenty of people taking a pop at, but that lovely maid – that had to be an accident."

Victoria thought of what Katie had said about Jessica's flirty nature and thought she could think of plenty of jealous wives, including Caroline, who'd happily shove a bit of cyanide into a sausage roll if they thought they'd get away with it, but held her tongue as she could see Albert was still very upset.

In a whisper she added, "I was wondering whether I should mention it to the police?"

Albert pursed his lips. "They won't want theories, maid, only facts. You should tell 'em what you saw, nothing more. They should be able to draw their own conclusions from that."

Before she could reply, the policewoman who had stared at her earlier came over to take her statement. Victoria smiled politely and organised her thoughts. Albert moved off to be interviewed by a young constable with bad acne.

An hour later, they were sitting, exhausted, at Victoria's kitchen table with Edwin seated opposite and Moss, snoring softly, draped across Albert's feet.

"So awful!" said Victoria for about the tenth time, her head in her hands. "And we have to go back and give fuller statements later. I expect I will have forgotten it all by then."

The reverend took his glasses off and polished them, a sure sign that something significant was about to be said. "I think we are all of the same mind – definitely foul play and, quite probably, poison?" Victoria and Albert nodded. "But how, and what?"

"In the food, and something like arsenic?" suggested Victoria, feeling as if she was taking part in a game of Cluedo, with the Reverend in the Kitchen with the Dagger well, breadknife, actually. Mandy Parkin would make a good Miss Scarlet, and perhaps Albert could be –

"You've been reading too many Agatha Christie novels," said Edwin gently. "Arsenic does not kill you instantly and it is pretty difficult to get hold of these days, you know."

"Oh, no, I didn't know that." She sighed and sipped her tea.

"Unless you're a rat catcher, of course," said Albert. "Old Janner Blackenford used to drive round with great tubs of it in the back of his van for killing off rats and wasps nests and such like."

"He did?"

"Yes, only stopped a few years ago. We used to joke that if he accidentally crashed his van in the river, there'd be enough cyanide in the water supply to kill off most of Westerley!"

"So what happened then? Why did he stop? Did he accidentally poison himself?" Victoria was fascinated.

"No, don't be daft, maid. They tightened up the rules and he had to hand it all in, but I reckon there's still quite a bit floating about in sheds and barns around these parts. Old Janner's still going strong, I believe. Isn't that so, Edwin?"

Edwin nodded. "It is, it is, and an old rogue he is, too." He finished off the last bit of coffee and walnut cake on his plate. "Delicious as always, Albert, dear boy. No, I think something altogether more subtle, a natural poison, a plant, say."

"Mushrooms!" cried Victoria with such enthusiasm that Moss woke up and gave a yelp.

"What's got into you, Victoria? Pipe down." Albert rubbed

his face. He looked tired and drawn. "No, course t'isn't bleddy mushrooms. They take hours to work as well. Nasty way to go, that is. You eat the things, feel fine, then hours later you suddenly realise something's awful wrong – and by then it's usually too late. They have to do something drastic like filter your blood or your kidneys or some such with charcoal, or, I dunno, too tired to think."

"There are a number of things it could be," said Edwin, sighing. "But really, isn't it all too far-fetched? I think we all need to go and sleep on it and we'll find it's all been some ghastly accident like plain old food poisoning." He got to his feet, ready to say his farewells.

Albert sighed. "Well, you'd think so, wouldn't you? But what about the brakes?'

"The what?" asked Edwin, pausing.

"Oh yes! Good grief, I'd forgotten that!" Victoria sat up suddenly, looking more awake. "When Giles crashed his Range Rover into the fountain last week, Tufty said that his brake pipes had been cut!"

The reverend shook his head. "Well, well… I'm afraid it really does look like murder then."

Chapter 4

"Whadya mean, you were too tired to cook? Who was going to be the one cooking anyway?" Albert grinned at her. "In fact, I'm not so sure as I recall the last time you cooked me a square meal. You'd let me expire, die of malnutrition, you would!"

Victoria slapped his arm and sank gratefully into one of the comfortable armchairs recently acquired by the Swaddle Arms. Trudy had decided that it was time for a revamp and had grandiose ideas of combining a coffee bar with a traditional pub. Some of her ideas had worked well, like the chairs that were so comfortable. Several of the other additions seemed somewhat surreal in the lovely old-fashioned building. The massive cappuccino machine sat uncomfortably beside the bar and the pictures of smiling Italian waiters in striped tops balancing large cups of coffee in one hand with cakes of some kind in another looked completely out of place, but nobody liked to say anything.

"Albert, Victoria, how delightful! Are you gracing us with your presence for a meal? Shall I check if we have a table?" Trudy smiled widely at Albert while Roger rolled his eyes.

"No need, Trudy, my love. I think we can take a rough guess on how many bookings we have for the next half an hour or so, something close to none! You two sit wherever you like! Now, what can I get you to drink?"

"Well, Victoria," said Trudy in her best sales voice, "I know you don't always want an alcoholic drink, so maybe you would like Roger to show his undoubted barista skills. He even has a custom-made Swaddle Arms stencil!"

Roger was pink with embarrassment, not helped by Albert roaring with laughter. "A Swaddle Arms stencil? I've got no bleddy idea what you're supposed to do with that, but in the meantime, we'll have a large red wine and a pint of the usual."

"So – no coffee then?" said a crestfallen Trudy.

"I would love to try one of Roger's specials after we have eaten, Trudy. They're all the rage, these special coffees now, aren't they?" Victoria glared at Albert and he stopped grinning.

"Well, we have Baileys syrup, almond, vanilla, mocha, oh, the sky's the limit here with Roger's barista techniques. I am the food specialist still, obviously, but Roger has really blossomed since we did our course at coffee HQ. I have picked up some delicious muffin and cupcake recipes, so any time you want to pop in earlier in the day for coffee and a cupcake, I'll be here!" With that, Trudy wafted away towards the kitchen.

"Roger, when did all this happen?" asked Albert.

"Oh when Trudy wants something to change it happens fast. It's all developed over the last two weeks. Once she had the idea she went in all guns blazing. Times are hard for publicans these days and it's important to diversify. Seems more folks buy alcohol in the supermarkets, while others decide to skip alcohol altogether and go for soft drinks and coffees."

"Promise me you won't let her dress you up like the Italians in the posters, though, Roger." Victoria smiled at him. She was a big coffee fan and could see that she might pop in and have a special coffee when she was visiting the shop.

"Think the whole thing is damn daft," came a grumpy voice from the far end of the bar. "Man can't even come into his local for some peace and quiet without being met by a barrage of I-talians and a bloody brastrapper." Bramley stared morosely into his pint as though the world were ending.

Suddenly the joke registered with Albert. "Ah, right, got it, brastrapper – barista. Good one, Bramley."

Deciding to ignore the second-rate humour, Victoria said, "OK, so shall we choose something to eat? I don't know about you, but I'm pretty hungry."

Roger brought over the red wine and beer and waited while they looked at the menu.

"I have no idea why you are looking at the menu, Albert. You know what you're having, you always have the same! Roger, I'll have some lasagne, please, and Albert here will have …"

Sheepishly Albert said, "Er, steak and kidney pud, if it's all the same to you."

Bramley came over to the table and pulled out a chair. They were obviously going to be honoured with his company.

"As you two seem to be the Cagney and Lacey of this village, what's happening with those murder jobs?"

"Not a clue really," said Albert. As he finished speaking the door blew open and in rushed Tufty, his red hair on end and looking particularly squirrel-like tonight.

"'Ere, you'll never guess!"

Roger looked up from the bar and Tufty had centre stage. "There's been a development in the murder case! Police reckon 'twas definitely something in the food, so they've taken Tom and Katie Brock in for questioning."

"Taken them in for questioning?" said Victoria. "What possible motive would they have?"

"Don't be daft," said Bramley, "they's perfect for it. 'Right, good fit', or whatever it says on those 'Merican series. Pay back, that's what it'll be. Smart of the coppers to see through their game. Always said that lot in Westerley were on the ball, no getting anything past them."

Victoria was confused. "I'm afraid you've lost me – what on earth could young Tom and Katie have against someone like Giles – or worse, their friend Jessica?"

"Well," said Trudy who had now come through the kitchen doors, having clearly been eavesdropping and abandoned preparation of their meal. "Young Tom and Katie would have a very strong motive, now I come to think of it. It was their family that owned the barn and had spent far too much on the conversion. Their dad had done all the work himself, but ran out of money before it was finished and they went bankrupt. Then, of course, the Peacocks come along and beat him right down on price as they knew he was desperate to get what he could for the barn. Old man Brock couldn't take the shame and hung himself. Ghastly times. The whole family must hate Giles and Caroline with a passion. Oooh, maybe their mother bought some Mickey Finns and dropped them into Giles' drink."

"You're getting carried away there, young Trudy," said Albert firmly. "Firstly, Mrs Brock wasn't even at the party, and secondly, I think Mickey Finns aren't that easy to come by in English backwaters."

"Well, that is very odd," said Victoria. "I thought Giles and Caroline had all the building work done on the barn conversion, and that it was all their idea?"

"Ah well, that's as maybe. They put in all that glass – murderous for all the local birdlife, I can tell you, and all the fancy decoration and the landscape gardening – but old Brock had bust himself doing the bulk of it, and then they beat him down and bought it for a song," said Tufty, and he and Trudy nodded emphatically in unison.

"Well, who knows what's the true story?" said Roger. "Meanwhile, how are their meals coming along, dear?" Trudy looked puzzled, then seemed to remember.

"Oh, they'll be just about ready by now, I reckon." She disappeared back into the kitchen.

"The usual, Tufty?" asked Roger, his hand already on the cider tap.

"Reckon," said Tufty and hopped up onto a bar stool.

"Well, I still think the police know what they're doing," said Bramley. "Not going to tell me the brains of the Westerley CID aren't a force to be reckoned with."

"Possibly," said Albert, "but we don't know they kept them in custody. All we know is that they were taken in for questioning. Everyone at the party will be questioned. It could be Victoria and me tomorrow."

There was a short disappointed silence while they all digested the fact that the exciting news might well mean nothing.

"One lasagne, one Swaddle special, local steak and kidney pudding!" Trudy swooped out of the kitchen with two very good platefuls of food and both Victoria and Albert perked up.

"Now here's the new coffee menu. Obviously you can confer with your barista once you have finished your meal, but may I just recommend the Brazilian with the Swaddle Arms stencil or the Columbian latte and a little shot of hazelnut syrup, just divine."

Albert picked up the small laminated menu that listed all the types and flavours of coffee. "I'm going to have to have one of these darn things, aren't I? No escape."

"I think you can face a good cup of coffee after your meal, Albert, so don't look so hard done by."

Victoria's phone rang in the depths of her handbag and she

silently cursed the caller. "Why do people always ring just as you are about to eat?"

Albert's mouth was too full to do anything except nod in agreement.

"Hello?" said Victoria a little curtly. "Caro, oh my goodness, you poor thing, how are you? Um, yes, we are out, just having dinner actually. So sorry, yes I know, oh dear, I'm so sorry you don't have anyone to have dinner with. Tomorrow morning? Why... er yes, I guess so. I am always happy to have a coffee with you." At that word Roger and Trudy looked up like a pair of expectant hounds being offered a dog treat. "At your house, yes, of course." Both looked down again with glum faces. "Tomorrow, at eleven. Why, of course, I'll see you then."

"That's OK with you, isn't it, Albert?" Victoria looked across at him. Albert's expression was somewhere between non-committal and pensive.

"Well, I'd be a deal happier if I was coming with you. Do you think she'd mind?"

"You come, too, but why?"

Bramley and Tufty picked up their pints and shook their heads. "Dodgy going round there, murderers lurking and gawd knows what." Bramley was in his element.

"Seriously, though, Albert, there can't be any harm in me going round to cheer her up, surely?"

"Mebbe, mebbe not, but I'll be happier once you're back home again."

* * * * *

Albert tried several times over breakfast to persuade Victoria to cancel her visit, let him accompany her or at least let him wait in the car. The more he mentioned it, the more determined Victoria became that a quick visit to a damsel in distress, so to speak, was not going to cause this furore. So just before eleven she set off to Caroline's. Her friends had comforted her on plenty of occasions. After all, that's what friends were for and although it was stretching it somewhat to call Caroline a friend, it must be horrific to be fine one day with a husband and excitement at the upcoming housewarming party and then to be alone like this.

Victoria parked right outside the barn. No valet. She smiled to herself. She rang the doorbell and waited. After a while she became concerned. Had she mistaken which day Caroline meant? Then worrying doubts crossed her mind: had Caroline been so depressed that she should have rushed to her side the previous evening when she got the call?

Eventually, just as she was about to give up and call for help, the door was flung open and a fully dressed, immaculately made-up Caroline flung herself into Victoria's arms.

"Oh my God, Victoria, my saviour! I thought I would go stir crazy left alone to deal with the fear, the horror …"

Victoria stumbled back a little as the full weight of Caroline's body fell against her, something for which she had been unprepared.

"Oh Caroline, I'm sorry, I should have come round sooner. You should have called me. I hadn't realised quite how devastated you must be by Giles' death."

Caroline stared at her wildly. "What? Have you any idea what it has been like living with the terror – never mind Giles dying! The fear that there's a gang outside waiting to murder me at the first opportunity. That's why I took so long to answer the door. I have to use the CCTV to check that I know all visitors before opening the door. I haven't slept a wink!"

"Shall we get the kettle on, help you to calm down and feel

more yourself?"

"Feel more myself? I may never feel the same again. And tea, an infusion, please – I couldn't possibly drink coffee. It is poison, you know, pure poison."

Victoria wondered which way to play this and what the correct words were in this situation, then decided there were no correct approaches. This was unique, at least in the etiquette book in her head.

Caroline allowed herself to be helped into the kitchen and stood moaning, looking furtively around her as though expecting an SAS attack at any given moment. Victoria looked longingly at the fancy coffee machine and then tore her gaze away to survey a matching collection of glass jars containing different coloured dried things that looked like sweepings off her kitchen floor. She opened the first three and sniffed them tentatively. Odour of bonfire, old socks and, thankfully, mint. She opted for the last and brewed two cups of pale green mint tea.

As Caroline sipped the infusion, she winced. Obviously Victoria hadn't got it quite right. Should she have added sugar? But Caroline bravely sipped on.

"So Caro, what has happened, have the police got any further?"

Caroline put down the cup and stared at her. "My God, you haven't heard?"

"No, haven't heard anything."

"Oh that's why you braved it over here, despite everything. I am so grateful." Caroline held her hand to her chest and Victoria tried very hard not to laugh. This was not even amateur dramatics standard.

"What has happened?"

"The police…" Caroline trailed off for dramatic effect, "…the police have decided that I was actually the intended murder victim.

I realise now I have a mortal enemy and my days may be numbered."

"They think you were the intended victim? Goodness, I can see how upsetting that must be. What is their thinking behind that?"

Caroline dropped the mask of tragedy for one of intense irritation. "What do you mean, what was their thinking? It was obvious the moment they mentioned it. That girl Jessica had no enemies and no connection to Giles – the poison, and I am sure it was poison – was obviously meant for me and, with my luck, Giles was the unintended victim and it was all aimed at murdering me. I'm frightened, Victoria." The wide-eyed desperate look returned.

Caroline's phone rang, vibrating and skittering noisily across the counter top. She jumped and then snatched it up with a desperate swipe of her hand.

"Hello, Caroline speaking." Her voice, suddenly weak and tremulous, sounded as though she were on her deathbed.

"What do you mean? I don't need to come down to the station." Caroline paused, looking very cross and her tone switched from pathetic to sharp. "No, no, officer, I insist I need round-the-clock protection or the loss of my life will be on your head." Caroline's hand lay flat across her chest again in a pose of martyrdom. "What do you mean, no officers can be spared? But I am in danger – and I am a higher rate taxpayer. I have a right to expect the police to protect me." Her stance was now one of annoyance and the 'poor me' look on her face was replaced by one of utter fury. "And who has decided that I am not at risk, hmm? Tell me that!"

Victoria was biting her lip and looking at the lovely view out of the kitchen window. Caroline had always been somewhat volatile, but this took the biscuit.

"Well, it's completely unacceptable, rural policing at its worst. I disagree totally with your detective's hypothesis and I only hope he doesn't live to regret a very poor decision. Once you mentioned it, it was obvious to me that you were correct and indeed I am a murder waiting to happen and I object most strongly to your change of heart." Caroline flicked her hair back and stood a little straighter. "Yes, I will indeed be taking it further. Your senior officers will hear about this. I may even write to my MP. I just hope it will be in time." Caroline slammed the small phone back onto the worktop.

"Well, of all the incompetent fools I have ever dealt with, that man is the worst!"

"That man? Do you mean Inspector Amery?"

"The one handling the murders, obviously, stupid little jobsworth." Caroline huffed.

"They have changed their mind now, then?"

"Hah! Not only have they in their wisdom decided I was not the intended victim, they apparently have no manpower to protect me. I was expecting twenty-four-hour surveillance and, as a citizen, an acceptable level of safety. I will have to ring Freddie."

"Freddie? Why Freddie?"

"Oh Lord, you might as well know. Freddie and I have been having this on/off passionate sort of thing. I just find him completely irresistible." Caroline laughed and looked at Victoria from under her eyelashes. "A girl has needs, you know."

Caroline picked up her phone again and pressed a button, a coy smile crossing her face as she twisted a strand of hair in her free hand.

"Freddie? Yes, hello, sweetheart, look there's no alternative, you're going to have to come down and move in just for a while. Damned police have abandoned me completely. Now what do I do? That's fantastic! Thank you, sweetheart. Yes, I do, too."

To hide her surprise and irritation, Victoria took her cup to the sink and rinsed it out, not waiting for a refill.

"Well, I think I'd better be getting back now. I have a deadline which has been hovering over me for a while. I will feel much better once it's sorted and of course Moss will be wanting his walk. You'll be OK for a while now, at least till Freddie comes. I assume he is coming?"

"Well, of course, he wouldn't refuse me anything! Sorry you don't find me in happier times, Victoria. We must catch up again properly. Meet at one of the better restaurants in Westerley perhaps?"

Victoria was despatched with a couple of air kisses and as she sat in the car and fastened her seat belt, she grinned. Maybe if the West End was short of a female star, Caroline should audition. She did a three-point turn and smiled at the prospect of a nice relaxing walk around the farm with Albert and Moss.

Just as she left the gravel sweep of the barn and drew level with the Podgers' pot-holed driveway, Victoria had to brake suddenly as the glowering figure of Morris Podger stepped right into her path. With a squeak of alarm, she braked sharply. With his eyes fixed on hers, Morris walked slowly round to the driver's side of the car, a shotgun slung carelessly over his shoulder. He tapped gently on the window. Reluctantly, Victoria lowered the window and heard herself say stupidly, "Oh, hello, Mr Podger!"

He leant on the car door and gave a slow smile. "Hello, to you too, maid. Nice to see you again. You're that Albert's piece, aren't you?"

Victoria had never thought of herself as a 'piece', but felt Morris wasn't someone she could engage in conversation about a woman's standing within a relationship, so she merely smiled and said, "Yes, that's right."

He leant in at the window and she could see his five o'clock shadow, the dark chest hair curling from the top of his open-necked shirt and could smell a strange, not entirely unpleasant, muskiness.

He had very dark brown eyes and the most amazingly long black eyelashes. "You wanna come in for a cup of tea or something?" His teeth, she was pleased to notice when he spoke, were most definitely a turn-off, being irregular and stained. And – horror of horrors, she noticed his eyebrows met in the middle.

Brought to her senses by this terrible revelation, Victoria put the car in gear and said, "Thank you so much, but I'm afraid I must be getting back."

"Now come on, maid, you'm in no need to hurry off." He rested his hand gently on her arm and gave it one long, gentle stroke, before reaching in and turning off the ignition. Victoria swallowed and took the now silent car out of gear and applied the handbrake.

"So, you'm friends with they Peacock people then?" He jerked his head in the direction of the barn. "Bit of bad luck they've had then? Crashing cars and dying and all." His accent was so strong, and his speech so slow it was almost like a Southern American drawl. Despite this, Victoria felt that he was most certainly not a stupid man. There was a very definite glint of intelligence in his dark eyes.

"They London types, always thinks they knows everything. And that they might, up in their own patch, their own little pond. But down 'ere, see, they gets out of their depth, 'cos they're in my pond now and I'm the bigger fish in these parts. I'm the big old pike, I am!" He laughed huskily at his own rather strange analogy.

"And he were a strange fish, that Peacock, or mebbe I should say strange bird!" He laughed at his own joke again. "I didn't care for him much, bit of a short fuse. Peacock was a good name for 'e. Always going around with his chest puffed out and showing off like. Much good it did 'im." He chewed his index finger. "He hadn't been too nice to my old mother, you know. Not respectful like, not to an elder like Mother. He'd shouted and bawled and gone red in the chops, silly bugger. But course, he didn't know Mother, didn't know who he was dealing with!" Another low chuckle. "Thought her was some poor old timid granny, got the shock of his life when her come right back at him. 'Twas brilliant to see. I never laughed so much, bleddy funny!" He chewed his finger again. "But I didn't like he. Shouldn't never of spoken to Mother like that, not right. Still, things has a way of turning out right in the end, don't they, and people gets what they deserves, I reckon." He leaned in towards Victoria suddenly. "Bet 'e told you 'e had loads of money, didn't 'e?"

Victoria felt the need to say something before the situation became even more bizarre. "Well, no, not exactly, but, of course, they do still have their flat in Chelsea and –"

"But I got lots of money too, see? Did you know that? We sold they Peacocks some land for that there big garden of theirs." He shrugged the shotgun into a more comfortable position on his shoulder, and Victoria wondered if it was loaded. "And I sold the barn in the first place to that builder bloke, Brock, the one what hung hisself. So I've got money, I have." He leant into the window again. "You ever fancy a trip to a club down in Torbay, my lover, you just let Morris know. We could have a right proper night out, you and I. I reckon we could purr along something pretty."

Victoria goggled at him, unable to think of anything to say. The prospect of a night out with Morris Podger in the bright lights of Torquay and Paignton was too much to contemplate.

"I got plans, I have. I reckon I can develop this area and get permission for a theme park. Yeah, straight up!" He grinned and nodded, assuming Victoria's look of amazement was one of admiration. "Nothing cheap, though. Something classy, a bit Las Vegas, you know the sort of thing. All themed, and that."

Victoria nodded and tried to look impressed.

"I'm thinking country and western maybe, rhinestones and

fringes, Stetsons and spurs – yeah? Am I paintin' you a picture?"

Victoria nodded mutely, fascinated as much by his fantasies as by the addition of a strange American lilt and the introduction of American slang in among his broad Devon accent.

"And then, course, we could have rodeo with bucking broncos and stuff. I reckon it would be a real money spinner in these parts, y'all."

He pinched his bottom lip between thumb and forefinger and narrowed his eyes. He lowered his voice., "I've heard you does writing for magazines, publicity, photos. I reckon you must have good contact up in The Smoke." He took the shotgun off his shoulder and propped it against the front wing and leaned in close. "So I was thinking, see, there could be a real opportunity for you here to make some big bucks, working with me. Working closely with me. You see where I'm going with this…?"

Completely round the bend, was Victoria's unspoken opinion, but she merely looked contemplative and said, "Hmm, interesting."

A door banged, and Victoria looked in her rear-view mirror. She saw Morris's girlfriend, Sylvia, stumping across the farmyard with a large bowl of something cradled in her arms, possibly feed for the chickens, she thought. The woman glared malevolently in their direction.

Morris gave a throaty chuckle. "Ah look at her, that's my woman. Do anything for me, she would. Jealous as hell. Look at her!" He laughed and shook his head. "Starin' like a conger. She wants to know what we be talking about."

"Well, not to worry, I need to be on my way now anyway," said Victoria brightly, reaching for the ignition key.

"Not so fast now, missy." Morris's moist, meaty hand clasped hers in a firm grip. "You don't need to rush off just yet. I was hoping you and my woman might get to know each other a little. I always like my women to get along, makes things easier."

Victoria felt a mix of indignation and laughter forming, and cleared her throat to calm herself. The man was preposterous! But she felt that she needed to tread carefully and not mock him. "Oh, do you think so?" she asked politely. In her mirror, she saw the other woman approaching, now wheeling what looked like a wheelbarrow piled high with farmyard muck with a pitchfork stuck in the top.

"That I do. You need a cockerel in the coop to keep all the ladies in order and," he added with a smirk, "to keep 'em happy. They tends to fight otherwise. Now my Sylvia, she's a wild one! But do anything for me, she would." Seeing Victoria's face, he added, "No, really, I mean that her would. Worships the ground I walk on. A passionate maid, know what I mean?"

Feeling this had gone on long enough, Victoria smiled brightly again and, shrugging off his hand, she turned the key and started the engine. "Well, it's been absolutely fascinating talking to you, Morris. Your plans sound really, er, interesting."

Just as she selected first gear, she saw a movement out of the corner of her eye, and then everything went dark as the windscreen was suddenly smothered in straw, and mud and muck. "What on earth…!" Victoria jumped out of the car, just in time to see Morris wrestling with Sylvia.

"Hey now! You mad woman! You crazy chick!" He was fighting Sylvia for control of the pitchfork before she could hurl another load of muck onto Victoria's car. Sylvia was red in the face and grunting with effort, while Morris laughed and twisted the pitchfork handle from side to side, playing with her with his superior strength. Glancing over his shoulder and grinning hugely, he said, "See, I told you! She's a wild cat, she is! I like a woman with a bit of fight in her!" He laughed again and began pulling Sylvia from side to side.

The woman was crying with frustration and swearing at him under her breath.

Victoria got back in the car, closed the window and flicked the central locking. She started the engine, putting the wipers on until the smeared mess across the glass cleared enough for her to be able to drive carefully past the warring couple.

"Don't let me see you back here again!" yelled Sylvia. "Or next time it won't just be chicken shit I throws at you!"

Victoria shot off up the road, or 'hightailed it out of there' as Morris would very probably have said. She pulled over in the first gateway she came to. She took a deep breath and wasn't quite sure whether to laugh or cry. Eventually, she laughed and imagined what Albert would have to say about the whole ridiculous scenario. There he was fretting about her visiting Caroline in the murder scene barn when she'd been in far more danger in a tatty farmyard with a pitchfork-wielding harpy!

She took another deep breath and checked her mobile: no signal. Never mind, she'd be home soon enough and could tell Albert all about it then.

She frowned. It was a nuisance, though. She had been rather hoping to go back and interview Martha Podger about her chicken breeding. It would make a really interesting article and blog. Perhaps she could go back when she knew mad Sylvia wouldn't be around to shower her with unmentionable muck, but then there was Morris to contend with, too. She slowed at a crossroads and then turned towards home. She wasn't sure who was the more worrying, Morris or Sylvia. Why did she seem to meet so many bonkers people in this part of the world? Honestly, sometimes she thought she'd felt safer up on London, or 'The Smoke', to quote Morris.

As she approached the village shop, she decided to pull

over and buy something for supper. Her culinary skills were not developing and she was either spoiled by Albert's cooking or eating far too often in the pub. One was bad for her conscience, the other for her bank balance – and neither was good for her figure.

"Afternoon, Miss West," said Dahlia from behind the cheese counter, "and how are you this fine day? Oh my word!" she said, catching sight of Victoria's car through the window. "Where have you been, dear? It looks like your car is covered in – "

"Yes, well, let's just say I had a close encounter in a farmyard," said Victoria. "Now, what can I prepare Albert for his tea, do you think? What would he like?" She realised that throwing open the subject for debate would cause a huge amount of interest, and probably gossip, in the village.

"Well, now," said the second triplet, Iris, suddenly popping up from behind the vegetable stand where she had obviously been cleaning. Her hair was now delicately draped with cobwebs and a small piece of parsley and she was pink in the face from her exertions. "Not wishing to be rude, dear, but I gets the feeling that cookery possibly wasn't one of your best subjects at school. Would that be a fair comment?"

Victoria resisted the urge to argue the point and said, "Well, perhaps so, and I never really had time when I lived up in London and – "

"But of course, we all know you can bake a good cake," said Dahlia with an exaggerated wink to Iris, and the two of them started tittering. The subterfuge organised by Albert, first with Victoria's Aunt Edith and now with herself, that they baked award-winning cakes when really it was Albert all along, no longer seemed to fool anyone, if indeed it ever had.

"But cakes aside, why don't you rustle up a nice shepherd's pie for him?"

"Isn't it a bit warm for that?" Victoria didn't in the least fancy cooking mince and potatoes. That was a winter dish in her opinion and, frankly, not something she liked.

"Well, perhaps," said Iris. "I know, what about a grilled gammon steak with a nice side salad and chips?" Seeing the doubt on Victoria's face, Dahlia dived into the freezer cabinet and emerged clutching a bag of frozen potato wedges. "There we are! No need for a deep fat fryer. Just stick 'em in the Rayburn while you griddle the gammon."

Victoria considered, decided not to tell them she had yet to even light the Rayburn and then smiled. "Do you know, I think you've got it spot on! I know he likes gammon and that seems quite quick and easy."

Iris was picking out two very nice if huge slices of gammon from the meat section and wrapping them in greaseproof paper. "Proper they'll be, come from just up the road out Moretonhampstead way. Snip the rind in a few places so it doesn't curl up and – " she picked out a tin from the back of a shelf, "here's some pineapple rings. That'll be like the icing on one of Albert's, I mean your, cakes!"

Victoria handed them a ten-pound note and, as ever, was amazed to receive change. "No Lavender today?" The third triplet, very much a free spirit, was obviously off on one of her jaunts.

The two triplets exchanged sad glances and Dahlia said, "No, dear, she's been terrible upset about those murders over at Burntwood."

Victoria hid her surprise and asked, "Oh dear, did she know the Peacocks or Jessica perhaps?"

"Well, no, but it's the vibes, you see. She's ever so susceptible to things like that. Hits her proper bad," said Dahlia.

"I'm sorry to hear that. Poor Lavender,"

"We know it's one of the many crosses she has to bear, poor

sensitive soul. And, talking of Burntwood, I hear you and Albert were in the thick of it – again!" said Iris, her eyes gleaming behind her spectacles. "Proper Jekyll and Hyde, you two are!"

"No, no," tutted Dahlia, "you mean Holmes and Watson. Jekyll and Hyde was a different kettle of fish altogether."

"Really? Who were they then?"

"No, not a they, 'twas just one person with a bit of a split personality," explained Dahlia rather crossly. "But never mind all that – we've heard it was poison. Is that right? You were there. In fact, I heard that poor young maid actually expired in Albert Moreton's arms!" They gazed at her intently and waited for her reply.

Victoria did not want to find herself the centre of attention again and she knew Albert would be absolutely furious if he himself were put centre stage. "Well, I'm afraid I really can't say at the moment, ladies. You see, we have to go and make full statements to the police and, until we've done that, I don't know that we should really discuss it at all." As she said this she had put her left hand behind her back and crossed her fingers out of the pairs' view.

They stared at her open-mouthed. Her attempt at deflecting them only seemed to have increased their level of interest. "Oh, right, well… do you think you could pop in here on your way back from making your statements, while it's still all fresh in your minds, like?" asked Iris, a note of desperation in her voice. "We'd really like to hear it straight from the horse's mouth."

Victoria sighed. "The thing is, Albert is rather upset about the whole thing." Both their hands flew to their mouths in unison.

"Poor man!" whispered Dahlia.

"Poor man!" echoed Iris.

"Yes, well, it was all rather shocking, so I'm not too sure that he will want to say anything much about it," Victoria finished lamely.

"The poor, poor man," said Dahlia again. "You get off home and cook him that lovely gammon supper. And mind you remember to warm the pineapple rings through as well. There's nothing worse than cold pineapple on a hot gammon steak."

Victoria scuttled out of the door before they could ask her anything else.

Chapter 5

As she drove along the narrow lanes with glimpses of rolling farmland or a patch of blue sea appearing through gateways, Victoria reflected on how even driving to the big out-of-town supermarket near Westerley wasn't a chore when the landscape was so lovely. Trailing on a bus to the nearest 24-hour convenience store in central London and then lugging the heavy bags of shopping back home was not only tedious but very expensive. Victoria wasn't one for frequenting budget stores, but even the priciest choice in Westerley seemed reasonable against the shops she had been used to in her London life.

She parked easily and trotted into the store. She looked down at her list and started walking purposefully down the aisles. The store was cool and relatively quiet and so much less stressful than in the old days. As she reached the wine department she heard a loud "Psst!" and wondered if she had imagined it. She looked around, but couldn't spot anyone she knew.

"Pssst! Victoria!"

Hearing her name, she realised there must be someone she knew nearby, but she couldn't recognise anyone.

"Over here. It's me," said a female voice in a loud stage whisper.

Victoria looked around anxiously again. A female figure sporting large dark glasses, a Sophia Lauren-style headscarf and a macintosh with upturned collar was waving manically at her from behind a display of special offer Chardonnay.

"Tori!"

Victoria stopped and walked towards the 'anonymous' person with a sinking heart, already sure she knew perfectly well who it was beneath the 'disguise'

"Hello, Caroline," she said wearily.

"Well, how you can tell, I have no idea. I am in deep disguise. I was going to wear a wig, but this headscarf seemed a simpler solution. I simply had to get out for food. We are starving through lack of supplies."

Victoria smiled to herself, wondering just what supplies Caroline might have run short on, bearing in mind she was loitering in the wine aisles.

"I'm sorry, Caroline, I would have bought some bits for you if I'd known. Is there a problem?"

Caroline stopped looking around furtively and stared at Victoria. She removed her glasses. "For heaven's sake, Tori, I told you last time we met. I am targeted. My persecutor could strike at any moment." She donned the sunglasses again and turned her collar up even further as an unsuspecting pensioner wandered past, staring at the unusual sight.

"What exactly did you need, Caroline?"

"Oh, just absolute basics. We are just grateful to eat. One cannot afford to be picky when you are a virtual prisoner in your own home."

Victoria thought she was being ridiculously melodramatic. "Well, perhaps I could pop round after I've finished my shopping and bring you some bits and pieces?"

"Oh, you are an angel. We would be so grateful."

"By 'we', do I assume Freddie is still hiding in the house with you?"

"Yes," replied Caroline, sotto voce. "Freddie is being a dear. He brought some supplies down from London to calm my nerves, but of course men always need to be fed, don't they, in more ways than one!"

Victoria felt grateful that she had a coat collar and dark glasses between her and Caroline's eyes. Really, this girlish glee about having an affair with Freddie was getting on her nerves. The man seemed such a nasty piece of work and Victoria had no idea what the attraction was.

"Well, I'll pop over with bread and some bacon, or perhaps you'd like some of my eggs? They're always useful for a quick easy meal."

Caroline ducked and appeared interested in the items on display on the bottom shelf. "Camera! Security camera. Just noticed it. They could be recording us," she hissed.

"Right, well let's not worry about that. I'll bring some basics for you."

"Thank you so much. We are right out of Prosecco, and the smoked salmon is down to the last packet. If they have any brioches, they are so much nicer than toast for breakfast – oh and perhaps a pack of really fresh Parmesan would be so helpful – ready-grated if at all poss? I'll dash off and see you shortly."

Caroline crept away sideways, flattened against the shelves, her arms stretched out each side, looking from left to right until she reached the end of the aisle and disappeared from view.

Victoria found herself counting to ten and wondered why on earth she had let herself get involved in this mess. She collected the other items she and Albert wanted and then resolutely pushed them towards the back of the trolley so she could put Caroline's items through separately and ask her for the cash later on.

Victoria blessed the cool bag she kept in the back of the car and packed her chilled items in that. She took a deep breath and headed off towards Caroline's house, wishing desperately she had never bumped into her. How frustrating to do so on one of her very rare supermarket trips! Perhaps it was an omen and she should stick to the village shop and the eccentricities of the triplets.

At the barn, the door was opened by Freddie who looked Victoria up and down and gave her a slow smile. "So, the lady couldn't resist returning to the scene of the crime, or was it something more personal you had in mind?" His leer was so overt that Victoria felt faintly nauseous. He really was very creepy.

"Sorry to disappoint you, but I've brought some shopping for Caroline. I bumped into her in Westerley."

"Oh, right, so you're the delivery service she was just talking about, hah! And a very sexy one, if I may say so."

Freddie seemed over-animated and jumpy, his eyes a glittering black. Victoria wondered if he was on something; he certainly struck her as the type.

"Who is it?" came a shrill voice from inside.

"Your grocery delivery service by the look of it," replied Freddie with a silly, nervous giggle.

Victoria exhaled and tried to stay calm. This really was taking things too far, even by Caroline's standards.

Caroline came to the door. "Oh, Tori, you are an angel. Thank you so much for the emergency supplies. Come in for a drink, or a coffee? I've just made some. Frankly, I am so stressed at the moment I have even resorted to caffeine!"

Victoria wanted to turn tail and walk away, but decided that would make her feel even more like a delivery service and so agreed. "I can't stay for long, pressing deadlines, you know how that is…" Victoria heaved the bag of shopping past Freddie, who didn't offer to carry it for her despite her narrow-eyed glare.

She plonked the carrier bag down on the table and removed the separate receipt from her purse.

"By the way, here's your receipt, Caroline."

"Oh, sweetheart, you needn't have bothered. I never keep those damn things."

Victoria mulled over how to ask for the money again more pointedly, or should she just say nothing? She felt Freddie's hand brush across her bottom and knew in that moment she wanted her money back – no matter what.

With a deliberate side step away from him, she said firmly, "No, the receipt, Caroline, is so that you or Freddie can give me the money I spent on your groceries, just under thirty pounds, so not an insignificant amount."

Caroline looked over at her and a look of pity crossed her face.

"Oh you poor dear. Yes, I should have realised how terribly tight things must be for you without a job nowadays. Freddie, make sure you pay Victoria. It's not fair to expect her to feed us!"

Victoria sipped the coffee, even though it was so hot it burned her mouth. Ghastly woman! How she wished she hadn't done her a favour. She knew just what Albert would say. Why did she keep being so soft about things?

"Chop, chop, come on, Freddie, can't you see the lady is waiting for it?"

Victoria wished the floor would swallow her up.

After a theatrical sigh, Freddie said, "Look, I'm getting just a tiny bit pissed off with all this 'Freddie pay for this', 'Freddie pay for that' stuff. Just how long is all this vast amount of money you promised going to take to materialise, sweetie?"

Caroline's eyes widened and Victoria caught the flash of irritation she tried to convey to Freddie to shut him up.

Freddie obviously caught the look and fished in the pocket of his tight jeans for a wallet. It wasn't overly full and Victoria could see out of the corner of her eye that the twenty and ten pound notes he removed left very little else. He threw it down on the table and walked out of the kitchen.

"I'm so sorry, sweetheart. I should have gone to the cash machine. Silly of me."

Victoria didn't know what to make of the obvious money shortage, but decided to say nothing. Suddenly, she heard raised voices and the front door slammed with an almighty bang. Loud footsteps marched towards the kitchen.

"Of course I've got a bloody right! Dear God, who the hell are you anyway, you nasty-looking weasel, and where's Caroline? Not sporting widow's weeds, I'll be bound!"

With the force of a small, angry weather front, a short sturdy woman blew into the kitchen. Her iron-grey hair was pulled back into a tight French pleat and she looked, as Victoria's late father would have said, as if she had been poured into her expensive clothes and had forgotten to say 'When'.

"So what have you got to say for yourself?" she barked at Caroline, but managed to intimidate Victoria at the same time.

"Ahh, er, Victoria, this is my sister-in-law, India. She and Giles were very close," said Caroline in a simpering tone.

Victoria spotted an excellent escape route and stood up. "How lovely to meet you, India. I am so sorry it is in such sad circumstances. If you will forgive me, I must be getting back. Thank you for the coffee, Caroline."

Caroline looked at Victoria's coffee, which had barely been touched and said rather desperately, "Well, there's no need to rush off, Tori. I'm sure India won't be staying long."

"Hah! That's what you think! I intend to be around for some time. I have taken rooms at the village hostelry. I had no idea they did B & B, but they seemed reasonable and I can be on hand."

"On hand?" Caroline said.

"Well, my dear, someone has to sort out this unholy mess and it's usually best to have family around to do that. You can't rely on the police or lawyers to do anything."

Victoria almost stumbled in her rush to say goodbye and raced out of the house. Sitting in the car felt like a haven compared to the stormy atmosphere inside the barn.

Home felt even more like a sanctuary and, after giving Moss an extra loving cuddle, she positively enjoyed pottering round and putting away her goodies from the supermarket. What had that terrifying woman India Peacock to do with anything? And what was that nasty little worm Freddie up to?

Albert put his head around the kitchen door. "Hello, my beauty! I can't stop, in the middle of something, but Tufty reminded me it was the 'Curryoke night' down at the Swaddle Arms tonight. You up for us going?"

"Of course," Victoria said. "Any excuse not to cook!"

"Huh!" Albert gave a mock glare. "I'll be back soon, so make sure you're ready, my girl. We'll give the old Jag an outing tonight, so at least we can arrive in style."

Victoria smiled. Ah, this was the life! She had no idea what Curryoke was, but it sounded fun.

* * * * *

Trudy was in fine form to host her first ever Curryoke night. She had obviously decided to take the Indian theme seriously and, apart from serving a wide variety of interesting-sounding curries and nibbles of poppadoms and dips on the tables and bar, she had dressed for effect, too.

At first glance, one would have thought the theme was 'Mata Hari' rather than 'Curryoke' but she looked every inch the part. Her eyes had been made up with large amounts of kohl, and she had wrapped herself up in what looked like sari material bought from a recent trip up to Bristol. Roger was similarly attired in a professional manner and had donned a turban decorated with a large feather, held in place by a heavy bejewelled brooch. Unfortunately, the brooch was slightly too heavy for the headdress and the feather kept flopping forwards, so Roger was constantly blowing upwards to remove said feather from his nose.

Trudy, determined to make the Swaddle Arms a success all year round, was mad keen on themed events. The bar had been beautifully decorated with twinkling fairy lights and, apart from being a little over the top, it was pretty to see them glittering away.

It seemed that 'Curryoke' meant what it said, a heady mix of curry and karaoke and Victoria was impressed with the landlady's enthusiasm and originality. There was a good turnout and, judging by overheard snippets of conversation, plenty of the villagers seemed keen to take part in the karaoke aspect, while also tasting the Indian delights that Trudy had been busy creating, inspired by much research on the internet.

Victoria couldn't assess Albert's mood. He must have been keen to come, after all he had suggested it, but he did look rather apprehensive as he sat at a table as far as possible from the microphone and screen that had been set up centre stage.

"And don't you dare, miss, don't you dare think I am singing one note tonight. I came because I thought you would have a bit of fun, but I don't sing, not never."

"Fine, OK, I won't suggest it for a moment, so long as you don't suggest I sing either. You know it's not one of my many talents!" They shared a conspiratorial grin, remembering Victoria's performance at the village show earlier in the year.

They had a choice of either lamb, chicken or veggie curry and these arrived in huge portions with poppadoms balanced on the top. Rather too English in style for Victoria's more cosmopolitan tastes, but tasty nonetheless. Albert declared it 'Damned hot!" and wiped his brow a lot, although Victoria felt this was more for show than anything else. Praise was given to a flushed-looking Trudy, and the plates were removed.

"Ladies and gentlemen, ladies…" There was a lull in conversation while they all sat waiting with bated breath for the announcement. Trudy, still looking rosily aglow, certainly seemed to enjoy being centre stage and waved the microphone about like a professional. "Ladies and gentlemen, I am sure you are all keen to join in and give us your renditions, but we have to be firm and have a running order tonight. I apologise in advance if this means that you have to wait a while, but as you can see from this massive turnout, we are victims of our own success here at the Swaddle Arms."

Victoria looked around at the smiling, eager faces and felt pleased for Trudy, who must have spent many hours making all the arrangements. Just then, the reverend came in through the door and made a bee-line for them. "Aha, Albert, Victoria, excellent. May I join you?"

"Please do, Edwin, we'd love your company." Victoria felt sure his dry wit would add to the evening.

"Hush, hush, now. If I could have your attention again, please? We felt it might be best if we started the evening off. As you know, Roger and I have been part of local singalongs and musicals for many years and this we felt might just set the tone for everyone. I apologise for the slight lull in the availability of your barman but, of course, it is all in a very good cause. All proceeds from tonight

will be going to the Newton Abbot home for distressed hedgehogs."
Trudy bowed theatrically and beckoned to Roger to come out from
behind the bar.

Victoria had never seen a husband look more hen-pecked than
the sad specimen who puffed ineffectively at the feather constantly
tickling his nose and walked ramrod stiff up to the microphone.
Trudy was always full of wonderful ideas, but they were not always
fully fledged before they were launched skywards and sometimes
sank like stones. Victoria hoped, for poor Roger's sake, that this one
would at least have legs, if not wings.

"Now we have such a wide repertoire of much-loved songs that
we could sing for you, but we are aware that we need light and fun
tonight and so I was thinking more Bollywood than opera. One of
our favourite films of all time is Grease. I won't bore you with tales
of when we were courting…" Trudy paused and looked around.
Victoria noted the distinct lack of encouragement from anyone to
hear further revelations of their courtship.

"Anyway, if you feel you want to dance, that's fine and let's
have a good old time – Roger, the music please!" Roger trailed
disconsolately towards a CD player and then returned to the
microphone as the familiar refrain began.

The introduction to 'You're the one that I want' began and
Roger sang in a faltering voice. "I've got chills…" and Victoria rather
thought she had chills, too. Roger's strangled voice continued, the
American accent as painful as the tone. Victoria gazed intently at
the grain of the wood on the table's surface and bit her bottom lip.

By the time they were singing the chorus in harmony, well
almost, she and Albert were gripping each other's hands in an
attempt to stop the mirth.

"Luckily," said Edwin matter-of-factly, "I have had many years'
practice at keeping a straight face in a multitude of situations and I

would say in this case I am probably very blessed to have had such training." His poker face was a marvel.

"Thank you, thank you!" said Trudy in response to the desultory clapping. "Now who's next? I've started a list so none of you will slip through the net and be left disappointed."

A small man in a bright green sweater marched up to the microphone and, after a brief discussion with Roger, he gave a passable rendition of 'The green, green grass of home.' "Nice of him to dress appropriately," whispered Edwin, with a wink.

"Fantastic! Thank you, Dougie! So, who's up next?" enthused Trudy, frantically scanning the scribbled list she clutched in her hand.

Jean Burnicombe had been sitting at the end of the bar with one of her pals, both of them downing sweet sherries as if they were on a two-for-one offer which, for all Victoria knew, might have been the case this evening. Now she raised her hand and waved frantically to attract Trudy's attention. A woman in her late fifties with bucked teeth and large-framed pebble glasses, Jean was Victoria's cleaner, inherited, along with the cottage, from her late Aunt Edith. Sliding inelegantly off her barstool, Jean walked quickly over to the microphone.

"Oh Jean," Trudy looked round anxiously as if seeking rescue, "you're so keen. How lovely to have such support. You're not due on just yet, but if you want to sing now, well, I suppose… And you're singing on your own?"

"Deed I am, Trude. Not a stranger to singing, me. Used to be quite a star in the local amateur whatsits in my youth." Jean adjusted her bra straps and cleared her throat and looked over at Roger. "You got my usual, Rog?"

"Ahh, indeed I have," said Roger and reluctantly put on another CD.

The opening notes of the song 'Memory' from the musical Cats came out of the speaker and Victoria turned a squeak of surprise into a cough as she and Albert shared a look of part horror and part hilarity.

Jean seemed to have trouble getting up to the high opening notes and her wail, cat-like in the extreme, drew visible winces from the audience. Her own memory seemed to be at fault and she began la-la-ing by the second verse.

"Oh, good lord," said Victoria in hushed tones, "I'm not sure I'm strong enough for a whole evening of this."

"I'm sorry, maid, and they've only just started." Albert sounded desolate.

"Are you definitely not going to have a go then?"

Albert started back in alarm. "No way! As I said, definitely not one of my talents!"

"Oh, brace up, you two," hissed Edwin. "Things will pick up. You just wait until Bramley and Yours Truly get up there!"

Jean received polite, if not rapturous, applause and, smiling hugely, she reluctantly handed the microphone over to a man Victoria vaguely recognised from the Swaddlecombe Show committee. He gave a lacklustre performance of 'King of the Road' and Victoria felt quite relieved it had been so low-key. "Quite apt really," whispered Edwin. "He drives a milk tanker, you know." Victoria raised her eyebrows in a silent, 'Really, how interesting' expression.

Suddenly, there were whoops, and even a few cheers, as the substantial presence of Farmer Bramley loomed centre stage. "Right–o!" he cried cheerfully. "Let's give it some welly!" and, obviously primed in advance, Roger put on the CD and the strains of 'I've got a brand new combine harvester' boomed out of the speakers.

"Oh my Lord," said Albert, "'tis his party piece!"

The reverend was clapping in time to the music, laughing and stamping his feet.

"I drove my tractor up your driveway last night," began Bramley, acting the lyrics as he went. "I turned me phone off to be sure it was quiet."

Victoria spoke into Albert's ear. "I don't recognise those lyrics."

"'tis his own version."

"He's rather good!"

Albert pulled a face. "Takes all sorts."

"Don't be such an old grump!" She slapped his arm and he grinned.

Bramley roared into the chorus and the entire pub joined and clapped along and Victoria decided it was rather more fun than she'd ever had in a stuffy wine bar in London.

To loud cheers and whistles, Bramley took several bows at the end and Trudy grabbed the microphone. "Wow, well done! Now who can follow that? Reverend, come on, we know you're always good for a warble!"

Edwin coloured. "Well. Really, I'm not too sure after that…"

"Oh, go on!" said Victoria and dug him in the ribs. "You said you would earlier."

"Well, if I must." He crept shyly onto the stage and some wags shouted comments.

"Go on then, Vicar! What about some Meatloaf – 'Bat out of Hell'?"

"Or Black Sabbath?"

"Oh, you really are a rotten lot," he said, giggling into the microphone. He turned to Roger who was fiddling with CDs and winked at him. Roger saluted in return.

"Oh, how sweet," sighed Victoria as the opening notes of 'You'll never walk alone' began. "I think I might cry."

"Get a grip, Victoria, for goodness sake," grumbled Albert, but he slipped his arm round her, nonetheless.

Edwin began, eyes closed in concentration, swaying slightly from side to side.

"Oh, what a lovely voice," sighed Victoria.

Albert nodded and patted her hand. "A fine tenor, just as a good man of the cloth should have."

Edwin added more power as he reached the dramatic last section, arms held wine in true Pavarotti style.

"Have you got a tissue?" squeaked Victoria.

Albert rummaged in his pocket and handed her a crumpled piece of kitchen roll. "Here, that'll have to do. Now shut up!"

As Edwin soared to the climactic ending the entire pub rose as one to its feet and clapped and cheered and Victoria sobbed. As Edwin returned to his seat she hugged him. "Oh, that was wonderful! So moving! You have such a beautiful voice, Edwin!"

"Oh, goodness, well…!" He was pink and happy and sat down as people patted his back and shook his hand. Jean was in floods of tears and planted a huge kiss on his cheek and called for another sherry as she'd 'come over all weak'.

As the euphoria died down, Albert said, "I reckon I'll go and settle up and then we can head off home. All this excitement is exhausting for an old farmer!"

They waited patiently to pay as Trudy and Roger basked in the success of the evening and chatted and poured pints. A woman bustled into the pub and came and stood next to Albert. "Extremely busy in here. Is this normal?" she asked and before Albert could answer added, "Absolutely gasping for a G&T!"

"Albert, what can I get you?" Roger hove to, grinning from ear to ear and flushed with success.

"Well, Mudger, I just want the bill, but this lady here is need of an urgent gin and tonic, so I reckon you'd best serve her first."

"Ice and a slice?" asked Roger.

"Absolutely!" boomed the woman. "Awfully decent of you. Many thanks." She smiled up at Albert and heaved herself up onto the barstool that was both slightly too high and slightly too narrow for her build. "India Peacock," she said, holding out a large hand. "And you are?"

"Albert Moreton and this," he turned to include Victoria, "– is,"

"Oh, that's OK," Victoria said, "we met earlier this afternoon at Caroline's house,"

India's smile froze. "Actually, to be legally accurate," she said, "it's my late brother, Giles's, house. I suppose you are a friend of Caroline's?"

Victoria felt stung. "Well, yes. We used to work together in London, a few years ago now. I mean, we're not close friends, just – "

Clearly bored with Victoria's wittering, India ignored her and turned her big, handsome face toward Albert. "And you, Albert, what do you do? I'd guess local landowner?'

Albert seemed to swell with pride. "Well, you could say that. I have a farm on the outskirts of the village. Here, let me get that for you. Roger, add that G&T onto my bill, please."

India lowered her eyes and then glanced up at Albert over the edge of her glass as she sipped her G&T. Good grief, she was flirting with him! Victoria felt herself go hot and then cold and she had a terrible urge to push the horrid little tub of a woman off the bar stool, but knew she was being ridiculous. "Actually, could I have another glass of Sauvignon Blanc while you're at it," she said brightly.

"Righto." Albert looked slightly taken aback. "Well, I'll have another pint them, if we're staying. Roger, stick it all on the bill and I'll settle up in a minute."

Trying terribly hard not to sulk, Victoria gave India a forced smile and, clutching her glass of wine, marched over to Edwin, who was still surrounded by admirers and in particular Jean, who was sitting next to him and leaning heavily against him. "Moved I was, proper moved, Vicar, I don't mind saying! And I never even knew you supported Liverpool. I never knew you was a footballing man. You learns something new every day!"

"Liverpool?" Victoria was puzzled.

"Don't ask," hissed Edwin. "You'll only encourage her."

"Oi, Jean, you drunken old duck, if you wants a lift home get that sherry down you!" commanded an impatient skinny man in an anorak.

"Lord, ooh sorry, Vicar, I didn't mean – well anyway, better go. Don't want to miss my lift 'ome. Bottoms up!" She downed the sherry and, kissing the vicar sloppily on the cheek again, walked unsteadily after the receding anoraked figure and out into the night.

"Dear Jean, I am terribly fond of her," said Edwin, "but sometimes, well, you know."

Victoria smiled. "Yes, I think I do."

A booming laugh from the bar made Victoria glance around. India was rocking dangerously on the stool. She looked like a golf ball on a tee.

"Albert got a new friend?" asked Edwin.

"Hmm, do hope not. That's Giles Peacock's sister. I think she's come down to stir up trouble. Or, to be fair, perhaps find out the truth of what's really been going on. I met her earlier at Caroline's and there was certainly no love lost between the two of them."

"What is it they say – 'where there's a will, there's a family feud'?"

Victoria nodded. "I fear so, and that's without thinking about the circumstances. Have you heard any more about what the police are doing?"

Edwin shook his head. "No, not a thing. Well, that's her third drink since she arrived!" he added as he watched India at the bar over Victoria's shoulder.

"Oh dear, poor Albert. Perhaps I should go and rescue him?"

The rector chortled. "I think he can look after himself. He seems to be holding his own perfectly well and lending a friendly ear to the lady."

The booming laugh rang out again and India said, "I say, you are a card! I do like a man with a sense of humour."

Victoria scowled. "Honestly! I don't think I can sit through much more of this."

Edwin patted her arm. "Patience, my dear. Albert has it all under control. Talking of the police, they've asked me to go in and make a statement tomorrow, so I expect you'll be hearing from them, too."

"Goodness, that will be interesting. I do wish they'd hurry up. The longer they leave it, the more likely one is to forget some detail that might be vital. I wanted to tell them about our poison theory, but Albert said I shouldn't speculate and should leave it to the professionals."

"I suspect he is right, Victoria. I'm sure they will get to the bottom of it once they've got all the 'path' reports, or whatever they are."

Edwin touched her arm. "Actually, you might want to collect Albert. He is starting to look a little anxious. His companion is wilting."

Victoria turned to look as India half slumped against the bar and seemed about to topple off the high stool. Albert caught her arm and steadied her with a cry of, "Hup, my beauty!"

"Oh dear. Well, thanks for the tip-off, Edwin." She gave him a peck on the cheek. "We'll be off then. You must come and see how the new hens are settling in."

"You are my sort of chap – earthy, practical and with a certain je ne sais quoi!" India was saying as she waved her empty glass about.

"And that's exactly what I see in him, too!" said Victoria as she sidled up to Albert and put her arm through his. "Darling, we really must be getting back. Your cows and your hundreds of acres must be missing you." Albert gave her a look.

India was waving her glass at Roger. "I say, landlord, another please!" Roger looked disapproving, but couldn't turn down an order, so took her glass to refill.

"Well, India, it's been a pleasure to meet you. I hope I'll see you again while you're visiting these parts," said Albert politely, while simultaneously squeezing Victoria's hand to reassure her.

"I do hope so too, Albert. It's been an absolute pleasure, my dear." She planted a wet and wobbly kiss on his lips and patted his cheek and almost plummeted from the stool again, but Albert caught her and propped her back up. "Steady the buffs!" she cried and laughed uproariously.

Victoria pulled Albert towards the door and with much waving and, in India's case, the blowing of kisses, they finally made it into the car park.

"For goodness sake! Ridiculous woman! I do hope you haven't matched her drink for drink or we'll have to walk home!" Victoria sounded snappish and hated herself for it.

"Don't you worry, maid. I made my pint last. She had no idea what was going on. Poor woman."

Victoria snorted. "What do you mean, poor woman? Drunken

old hag. She had her claws firmly into you!"

Albert laughed as they climbed into the old Jaguar. "Don't be daft. She's a sad and lonely woman. Her's lost her brother who, God knows why, she was quite fond of, and she doesn't have many friends."

"I'm not surprised if she carries on like that!"

"Oh come on now, show some charity. Poor old bird, not a nice situation to be in now, is it? I reckon she's been under a lot of stress and that led to her having one or two too many tonight. I think we've all been there and done that at some time or another." He paused and looked at her. "Haven't we, maid?"

Victoria felt herself blush, which she hoped he couldn't see in the gloom inside the car. "Well, yes, I suppose you are right, but she was all over you!"

"And why not! Handsome landowner like me!" Victoria punched his arm. "Ouch! Don't be mean. While you were being all bitter and twisted, I was learning all sorts of interesting things, so there."

"Really?"

"Oh yes, nothing like a sympathetic ear when someone's had a few."

"You cunning old fox!"

Albert smiled as they pulled out of the car park. "Well, I don't know about that, but her took a shine to me, and she wanted to talk, poor old maid."

They drove on through the soft dark night towards the farm. Victoria waited. And waited. Finally, she burst out, "Oh come on, Albert! Stop teasing. What did she say?"

Albert swung the Jaguar into the drive and carefully steered his way around the potholes. "We're nearly home, maid. Let's get the kettle on and I'll tell you."

"Honestly!" Victoria huffed, and climbed out of the car. Albert went in and put the kettle on. Victoria grabbed a torch and, somewhat paranoid since the fox attack, went and checked the hens. Letting herself into the newly-fenced run, she opened the door to the coop. They were all neatly lined up on their perch, eyes closed, warm and content in their fluffed-up feather coats. She closed the door and lowered the access flap. They were safe for the night. Back in the kitchen, Moss was bouncing with enthusiasm, and Albert had placed two cups of tea on the table. The cake tin stood centre stage, as usual.

"Right, tell all," said Victoria as she sipped her tea and watched as Albert cut himself a relatively small piece of lemon drizzle cake.

"Funny old maid! But she's all right, is India. I think she'd always sort of kept a motherly eye on Giles and she's angry and upset at what's happened, naturally."

"Well, yes, naturally. But…"

With infuriating slowness Albert chewed a mouthful of cake, swallowed and then sipped his tea. "But she's no fool and, while he was her brother, she knew he was a hothead and in her words, 'a fool where women are concerned.'"

Victoria nodded encouragingly, still waiting for the really juicy snippets to be revealed.

"Her wasn't too happy when Giles inherited far more of the family money than she did. I wasn't too sure of all the details, but trust funds and all sorts of things. And probably all the usual stuff about the boy child automatically getting more than the girl and, as is so often the case, regardless of whether he's got the brains to use it wisely or not. I reckon India would have made a far better job with the family money. Sharp as a tack, that one. And shrewd."

He took another bite of cake, paused to nod silent appreciation of his own culinary skills and sipped more tea. Victoria thought she might throw the cake tin and contents out of the window if this prevarication went on much longer.

Finally, he swallowed and went on, "India is furious now as it looks like Giles has left everything to your friend Caroline. She had told Giles when they first got together that she thought Caroline was a gold-digger and only ever after his money."

Victoria considered this. "Caroline has always seemed quite well-to-do, but I'm not sure that she was, just good at putting on an act. I don't think she comes from a wealthy background, so perhaps that's true. I don't know her well enough, I'm afraid."

"India, not surprisingly, is highly suspicious about his death and thinks, to quote her again, he was 'done in'! She's already got the measure of that slimy Freddie character and says he's on drugs. Did you know that?"

"I suspected it," she said, "but I wasn't sure."

"India caught him shoving something up his nose in the bathroom or some such. Never understood all that stuff meself. And she also reckons he's got Caroline hooked."

Victoria sighed. "Hmm, she could be right there, too. She has been behaving very oddly, even by Caroline's standards. There used to be a lot of it about in the magazine world, so she may have been on stuff for years. It never interested me. I must have been very dull."

Albert grinned. "You? Dull? I don't reckon that'd be the case! Anyway, India is on the warpath and is convinced Freddie and Caroline have conspired to kill Giles. She's seeing the detective in charge of the case tomorrow."

"He's going to have a busy day then. He's seeing the reverend, too, and I wouldn't be surprised if they call us in as well."

Chapter 6

Victoria was brushing her teeth when she heard the distant trill of her mobile phone. "Damn!' She hastily dried her mouth and began rushing from room to room, eventually tracking it down to her bedside table. "Hi, Georgie! Oh dear, you're going to be mad with me. I haven't quite got it finished."

"What? Oh, don't worry about that!"

"Sorry? I'd just assumed you were ringing about the article. So, what can I do for you?" Victoria breathed a sigh of relief as she realised her editor was only after gossip.

"Well, I was talking to Colin, you know, Colin French the advertising chap, and he said he'd bumped into you in Devon and the most awful drama had occurred – I mean, I can hardly believe it. Is it true, or was he winding me up?"

"You were talking to Colin? Yes, I did bump into him just recently." It amused her to hold back the goodies she knew Georgie was after. Gossip flew around the magazine world in a flash and anything she said would be halfway round the globe in an instant.

"Well, wasn't it at Caroline's place? Fab barn conversion, he said – but anyway..."

Victoria grinned. "Yes, that's right. It was Caroline's housewarming party, Caroline Johnston as was. Caroline Peacock now."

"Yes, yes, I know who she is, but Colin said – well, he said there'd been a murder!" Georgie's voice had dropped to a theatrical hiss.

"Yes, there was. It was horrendous actually, a terrible experience and awfully sad."

"But Colin said you were right there, next to the person who died, I mean, was murdered!" Georgie sounded as if she might faint with excitement at any moment.

"That's true, we were very close. In fact, we are going down to the police station today to make statements as we were in the thick of it."

"God, how exciting! Real life DCI Rebus-type stuff!"

"Except that's Scotland and this is Devon. And well, no, it's not too exciting really, just an awful tragedy that two people are dead."

Victoria moved the phone away from her ear a little as a shrill "Two people?" nearly burst her eardrum. "Yes, sadly, a young waitress was killed as well…"

"No! So are there any clues? What do the police think happened?"

"Well, if they have any firm ideas they aren't sharing them," said Victoria, not prepared to discuss any of their own theories either, just in case they ended up as headline news in a daily paper. Georgie probably knew plenty of editors.

"Well, heavens, darling, do be sure to let me know the moment you hear anything, won't you?" said Georgie. "I mean, I don't want to sound nosey but, hey, it's not every day you know someone who's actually witnessed a murder!" Then as a rushed afterthought, she added, "And, of course, I am concerned about poor Caroline. We go back years, you know. I do care about her."

"No, obviously you aren't being nosey and yes, I know you always cared about Caroline. Deep down." Victoria wondered if Georgie's nose had grown about a foot as she'd said that, bearing in mind they had always been bitter rivals in the magazine world and rarely met outside work.

"Well, I really must make a move, Georgie. Thanks for ringing and I'll get the article to you tomorrow latest."

"Oh, there's no mad rush, Victoria. You can have another couple of days. But do let me know as soon as you hear anything juicy, won't you?"

"Yes, yes, of course. I will let you know if there are any developments." But not if I can help it, thought Victoria. Scandal and gossip were never the nicest things to fuel and she didn't want to be the source of any of it.

"You ready?" shouted Albert from downstairs, on his return from walking Moss. "That seems an awful long time to just brush your teeth."

"Sorry, Georgie, my editor called," Victoria shouted back.

"What she want?" came yet another bellow.

Frustrated by trying to carry on a conversation over this distance, Victoria finished brushing her hair and added a touch of lipstick to put on a brave face for the police – a meeting she was secretly dreading – and came down the stairs. "Just hang on, there's no point in shouting!"

Albert was cleaning and drying Moss's paws, which had obviously been used to dig furiously in mud, or something worse. Moss looked nonchalant, which was always a bad sign.

"What's he been up to?"

Now it was Albert's turn to look nonchalant and Victoria decided that if the pair of them were displaying the same emotion there had to be something really serious afoot.

"Albert?"

"Oh, nowt to worry about, nothing much. Soon been sorted anyway."

"And the nothing is?"

"Well, he was just checking that the new cabbage plants were in straight and was adjusting them accordingly."

Victoria folded her arms and looked sternly at both man and dog.

"So what you are saying is that this vile puppy has dug up all my new cabbage plants and that you let him, or weren't watching?"

Albert looked downcast. "Well, there may be some truth in that, maid. I was just looking at a tool catalogue with my tea and got a bit engrossed in seed drills and, before I knew it, chaos!"

Victoria glared at Moss. "And you, young man, you are a very bad dog!" She wagged her finger and he dropped to the floor and looked desolate. "But I can't entirely blame you as you were supposedly accompanied by a responsible adult who wasn't paying attention."

"They're all back, all planted again. No damage done really, apart from the mud on the path and his paws, of course."

Victoria rolled her eyes. "Men! Honestly! And you are a very bad puppy!" She had to try really hard not to laugh as Moss pulled an 'I'm just a puppy and it wasn't my fault' face.

Concluding that the storm had passed and that he and the dog would live to fight another day, Albert said, "Right, come on – we're due at the police station at eleven for interviews, so we need to get a move on. You, young man, are staying here in your puppy cage."

They parked easily, for once, in Westerley and Victoria tried not to feel anxious as she walked into the police station. The sergeant behind the desk looked up with a querying expression.

"We have an eleven o'clock appointment to give our statements about the Peacocks' party," said Victoria, though referring to the party seemed a bit frivolous. "I mean, the tragedy at the Peacocks. Or in fact, the deaths, the murders, erm…" She petered out and the desk sergeant looked at her impassively, then eventually said, "Take a seat over there, please, madam, sir," and gestured them to a row of seats along a wall.

Taciturn, she supposed, was a good description, but then it would have been worrying if he had greeted them with a big jovial grin and happy handshakes. They sat down meekly side-by-side and Victoria tried not to stare at the huge, heavily tattooed woman two seats to her left who was humming and swaying slightly, while chewing gum in a leisurely manner. Next to the tattooed lady was a man so thin he looked like a whippet, his skin a whitish grey, his left leg jiggling incessantly. Aware of her interest, Albert nudged her arm to stop her looking.

After scratching his ear with his biro, the desk sergeant put through a call. "Eleven o'clock are here … Peacock case."

He looked up at them and, raising his eyebrows, said, "Names?"

Albert replied as Victoria's brain seemed to have turned to jelly.

"Albert Moreton and Victoria West. I believe we are to see …" he trailed off as the police officer was already talking into the phone again.

"Yeah, yeah that's right. OK."

A plain-clothes policeman came through a door to the right of the main desk.

"Albert Moreton?"

When he looked at her as well as Albert, Victoria repressed her knee-jerk reaction to say, 'Do I look like an Albert?' But she was sensible enough to realise a police station was not the ideal place to get chippy about gender issues. Albert rose and she got up to follow him.

"No, Miss, just Mr Moreton for now, thank you. Someone will be out to see you in a moment."

Suitably chastened, she sat down again and wondered why she

felt so jumpy. Heavens, not only had she done nothing wrong, she was actually helping the police!

A woman with a round, friendly face and short, sensible hair came through the same door. She walked towards Victoria and, holding out her hand, said, "Miss West, I'm DC Mortimer. Thank you for coming in to see us. Would you come with me, please, so we can take a statement?"

DC Mortimer seemed much friendlier than the other two police officers she'd encountered so far and Victoria breathed a small sigh of relief.

They walked along an echoing corridor to a door marked 'Interview Room 3'. Victoria wondered which room Albert had been taken into and tried to keep calm. It would be fine.

They sat at a small bare table with a couple of institutional chairs of grey plastic with black metal legs. She tried to adjust her position and was surprised to find the furniture was screwed to the floor. She shifted a little in the fixed seat and wondered if she should start the conversation, but told herself to be sensible. This wasn't a social occasion.

"I will be recording this interview if that's OK?" DC Mortimer looked across at her and Victoria nodded. "So, Miss West, perhaps you could fill me in on the background of why you were at the Peacocks' on the 29th?"

"I used to be a work colleague of Caroline's. Caroline Peacock, I mean. Although she was Caroline Johnston back then. It was before she met Giles. Mr Peacock, I mean." Oh dear, she was rambling. She took a breath. "We were journalists working on a national magazine. Not close colleagues. It was a huge building with many magazines, but it was a pleasant surprise to bump into her again here. I got the impression she was relieved to meet someone from her London life as she was a bit lonely down here."

"So you hadn't kept in touch with Caroline in the recent past?"

"Oh no. We hadn't seen each other for maybe five or six years or so."

"Do you know any of her current friends? Did you know her husband?"

"No, I hadn't met Giles before the party and certainly hadn't met Freddie before. We had one friend or rather ex-colleague in common, Colin, who was at the party, too, Colin French, a local man originally. I'm not sure many of the other guests were actually her friends, just local acquaintances really."

"Oh yes, Mr French. We will also be talking to him. So run me through what happened when you arrived at the Peacocks' house."

Victoria started relating their arrival and she saw a suppressed smile cross DC Mortimer's face as she described the valet parking being offered.

"So the food was being passed around on trays. Was there any left around or as a buffet?"

"Yes, there were waitresses bringing round trays of canapés as well as drinks, obviously, and there was another room where the food was laid out on one long table with plates for you to help yourself."

"Was there anything unusual among the food? Oysters, sushi – mushroom dishes?"

Victoria paused. She could see where the officer was heading. "No, there was nothing more exotic than king prawns. It was just very well presented upmarket buffet food. Nothing surprising, but it was beautifully prepared. Quite a choice of drinks: champagne, wines, fruit punch, spirits, all manner of things. The Peacocks had obviously spared no expense."

"Can you give me an impression of Mr Peacock's behaviour at the party?"

Victoria looked down and then rubbed her chin. She didn't want to speak ill of the dead and she'd hardly known the man. But this was serious, this was a police station, so she must try and be as straight and honest as she could. "The main thing, I suppose, was that Giles was obviously already drunk when we arrived. He was behaving inappropriately as Jessica was a member of staff. I didn't really know him, but he was behaving rather odiously. I – well, I didn't really like him, if I'm honest." There, she'd said it.

"Can you expand on that? Did you dislike him because of things he said to you, or to someone else, or what?"

"Oh dear. Well, I just can't bear men who get drunk and leer at you. He was horribly touchy-feely and just a ghastly caricature of the country gentleman he clearly thought he was." She shuddered involuntarily. "Sorry, that sounds a bit melodramatic."

"You obviously feel quite strongly," said DC Mortimer.

Victoria shrugged. "He was just being rather offensive. I am sure it was largely because he had drunk too much, but I think when I saw him flirting with Jessica it really turned my stomach."

"Perhaps you could describe it for me?"

"Well, they both seemed to be rather drunk and his hands were just all over her. I do hate that, don't you?" Victoria looked across at the policewoman, who just nodded. "I hate being manhandled, when you know the man isn't even thinking of you as a person, just as an object." Victoria realised she was making far too much of things and sounding rather shrill.

"So yes, when I saw them both drinking out of the same glass in a very intimate way and Giles feeding Jessica with bits of food from his plate, it rather sickened me."

"And Jessica? Did you know her prior to the party?"

"Oh no, not at all. She seemed very sweet, though. Well, very pretty anyway."

DC Mortimer nodded and seemed to be about to wind up the interview. "Erm, can I ask something?" ventured Victoria.

"Yes, of course." DC Mortimer eyed her warily.

"Well, you were asking about the food, and whether it was at all exotic, or anything. Well, it wasn't. But, as I said, I did see Giles actually feeding Jessica from his own plate."

"Yes?"

"Well, I'm not sure, but I just wondered if that was how, or when, the poison was administered."

DC Mortimer narrowed her eyes. "I'm not sure I follow you."

"They were eating some stuffed celery, I think it was. I'm not sure what the celery was filled with, or even if it was celery, but I just wondered if…" She trailed off. The police officer's eyes had taken on a distant look and Victoria realised she wasn't really listening and clearly thought Victoria was slightly cuckoo.

She was asked several more questions about people that were in attendance at the party and the only people she was able to say she knew really were Colin and Mandy. The officer seemed to be losing interest in her statement and Victoria hoped it meant they would be finishing shortly.

"Just one last question, Miss West. Are you acquainted with Thomas and Katie Brock, the caterers?"

"No, I wasn't until I met them at the party, but again they seemed helpful and, of course, the food was wonderful, delicious."

The detective heaved a sigh and closed her book, clicking off the tape recorder.

"Thank you, Miss West. If you think of anything else we should know, perhaps you will get in touch."

DC Mortimer got up and held the door open for her and directed her back to reception, where she hoped she would find Albert. And there he was, chatting away to Tom and Katie, the

119

caterers.

"Hi," said Victoria.

"Everything OK?" asked Albert

"Well, yes, I think so. I'm not sure I told them anything useful, though. And when I did try to discuss our little theory it seemed to go right over her head."

"Similar experience to me then," agreed Albert. "You've met Tom and Katie before?"

"Hi, Tom, Katie. Well, we've only spoken very briefly. Look, I know it's not the right time, but I thought you did a wonderful job of the Peacocks' party. I do wish you lots of success. It's lovely to see young people giving things a go."

"Well, I suspect the business may be ruined," said Tom sombrely. "News travels fast and everyone thinks we poisoned half the party!"

"Come on, Tom, cheer up. We will have our names cleared, you know we will," said Katie briskly.

"Yeah, says you. I told you it was a bad idea to do work for those people in the first place. I can't even bring myself to be sorry he's dead."

"Sssh!" hissed Katie, looking round fearfully. "Someone will hear you. It's bad enough that we are suspects already."

"Come on, Tom," said Victoria in her best cajoling voice, "why would anyone suspect you?"

Tom looked thunderous. "Maybe because I would have killed the man with my bare hands if I'd the chance!"

"Oh," said Victoria, looking at Albert and hoping for some help extracting herself from what appeared to be a rather large hole.

"As far as I am concerned Giles as good as murdered my father." Katie tried to quieten Tom as the silent officer at the desk was clearly listening intently.

Now he had started, Tom didn't seem able to stop. "Not only did that man take advantage of the fact my father was desperate for money and screw him lower and lower on price, but he then came up with more and more things Father had to finish or they wouldn't buy it. Finally, he stretched the time he took to complete so long that my father had to declare bankruptcy. No wonder he had a heart attack." He ran his hands roughly through his hair. "I hated Giles and Caroline with every bone of my body. But as Katie said, why miss out on such a well-paid job and miss taking a load of money off them?"

"We really hoped all those local dignitaries would be impressed and would recommend us," said Katie, her chin wobbling slightly, although she kept the tears at bay.

"Cheer up, lass. Your dad was a fine chap and I was proud to have known him. This nonsense will be cleared up soon enough and you can get on with your lives," said Albert.

Just as he finished speaking, the door to the interview rooms opened and the same two police officers that had interviewed Victoria and Albert appeared and asked Tom and Katie to accompany them. The young siblings were pale but determined, and Victoria was touched to see Katie clutch Tom's hand tightly, before releasing it and walking ahead of him down the long and intimidating corridor.

"Well," said Albert preparing to get to his feet. "That's a bit of a rum do. Let's get home and have a nice cup of tea before we take that young pup out for a walk." But before he could straighten up, the main doors into the police station were crashed back on their hinges as a dark, wild-haired woman stormed into the reception area and stopped, centre stage, hands on hips. Even the stoic desk sergeant had jerked up in his seat and was looking slightly animated.

"So," she bellowed, "what bleddy fool has summoned me to this dump, eh?" Victoria wondered if the woman was about to slap her thigh and add, 'Me hearties!' as she had a distinctly theatrical air about her. Or was it more of a pirate theme, or perhaps gypsyish…? But before Victoria could follow through on this meandering train of thought, the woman turned her flashing eyes on Albert and her face instantly softened. "Albie!" she cried and took two steps towards him, arms flung wide.

Albert was on his feet in a flash. "Steady on there, Patricia!" he said, his own arms outstretched, but not so much in welcome, more as if ready to ward the woman off. Victoria snapped her mouth shut, suddenly aware that she had been gawping like a landed fish.

Patricia stopped in her tracks and seemed to deflate a little. "Well, Albert Moreton, I wasn't expecting to meet you. Mr Goody-Two-Shoes. What have they got you in here for then?"

Albert scratched his cheek, a sure sign of discomfort as Victoria well knew. "You see, 'tis all a bit unfortunate really. We were witnesses to a nasty incident and we've, er, been called in to give statements, and – "

"Who's 'we'? What you and 'er?" Patricia tossed her head contemptuously in Victoria's direction and her hair rose and settled like a much-used floor mop.

"Let me introduce you – Patricia Podger, this is Victoria West."

Patricia's eyes narrowed and she inspected Victoria minutely. "Is that so?" she said at last. "Not what I was expectin' after all what I'd heard." She held Victoria's gaze and then suddenly turned her eyes away and roared at the desk sergeant. "I 'aven't got all bleddy day, you know, Jim Pickworth. You find out who it is wants to see me and tell 'em to move their arse. OK?"

Suitably stung, Sergeant Pickworth climbed off his perch and disappeared out into the nether regions of the police station.

Victoria realised she'd been holding her breath, and thought it was a good time to exhale. The two other people sitting in the reception area were looking on agog. The skinny man was by now a mass of tics and fidgets and suddenly it all seemed to become too much for him and he bolted out of the swing doors, leaving the large tattooed woman to watch the unfolding drama with a bovine placidity, still chewing her gum like cud.

So this, Victoria mused, was Albert's old flame, Patricia, sister of the equally bonkers Morris. She could only marvel at what on earth Mr Podger senior must have been like to produce these two offspring. They had their mother Martha's stubbornness, but that was about it. Their looks and their dramatic temperament certainly came from the paternal line.

"So," said Albert eventually, "why are you here, Patricia?"

She blew out her cheeks as if it was all too, too boring. "Same as you, I reckon."

Victoria frowned. "Really? Were you at the party?"

Patricia rounded on her, mimicking her voice and accent. "Oh, absolutely, dahhhling! But I wasn't hob-nobbing it with your London pals, I was helping with the washing-up out the back with the lackeys, don't you know?" Victoria felt like she'd been slapped. What a vile woman.

"Now, now, Patricia, there's no need to take on so," said Albert with a smile. "I don't remember seeing you either. I went into the catering tent to ask everyone to come out and wait for the police to arrive, and you weren't there."

"Yeah, well!" She folded her arms, instantly defensive. "Actually, I'd nipped out for a ciggie round the back, and was having a chat to our Morris over the fence. Soon as I realised there was trouble afoot and the plods were being called, I was out of there. I'm no fool." She looked quite pleased with herself.

Victoria was having great difficulty in imagining how Albert had ever, even in his wildest youth, been attracted to, let alone gone out with, this harridan of a woman. But then, take thirty years off her and about four stone in weight, and she had to admit she may well have been an attractive wild wisp of a girl. Yes, she could see it.

"What are you lookin' at?" Victoria was jolted back to the present to see Patricia's dark and menacing face far too close to her own.

She managed a smile and swallowed. "Actually, I was thinking how alike you and Morris are. I had a nice long chat to him recently, and he mentioned you," she lied.

"You did? He did?" Patricia mulled this over. "Yeah, well I expect he was trying his charms on you. He likes posh birds."

Sergeant Pickworth returned to his seat. "Miss Podger," he said, "just take a seat and someone will be out to see you directly."

"Oh will they? Well, I might, or I might not still be 'ere." She flounced over to a seat near Albert and flopped down into it. "'Tis all a waste of bleddy time! I mean, I knew that red-faced git Giles. What a plonker! He'd been right rude to Mother, so I won't be shedding no tears over 'im. Fact, given the chance, I'd have smacked him right in the chops! But that young girl, what's her name?"

"Jessica," said Victoria.

"Yeah, Jessica, well, I never knew her. She was just another of the waitresses like me. So I dunno why they think I can have anything to say that will be of any help at all."

"Quite," said Victoria. Albert shot her a glance that very clearly said, 'Shut up!'

"I mean to say, I 'spect lots of folk would like to have poisoned 'im. It was poison, weren't it?"

"That seems to be what everyone is thinking, but they don't know what or how," said Albert.

"But I dunno why anyone would want to poison a young maid. Mind you, she were a looker."

"I thought you said you didn't know her?" snapped Victoria. This coarse woman was really trying her patience.

"I didn't know her, miss hoity-toity, but I knew what her looked like." She brushed back her unruly mane. "I reckon she had a bit of a look of meself from when I was in my prime. What do you reckon, Albert?"

"Right." Albert slapped his hands on his thighs and stood up decisively. "C'mon, Victoria, time we were heading back home."

"Home, eh? You living together then?" Patricia looked crestfallen.

"You could say as much," said Albert, with a contented smile, as he took Victoria's arm and steered her firmly towards the doors. "And how's your Gary anyway, Patricia? He at home at the moment, or still residing at Her Majesty's pleasure?"

The last thing Victoria heard before the doors swung shut was, "An' you can bugger off an' all!"

The journey back to Swaddlecombe was tense, with neither Victoria nor Albert speaking. Just before they reached the village, Albert pulled into a gateway and switched off the engine. "Well, I'm sorry, maid. You must think I'm a strange fellow."

Victoria looked at him, embarrassed that he knew her thoughts and decided to lie. "Not at all. Why do you say that?"

"Oh, come on! You must be thinking what the hell did he ever see in a rude, bloated, ignorant old trout like that!"

"Well," Victoria suppressed a smile, "that's possibly a little harsh, but I suspect she's changed somewhat since you knew her."

Albert sighed. "She has that. Can hardly believe it's the same woman. Her was dainty, black-haired, like a pretty little gypsy maid. Always had a quick temper, but generally, her was a sweet little thing and great fun. I reckon that Morris hasn't helped."

"What was their father like? They don't seem very much like Martha."

Albert snorted. "Old Frank? Daft as a bleddy brush! No side to him, though. Spent most of his life in the Swaddle Arms, or in the hedge down near the mill." Victoria was puzzled. Albert grinned at the recollection. "He used to cycle to and from the pub and he was usually so soused that he'd topple off into the hedge at the bend before the mill. Sometimes he'd stay there all night. Lots of locals still refer to it as Frank's corner to this day." He shook his head. "He were a dark and handsome youth, so they get their looks from him, but he was a quiet sort. I reckon it's all down to that Morris. He's not entirely right, you know."

Victoria sighed. "Yes, I did get that impression. He did seem, well, strange, in a weirdly compelling sort of way."

Albert started the engine again. "Yes, well, maid, you just remember he's a nutter, and you steer clear of him, all right?"

"Yes, sir!" Victoria gave him a mock salute and felt ridiculously pleased to have her knight in shining armour to protect her. "Oh, could we stop at the shop, do you think? I need some milk and bread."

"You never thought of buying a freezer and stocking up? You spend your life in and out of that place! I reckon you really only go in for the gossip."

"That's a rotten thing to say, Albert. But it is also mostly true!"

They parked outside the shop and both looked in puzzlement at the strange black arrangement in Lavender's bargain bucket. "Oh my," said Albert, "that looks a bad sign!"

"Goodness, is it some sort of gothic theme? Oh, hang on, do you think it's a tribute?"

"Tribute?"

"Well, the murders?"

Albert shrugged. "Knowing Lavender, it could be anything, but I suspect you're right. You'd better go and find out then."

"Aren't you coming in with me?"

Albert shook his head firmly. "Nope. I shall sit here in peace and read my copy of 'Farmer's Weekly', thank you very much!"

Victoria climbed out of the car and went into the shop, glancing at the black basket arrangement as she passed. It seemed to be an eclectic mix of items, all essentially black. There was an old-fashioned plimsoll, black ribbons, some black clothing Victoria couldn't readily identify, a black pen and several books with black covers.

The shop's doorbell clanged as she entered and, as usual, all eyes turned to see the newcomer.

"Oh 'tis Victoria!" said a familiar voice, and Victoria spotted Jean over by the veg section. The triplets were all in attendance, and Lavender was wearing black armbands, as well as black gloves and a black hat. The rest of her attire was much as always, multi-coloured and interestingly layered.

"We've just been saying what a tragedy it is," said Dahlia in hushed tones from behind the cheese counter.

"Indeed," said Victoria, not entirely sure where the conversation was heading, but assuming it concerned the Peacocks' tragedy.

"That poor young thing. In the prime of her life," said Iris, arranging tins on a back shelf.

"I don't think she'd even reached her prime. Her was only just eighteen," added Jean, shaking her head. "Poor young thing."

"Did you know her well then? Had she grown up in the village?" Victoria really knew nothing about the girl.

"Well, sort of. She didn't attend the local school, of course, she went to Lady Mary's in Exeter." Dahlia's tone was confiding.

"Oh, I see. You knew her parents then?"

Iris chewed the end of her pen as she noted down the stock of tins precariously stacked in every available space. "Well, no. They didn't come in here much. More your Waitrose sort of people, I think it's fair to say. Wouldn't you, Dahlia?"

Dahlia nodded. "Oh yes. Definitely Waitrose, dear, without a doubt."

As so often happened Lavender, with her deep voice and uncomplicated delivery, summed the whole thing up. "They were snobs, you know. But they went to our church so that makes them one of us."

Iris fluttered and coughed. "Well really, dear, I don't think you need to be quite so, er, blunt about it."

Lavender gave a huge slow shrug. "I'm only repeating what you say. It's nothing new." Her eyes, made large by her steel-rimmed spectacles, were owl-like when she turned her gaze on Victoria. "I saw you looking at my tribute. Did you like it?"

"Oh yes," said Victoria earnestly. "I assume all the items have some special relevance."

Lavender nodded. "Of course. She was very good at sport, was Jessica." Jean made a squawk of agreement, but not in a good way. "I mean gymnastics," said Lavender firmly.

"You could certainly say that!" tittered Jean, and covered her mouth.

"She represented the county, so there's the plimsoll. She was a keen reader, so there are books and she had long hair, so I put in the ribbons."

"Ah, I see," said Victoria, and hoped that was the end of it.

"Now the clothing –" continued Lavender, but Dahlia had heard enough and shushed her sister and asked Victoria what she'd come in to buy. "That's all very well Lavender, dear, but we are a

128

shop and I am sure Victoria came in here for a reason."

"I know I did, but it's completely gone out of my head," she confessed. "Oh, hang on – bread and milk – that was it!"

"I'm afraid we haven't got any of the skinny stuff in. There's no call for it, you see, dear," said Dahlia, as she said every time Victoria asked for skimmed milk.

"Oh well, semi-skimmed will do. And any bread that you have left. I realise it's a bit late."

"You're in luck. We've got a nice granary left and a crusty white. Which would you prefer?"

"I'll take both as Albert can always freeze one of them for later." She pulled out her purse and paid.

"I can see him in the car," said Lavender in her dulcet tones. "Doesn't he want to come in?"

"I think he's a bit tired. We've been down at the police station making our statement and – "as soon as she'd said it, she realised it was the wrong thing to say. There was a collective intake of breath and four pairs of eyes bored into her.

Before the inquisition could start the shop door flew open, sending the bell into a further frenzy of jangling. "So!" boomed India. "We meet again. Or are you following me? I seem to bump into you everywhere I go."

Victoria scowled at the woman. How very large and loud she was. "Well, considering I was here first, I don't see how I could be following you and actually, this is the country. It's called a 'community' and it is quite common to bump into your neighbours on a regular basis." If the triplets and Jean didn't breathe soon, Victoria thought, they'll be going down like skittles.

India looked at her for a moment and then her face broke into a wide and rather attractive toothy grin. "Well said! Sorry, you're quite right, of course."

Chapter 6

There was a sigh as the triplets breathed again, although their eyes continued to look like organ stops. "This is India Peacock," explained Victoria. "Giles Peacock's sister." It seemed impossible for their eyes to get any larger, but they did, with their mouths now turning into equally round shapes as they all said, "Oh!" in awe at this new piece of information.

India gave them an uncertain smile. "Well, yes, my poor late brother, that is." She turned to Victoria. "That friend of yours is an absolute gold-digging bitch, if you don't mind my saying."

Now it was Victoria's turn to goggle, while the triplets were nearly fainting from excitement. "Is she? Oh, right, well I haven't really seen her for a few years, so I'm not actually that au fait with the situation and –"

"And as for that bloody Freddie character – Christ! We can all see what's going on there!" she snorted. "Got 'criminal' tattooed across his forehead, that one."

"No! He never has?" gasped Jean. "Well, I never!"

"No, not literally, woman – metaphorically!" India snapped. "And if they think they are going to get all the family's money, they can think again!" She banged her fist on the counter and Dahlia gave a little shriek. India looked at her as if she were mad. "Do you sell whisky?" All three of them shook their heads in unison. "Damn."

"If you pop over to the Swaddle Arms, I'm sure Roger Mudge will sell you a bottle," said Victoria, hoping this would make her hurry up and leave before she gave the triplets any more juicy gossip.

The doorbell clanged again and Victoria groaned inwardly. It was Sylvia, mad Morris's lady friend. Could things get any worse, she wondered. Dahlia cleared her throat and said, "Sylvia Black, what do you want?" snappishly. Victoria had never heard her address anyone like that before.

"What's it to you?" Sylvia sneered back, rather idiotically Victoria thought.

"It's my shop, that's what it is, and you are not welcome here."

"Ah, shut up!" said Sylvia, which set off a great deal of clucking and tutting from the triplets. "Anyway, I don't want none of the junk you sell in here. I only come in to say to you," she prodded India in her well-upholstered chest, "to keep away from our farm and my Morris!" Victoria wanted to run for cover and contemplated hurling herself behind the counter rather as they did in westerns when the shoot-out began.

"How dare you!" India seemed to swell in size. "You common little tart! How dare you touch me and what the hell are you talking about? Who are you?"

"Don't you call me a tart, you – you…" the need for a suitable word seemed too much for Sylvia, so she opted for an easy one, " – cow! I seen you at the stuck-up Peacocks' place! I seen you! Me and my Morris, we live in the farm next door and – "

India sneered into the slighter woman's face. "Oh, now why doesn't that surprise me? That absolute eyesore, that apology for a farm, that junkyard of trash. Get away before I call the police, coming in here, making threats – get out!"

To back up India's words Dahlia, closely followed in formation by Iris and Lavender, now appeared brandishing a broom. "Be off with you!" shouted Dahlia. Knowing when she was outnumbered, Sylvia glared at them all and stalked out of the shop, slamming the door so hard that the bell fell off and landed in a box of carrots.

Chapter 7

"Come on, come on, write, write, write," muttered Victoria to herself, "and you, Moss, can just wait. You've had one walk today. Now sit quietly and behave while I get this wretched thing done, then maybe we can play."

Moss gave her an enormous guilt-inducing look, huffed, then puffed and lay down with a resigned "Wuff".

Victoria's latest article on candle-making in rural Devon was nearly complete. A local company called 'Wee Willie Winkie' had been very helpful and the photos were looking amazing. The light had been just right that day and their wonderfully rustic premises had lent themselves to lots of very artistic shots. She hoped the editor would use at least some of the clever ones, not just boring product shots.

She had been amazed to discover how alive and kicking candle-making was in the south-west. Somehow she had assumed candles were mainly made by machine nowadays and in dull factory settings. Not so, it seemed. The idyllic farmstead had barns and outhouses all given over to the manufacture of wonderful herb-scented candles and these were very much handmade. The team running the company ranged in age from sixteen to seventy and all seemed equally enthusiastic.

As the last few words were checked and an email composed, she had her finger poised over the send button and jumped when the phone rang. Hastily pressing send, she picked up the phone.

"Hi, Tristram, is that you?" The phone number of the interior designer she was using had come up on the phone, but she was often contacted by his assistants if he was too busy to bother with such mundane things as her cushions and spare bedroom curtains.

"Sweetheart, darling, it is indeed. The most divine range of country florals has just swooped in and obviously I immediately thought of you and your fabulous cottage. My dear, your back bedroom is positively screaming for the elderflower and bramble colourway."

Victoria had got used to his superlatives or, as Albert unkindly put it, drivel, so she just said, "Tristram, I love the small floral ditzy print we chose, really. I am very happy just as I am. When are they going to be ready?"

"Ahh, well thereby hangs a tale. The company has decided to discontinue that print and I am struggling to get stock for you, so perhaps a change of plan?"

Oh, I see, thought Victoria, you mean you can't get the fabric so how about this new lot that just came in? She smiled. Maybe her spare room was screaming for elderflower and she just hadn't noticed.

"Why don't you pop a sample in the post, then I'll get back to you?"

"Oh my dear, such poor service, I wouldn't dream of it. I am en route to a house not too far from yours. Do you know the Peacocks?"

"What, Caroline Peacock? Are you sure? I wouldn't have thought she had time for interior changes right now."

"Oh, my dear, Caroline and I go way back to our Chelsea days. I just drop in without an appointment. She always understands and I need to deliver the last of her silk cushions. Truthfully, they are simply to die for. If you know her then do ask to see the third guest bedroom next time you are there – very 'you', I would have said!"

"Tristram, can I ask, you do know what has happened recently to poor Caroline? You really don't sound as if you do."

"Oh, you mean the Freddie thing? Yes, she told me all about it. Much like being a hairdresser my job, you know. Clients always confide. I do feel sad for Caroline, disliking her husband as much as she does, but there's nothing she can do about it really, poor baby. He is a rather hateful man! Mind you I have my doubts about Freddie. I'd say he was after her money, but what would we know? They may be star-crossed lovers."

Victoria took a deep breath. Obviously Tristram was not up to speed with recent events and she braced herself for an emotional storm. "Actually, Tristram, I think you might want to rethink your visit. Caroline has been through a lot recently, erm, perhaps you don't read the local paper? Giles was murdered at their house not long ago and the police are being, well, difficult. It's too long a story to relate over the phone, but I don't think now is an ideal time for silk cushions."

There was a pause on the other end of the line and then a measured "Oh... My... God" and another pause. "What – murdered as in 'dead'? I don't believe it! You're kidding me!" His voice rose to a squeal.

Victoria felt faintly annoyed at his response, but it was really no less than she'd expected. "No, I'm not kidding Tristram. Albert and I were there when he was killed. It was awful, actually, and they are no closer to finding out who did it. Very difficult times for Caroline, although I must say, I think she is rallying well. Currently she believes she was the intended second victim, and not the poor young girl that died with Giles."

"Someone else died, too?" he hissed excitedly down the phone.

"My God! I think I'd better bring the fabric swatches over to you, sweetheart. It sounds as though you could do with a cup of tea and a chat about curtains. Are you in this afternoon? No, no, sorry, damn, make that tomorrow morning – are you there mid-morning time?"

"Yes, Tristram, I am. You come on over with the elderflower and bramble. I'm sure it will cheer me up no end." Victoria smiled to herself at his pathetic excuse to get all the gossip under the guise of studying fabric swatches.

She heard the back door close and Moss began a torrent of barks and Victoria jumped. "Got to go, Tristram. Someone's arrived – see you in the morning – bye!" She turned in her chair and was relieved to see the reverend. "Saved by the bell. Thank you, Edwin!"

"I'm so sorry, I should have knocked rather than just barged in. I didn't realise you were on the phone."

"No problem, I was keen to end the call anyway. Shall I put the kettle on? Can you stay a while?"

"That would be marvellous, Victoria. I'm rather keen to ask your opinion about something."

"That sounds intriguing. Come and have a seat. Moss, no Moss, down!"

"Don't worry. Moss and I are great pals, aren't we, old chap?" The rev stroked Moss's ears and the puppy closed his eyes in ecstasy.

They all settled at the kitchen table. Victoria felt much happier having sent off her article. It always preyed on her mind until it was done each month, and she always enjoyed the reverend's company anyway.

"So how are you keeping, my dear?"

"Not too bad. I feel particularly good today as I am up to date with all my articles and blogs and so sunshine and no work makes me a happy bunny!"

"Marvellous! I know the feeling well! I have the same weekly battle with my sermons. Sometimes inspiration just will not come. Very trying."

"Anyway, what can I do for you? You mentioned you wanted to talk about something?"

"Yes, I hope you won't think this odd, but I seem to remember a wild plant book in your aunt's collection and I wanted to refer to it to follow a hunch that I had. It's, er, half-remembered botanical stuff and it's been niggling me all morning. Would it be possible to have a look?"

"That's easily sorted. Just hang on a second." Victoria went to the bookshelves under the stairs. She had tried to sort her aunt's reference books into this area of the house, although she was never quite sure why she might want pages and pages of out-of-date information when she could look anything up on the internet in a moment, but they were lovely books despite their age and rather quaint inaccuracies.

Britain's Wild Plants and Their Dangers. She checked the date of publishing and raised her eyebrows.

Victoria returned and handed the large, rather dusty book to Edwin. "A bit rusty and out-of-date, 1903 to be precise, but hopefully not too many extinct variants!"

"Ah, now then, let me see…" He consulted the index and riffled through the pages and then said "Ah!" He turned the book round to face Victoria and, with a pudgy forefinger, pointed to Water Dropwort.

Puzzled, Victoria said, "Why are we looking at Water Dropwort in a book over a hundred years old?"

"Because I think it is the plant that killed Giles. This one," he tapped the page, "Hemlock Water Dropwort – Oneanthe crocata – looks just like cow parsley to me. Here, read this, Victoria."

"The water dropworts are a genus of plants in the family Apiaceae. Several of the species are extremely poisonous, the active poison being oenanthotoxin. The most notable of these is O. crocata, which lives in damp, marshy ground, and resembles celery. One root is sufficient to kill a cow, and human fatalities are also known. It has been referred to as the most poisonous of all British plants and is considered particularly dangerous because of its similarity to several edible plants."

Victoria sat back. "Well, I never knew there were such dangerous things around! What makes you think this is the plant? Or indeed that it was a plant?"

"Well, I remember you saying that they were both nibbling away at opposite ends of a piece of celery, which stuck in my mind as it seems quite a feat to achieve. Also, it seems other people have said that they were feeding each other and I believe several have mentioned the celery boats. Now the stems of this plant do indeed look just like celery and are extremely poisonous. It doesn't take too much to cause a fatality and they certainly chomped through quite a bit in their ill-fated flirting."

"Good grief! But who would know where this stuff grows and that it was poisonous?"

Edwin chuckled. "Oh there are plenty of locals that have this level of plant knowledge. Hemlock is really quite well known and that's the same family; lots of it growing around the area, I should think."

Victoria was intrigued but not utterly convinced. "Well, perhaps you should take the book to the police, see what they think?"

Edwin looked dismayed. "Oh dear, I was rather hoping that you would."

Victoria sighed. "I don't think they would appreciate me

sticking my nose in with 'helpful' suggestions. Of course if we came across something really concrete – but as we aren't sure, I think it would be much better coming from you. You have gravitas, Edwin, and are a pillar of the local community."

Edwin laughed. "Well, it sounds as if I will just have to 'man up' as the youngsters say, and drop in on my way home. I just thought this might be a clue to help solve the case."

Victoria shrugged. "Who knows? You could be right. I suppose it's better to mention it than not."

Edwin 'accidentally' managed another slice of the chocolate cake that Victoria had laid out and they were chatting amiably when the phone rang just as Albert came through the back door.

"Oh, for heaven's sake, no peace," said Victoria. "It's been like Piccadilly Circus here this morning."

"Well, I'm pleased to see you, too!" Albert sat down at the table and cut himself a large slice of cake.

"Hello?" said Victoria into the phone, "Caroline? How nice to hear from you... so soon."

"I'm sorry to be a pain, Tori, but I have no other friends to turn to." Victoria wondered how empty her life must be if their relationship amounted to her main friendship. "Would you mind, I know it's a nuisance, but the police have just left and I really need a girly shoulder to cry on. It's all so terrible just now." Caroline sounded genuinely low.

Victoria couldn't stay hard-hearted for long and Caroline's tears seemed less fabricated than some of her recent behaviour. "Shall I pop over for a cup of tea this afternoon, Caroline? I'm afraid I can't stay long. I may have to bring my dog Moss with me as I really can't leave him for too many hours."

"Oh, that's no problem, Freddie adores dogs and I am sure they can whizz off into the fields and do whatever people do with dogs in fields." Victoria made a mental note to ask Albert to dogsit instead and was annoyed, having said she would visit, to find that the dreadful Freddie was still there.

"I'll be over about two, just for a quick cuppa and a chat."

"Thank you, thank you. I just don't know how I would have coped without you these last few days!" she said and hung up. Victoria was sure this was a slight exaggeration, but she found it hard to say no to anyone.

Albert was more than happy to take Moss with him for an afternoon on the farm, so Victoria left on her own to visit Caroline. They had never been particularly close friends in London and she had no desire to spend a great deal of time with the woman now, but with the recent tragedy, she felt she should try and be supportive.

Caroline was waiting for her at the front door and welcomed her as though they hadn't seen each other for years, not hours or days.

"Do come in. I have made the most amazing Long Island tea – knocks your socks off but tastes divine!"

"Sorry, Caroline, I can't drink, I'm driving."

"Oh don't be such a bore. Do you fancy staying the night?"

"Erm, no, I'm sorry, plans already made for this evening. But I'd love a long cold lemonade or something."

Caroline pouted and Victoria followed her through into the enormous kitchen. Much as Victoria envied Caroline the large American style-fridge and the acres of worktop, bearing in mind the minuscule amount she cooked, it would be rather pointless.

Caroline flung open a fridge entirely filled with bottles of wine, champagne, beers and, much to Victoria's relief, bottles of mixers including lemonade and tonic. "Oh marvellous. Thanks, Caroline, I'll have a lemonade with ice, please."

"Fine, be a party pooper, but you won't mind if I have some of my exquisite Long Island cocktail?"

Caroline took a half full bottle of lemonade out of the fridge and put it on the worktop. "The ice comes out of that dispenser on the door. Do help yourself."

Victoria realised she was truly being sulked at, but she smiled to herself and added ice to a glass and poured the lemonade.

"Come on, I have the garden furniture out. It's still lovely and warm, and the umbrella always reminds me of the south of France."

They wandered out to the garden and despite herself, Victoria felt relaxed as the autumn sun warmed her face. The view, now starting to turn from rich summer green to deep autumn gold, stretched ahead of her. The British countryside was magical all year round, but the start of autumn was always something special.

"You said the police had been and that it was a difficult visit?"

Caroline clutched her forehead dramatically. "Oh God, it was. They're horrible people. I'd hate to be such a suspicious person all the time. They have got it into their heads that just because it wasn't long ago I increased Giles' life insurance policy it means I must have had awful things planned! Complete nonsense. I didn't even realise we had increased his policy. Freddie has been handling all that kind of dull stuff." She waved dismissively. "Life's too short, I say!"

"Sorry? Freddie increased Giles' life insurance and you didn't know?"

"Not really, no. I don't listen to half of what Freddie says." She gave a low giggle. "Wasn't really what I got him for, if you get my drift."

"Well, frankly, Caroline, I'm not surprised the police have their suspicions! If your lover ups your husband's life insurance policy just before he is killed, it does seem a little bit suspect to me."

"Oh,. Freddie wouldn't hurt a fly. He isn't even in the same room as people, mentally, at the moment. He's far away on his Shetland Island making plans for his big adventure."

"I'm not with you, sorry," said Victoria, thinking this was all sounding rather odd.

"The Shetlands, Freddie's dream destination. He has a company up there that's going to make millions before long. Brilliant ideas man is Freddie – well, and brilliant at a few other things, too!" Caroline gave a breathy laugh and swallowed the rest of her Long Island tea.

Although not wanting to be prudish, Victoria was beginning to feel the whole Caroline and Freddie thing was really quite distasteful.

"What on earth has Freddie found to do up in Shetland to make a fortune? I can only think of sheep, tiny croft houses and beautiful scenery, none of which would earn you much."

"Ah, but that's why he's such a genius, Tori. It has nothing to do with the land. Oh no, this is the sea."

"What, natural gas? Surely not oil?"

Caroline frowned as if she couldn't make the connection. "No! Diving – there are thousands, well make that hundreds, of shipwrecks laden with gold and jewels at the bottom of the sea up there. Freddie has a diving school where he teaches people to dive and then once they are trained, organises dives out to the sites of wrecks he has found. They'll be up there in their droves once he has all the facilities built, even a hotel apparently."

Victoria paused before making a calculated guess. "Don't tell me, he would like you to invest in his business."

"Oh absolutely, and I am trying to think of some deserving friends that I ought to rope in, too." She laughed. "Rope in, that's clever as it's going to be money for old rope. We'll be rolling in it before long. Freddie really is a whizz kid."

Victoria thought that far from being a whizz kid Freddie was probably a complete con artist. Despite her reservations about Caroline, she felt sorry for her. She'd obviously been so bullied and belittled by Giles that she believed all the nonsense Freddie was telling her, thinking she was in love. To anyone outside their sorry little affair, it was obvious that all he saw was a sad, moneyed, middle-aged woman.

Caroline poured herself another drink and proceeded to wave the glass about as she talked about the wonders of Freddie, her distress at the police questions seemingly forgotten.

Victoria sneaked a look at her watch. This was pointless and she ought to be getting on. In the distance, she heard a cock crowing and surreptitiously glanced over at the Podgers' farm next door. She could just glimpse the odd flash of colour as various chickens scratched about in their runs. Hmmm, perhaps her journey might not be a complete waste of time. Her nose for a story was twitching and she chose to ignore Albert's warnings about steering clear of Morris.

Caroline, now on her third Long Island iced tea, was becoming distinctly slurred and Victoria found making her excuses and leaving not too difficult. With much waving and promises of popping in again soon, she left Caroline, who was already starting to look drowsy, reclining under the sun umbrella. Victoria drove out of the drive and turned into the Podgers' almost immediately adjacent.

Parking her car next to the barn, and out of Caroline's view, Victoria felt rather deceitful, but it wasn't her neighbourly feud and she wanted to source her next blog. She was relieved not to see either the awful Morris or the bonkers Sylvia and soon spotted Martha's stout figure in the distance, trotting between various sheds and hen houses.

Martha saw her just as she came out of one of the chicken coops, clutching a basket almost overflowing with eggs. "Hello!" said Victoria brightly, but determined not to come across as the townie idiot she had done on previous occasions.

Martha squinted at her, brows knitted, and then eventually said, "Oh, it's you again."

Not put off by this less than rapturous welcome, Victoria ploughed on. "I'm sorry for just turning up unannounced, but I wondered if you could spare some time to talk to me about your hens? I'd like to write an article for my magazine."

Martha stopped in her tracks and fixed her with a beady eye. "Would you now?" She started off towards the house, her stumpy legs in their wellingtons moving at a surprisingly fast pace. Victoria trotted alongside, feeling like some door-stepping journalist after a scoop. Suddenly the woman stopped and Victoria had to swerve back to face her again. "What's in it for me? A fee? Publicity?"

Right, thought Victoria, now we are talking turkey, or more accurately, chicken. "I don't have a budget for a fee, Mrs Podger, but you would get a lot of publicity. I can include a website address, err, if you have one, or an email or…"

"I'm not a complete bloody moron. While it's true I don't have a website, I am on email, I does Facebook and I've even been known to tweet," she snapped. "And don't make no smart comments about tweeting and my hens, neither."

Victoria grinned. You had to admire the old girl; she was no slouch. "Well, that sounds good. I'd reference your links at the end of the article. 'Country Days', the magazine I write for, is published monthly and has the highest readership figures in the country lifestyle market." She was trying hard to sound the professional journalist.

"I reckon I've seen it in Westerley, in that big newsagent in the precinct. Course, it's mostly twee nonsense, but I reckon people with more money than sense buys the thing and if they wants to spend their money with me, that's fine."

Thanks for the endorsement, thought Victoria. "There is also an online edition, so people could link directly through to you and – "

Martha had started walking towards the farmhouse again. "You come in and have a cup of tea and we'll discuss it."

Victoria hesitated, remembered her previous visit and the smells and unidentifiable detritus on the floors and hoped she had the stomach for it. "Oh, right, thank you." She hastened after the receding figure and took a deep breath before she entered the hallway after her.

"Keep yer shoes on, 'tis all muck and grime out here. That Morris is a pig!" she said over her shoulder. "Kitchen is altogether safer. I had a good old muck out last weekend, so it's not too bad now."

Once Victoria's eyes had adjusted to the shock of the colour scheme, it was indeed, not too bad. Almost every surface of the kitchen had been painted in bottle green gloss paint, while the walls were a paler green. It looked like a cross between an operating theatre and the local council offices. Victoria thought of Tristram and his elderflower and bramble colourway and suspected he would quite possibly faint if he were with her now. But then again, perhaps it would be classed as 'rustic retro 'and be the focus of his next window display. On balance, she thought probably not.

Martha shooed the large ginger cat off the table and tipped an elderly Jack Russell out of one of the two sagging armchairs next to the Rayburn. "Go on, Nipper, bugger off!" she said to the dog, but in quite a gentle way. She filled a blackened kettle and slapped it down on top of the Rayburn with a clang. Victoria thought of her own Rayburn, as yet still unlit, and knew that she would soon have to grapple with it as autumn drew in.

"Tea all right?" barked Martha. "I don't hold with coffee."

"Oh yes, fine, thank you. Not too strong, though, please." Martha shot her a withering glance that said 'of course not, you namby-pamby townie' as clearly as if she'd spoken aloud.

Victoria gazed at her surroundings, her writer's magpie eye taking in the details of old enamel utensils, much like her aunt's, and weird bits of tubing and pieces of metal that she guessed were to do with farming, and storing them away for future use.

"Bet you've never seen a kitchen like this before?" said Martha, following her gaze.

"Er, no, not exactly."

"He's an idiot in many ways, but my Morris knows how to wield a paintbrush, I'll give him that. Inherited that from his father, he did. Lovely smooth finish." She ran her hand appreciatively across the worktop. "Hell of a durable as well, this here paint. Chose the colour meself." She beamed at Victoria. "It's not just you posh lot that does all this interior design stuff, you know!"

Two large mugs of tea were plonked onto the table and Victoria was relieved to see hers was of a pale gold while Martha's looked more like treacle. "Thank you," she said and took a sip. "If I could arrange to come over for half a day and interview you, take notes and so on. I don't need to hold you up, just follow you round, if that's OK?"

"'Spect so," said Martha and sucked at her tea with an extended top lip, rather like a chimp.

"If I can, I'll take photos at the same time, but I might have to come back again later." A sudden crack of gunfire, alarmingly close, made Victoria yelp and leap out of her chair, her tea slopping onto the table.

"My, you'm jumpy!" said Martha. "That's just our Morris taking a pot shot, fox or rabbit, I 'spect." She grinned at Victoria, who, pink and flustered, was trying to mop up her spilt tea with a tissue. "Don't you worry about that, maid. Duke will lick that up later." She nodded at the ginger cat before continuing. "Our Morris is either shootin' or poisonin'. Goes with the territory when you've got fowl, lots of vermin and pests. I don't reckon you'll want to say too much about that in your article for your genteel readers, will you, maid?" She gave Victoria a gap-toothed grin and her old eyes glittered with mischief.

"Well, I think we've probably covered everything," said Victoria hastily, keen to avoid another encounter with mad Morris, now identified as both a shooter and a poisoner. "What day would suit you next week?"

"Let's say Tuesday, 'bout eleven o'clock?"

"That will be fine." Victoria tapped the date and time into her phone and prepared to leave.

"You brazen hussy!" yelled a male voice, Morris's, Victoria realised with alarm. An answering unintelligible female yell, presumably from Sylvia, was followed by another gunshot. My God, she thought, he's killed her!

"You all right?" Martha was peering at her. "You've gone a bit pale."

"I, er, yes, yes, I'm fine, thank you. See you next week." She scuttled towards the front door, past the tottering piles of papers and magazines, watched by Duke and Nipper. She wanted to get away, but was terrified at the prospect of Morris, now firmly entrenched in her mind as a murderer, lurking outside.

Feeling like a player in some American murder mystery, she slunk out of the farmhouse and ran quickly across to her car, fumbling with the keys in her agitation. At last, she was safely in the driver's seat and she fastened her seatbelt. As she raised her eyes to the wing mirror, preparing to reverse, she screamed. Morris, reflected in it, was smiling at her and waving his hand in a friendly manner.

"Hello again, then," he called through the closed window. Behind him, Victoria could see Sylvia, sullenly sweeping out one of the sheds. So she wasn't dead after all. Victoria took a deep breath and told herself to get a grip. She was becoming hysterical. She lowered her window, just enough to be able to speak to him.

"Hello. My goodness, you made me jump!" She knew she sounded shrill, but managed a fixed smile of greeting and hoped that it passed muster.

"Well, didn't expect to see you here again so soon. Can't keep away?" He leered at her through the window. "Is it my animal magnetism, or my money, I wonders?"

"Morris?" Sylvia called from the distance.

"I'm busy, woman," he snapped before turning back to Victoria. "Well now, I heard you've been helping the police with their enquiries."

Victoria felt her heart skip a beat. "Well, yes, Albert and I were asked to give statements…"

"Albert and I!" He mimicked her voice and accent and moved close to the window again.

Finally, her petrified brain realising how he knew, she added, "Of course, your sister was asked to make a statement, too. I met her at the station. Seems like we are all doing our best to help solve this terrible crime."

"A crime, is it? Well, some of us may see it as a good thing!" He laughed and showed his hideous teeth. "Giles Peacock is no loss to no one, I don't reckon. Not even his snooty wife!"

Victoria was appalled, but kept her outrage firmly under wraps and simply said, "What about young Jessica? Was that a good thing, too?"

He stared at her and rubbed the side of his nose. "Well, no. That was a tragedy, that was." He straightened up and glared off into the distance. "They come to see me, too, you know, the police. Rambling on about poison. I ask you!" He snorted. "Wanted to see if I had any. Me? 'Course I have. Tons of it! Rat poison and all sorts. I said to 'em, you don't know what you're talking about, there's nothing here that would polish off that fat, red-faced pillock like that in the middle of his party." He shook his head and then bent in close to her again. "Rat poison takes time. Nasty stuff. Makes you bleed on the inside, takes days. Agonising, I reckon." He smiled slowly and Victoria found she was holding her breath.

"Anyway, I said to 'em, I said – poisoning, that's a woman's crime! I wouldn't do it like that! I'd've shot the bugger!" He laughed again and shouted across the yard. "Haven't you finished that sweeping out yet, woman? When you've finished, I'll have a bottle of beer. From the fridge, mind, I don't want it warm."

Victoria started the engine and selected reverse. "You off then?" He looked surprised.

She let in the clutch, slowly inching backwards. "I really must get on, articles to write, you know…"

"That offer of a trip to that club in Torbay still stands, I reckon you'd enjoy that, fine woman like you, up on the dance floor, like." He cocked his head towards the house. "That Sylvia, you don't need to worry about her. She does as she's told, no problem, that one. I got 'er right where I wants 'er."

"I'm sure you have, Mr Podger."

"Call me Morris, 'tis more friendly like. And we are friends, aren't we?" His fingers were gripping the top of the window and Victoria feared it might break in the grip of his meaty paw.

Victoria heard the approach of brisk footsteps and Sylvia's shrill voice. "Here you are then, you swine! Here's your bloody beer!" and she emptied it over his head, some of the liquid splashing in through the window and onto Victoria's jeans. "I 'ope it's cold enough for you!"

Victoria shot backwards as Morris roared and turned on Sylvia. As she left the yard she could see them in her mirror, not fighting as she'd thought, but locked in a passionate kiss, Morris like a great bear hunched over the wilting and adoring figure of Sylvia. Dear God, those two were dangerous. They seemed to spark off each other, one of those terrible relationships fuelled by jealousy – lots of rows and fall-outs and then lots of passionate making-up. Thank goodness she had found kind and sensible Albert, her rock.

As she drove carefully home along the narrow lanes, she thought she'd probably phone Martha and cry off their meeting. She didn't think she could deal with Morris for a third time. It seemed to be tempting fate.

Chapter 8

"Is that the mad chicken lady of darkest Devon?"

"No, Gray, it's me!"

"Well, poo to you, you're no fun! Sebastian is shouting 'hello' from the other room, by the way."

"Hello, Seb in the other room! And how are things with you two?"

"Oh, we're both fine, fine. Horrible work levels, but hey, that's the price you pay for being indispensable, or so Seb says. Frankly, I think he's just found a bit of totty at work and lies horribly about working late every night."

Victoria smiled; no change there then. Gray and Sebastian had been such good friends to her during the darkest days while she'd fought breast cancer and they could still cheer her with a quick phone call. Now that the chickens had been replaced and life in the poultry wing of the cottage was good again, they could come down any time, which was a distinct improvement on the last time they rang when she had been panicking they would arrive and there'd be no chickens.

"So when are you coming down then, Gray?"

"Well, that's the point of the phone call, sweet girl. A boring old work thing has come up and so the weekend we thought we were coming down is off and things are looking tight, so it could be another few weeks yet, if that's ok?"

"Gray, it's fine. We will be here whenever. I am looking forward to introducing you to Albert and showing you the village."

"Ooh, he's still the main man then? Exciting! Yes, we can't wait. · I'm sure we won't be able to resist his charms."

"Not sure he's your type, Gray."

"Pah, spoilsport, take away a man's dream, why don't you? Right, I have to get going, hand-shaking, sincere expressions and much grovelling at an Arts Council funding thing tonight. So we'll see you in a few weeks at the outside?"

"Whenever is just fine. Ring me beforehand but, yes, I am usually here."

"I do worry about you mouldering away in the country with all that greenery and nothing ever happening – ugh! But never mind, we'll brighten things up shortly. Bye, sweetheart."

"Bye, Gray and…" but Gray had put down the phone first as he always did. Nothing was ever done at normal speed. He was full of bounce and self-assurance.

Moss started barking as Albert came through the back door.

"Hello, maid, how's your day been?"

"Oh fine, enlivened by a visit from Tristram and his fabric swatches." Albert frowned, confused. "Oh, don't worry – anyway, how was your day?"

"Enough trauma up in main meadow to write a soap opera. Badger tunnelling for England and making a right mess, a stupid bleddy sheep got its head stuck in the fence, as per usual and the latch on the main gate has fallen apart so got to replace that tomorrow. But, other than that, it's been plain sailing all day!" Albert slumped down into one of the kitchen chairs and Victoria took the hint, put the kettle on and retrieved the cake tin for restorative purposes.

"So who was that on the phone?" mumbled Albert through a large mouthful of cake.

"Just Gray, as in Gray and Sebastian. They are both fine, but it'll be about another month before they come down. I guess it doesn't matter really, but I was looking forward to seeing them. Anyway, they have a gap in their calendar coming up soon. So glad we got the chickens sorted!"

"So I'm guessing, maid, that if I said what's for dinner, you'd say 'I don't know – ask Albert?'"

Victoria felt a bit guilty. "I'm sorry, but I have been focussing so much on work today, food, and preparation of same hasn't really been on my mind."

"'Tis OK I guessed it would be that way. We'll go down to the pub."

Victoria sighed. "Shame we haven't got a takeaway nearby that delivers. Reckon it'll be the next century before we get any food delivered here. Would be nice just for once to stay in and get food brought to us." She thought back to her London flat where she was deluged with flyers from assorted takeaways every single day and could probably have ordered and got deliveries from tens of places, if not hundreds.

"But then," she mused, "that's one of the many joys of the countryside – no takeaway and fast food litter ruining the place. Trudy will cook you something nice at the Swaddle Arms, you know that." Still, Victoria did feel rather guilty. Albert looked dead beat and a trip to the pub was not always the most relaxing evening. It rather depended on who else was there.

Victoria need not have worried. The pub was close to empty with nobody to bother them and, after a pint and a chat with Roger, Albert was looking more relaxed. Trudy had flapped round them for a while trying to promote her coffee machine again, but once they had ordered she was off to the kitchen to get cooking. Albert had broken with tradition and had ordered from the specials board and was having a pheasant dish as it was shot locally and this, as Roger had patiently explained to her, was now the open season for pheasants. Victoria decided to be contrary and go vegetarian. Somehow, the thought of tucking into a local pheasant, possibly one she had carefully avoided in one of the lanes, did not appeal to her, so she chose goat's cheese and red pepper pizza.

The door opened and a scattering of autumn leaves blew in ahead of the next customer. The wind must have got stronger since they arrived. Victoria looked over at the newcomers and saw to her horror it was Caroline and Freddie.

"Coooee, Tori!" Caroline hailed them loudly across the near empty bar.

Victoria groaned and murmured, "Oh no, I'm so sorry Albert!" under her breath.

"Don't worry, maid. Our food'll be along soon. We can just chat for a moment," said Albert and squeezed her hand in solidarity.

"Well, what a coincidence meeting you here! Regulars, are you?" Victoria wasn't sure that she believed the display Caroline was putting on. She was overly chatty and her eyes looked too bright. It was the only pub in the village, so it was quite likely she'd be a regular, surely?

"Yes, it's been a busy day. No time to cook and, well, Trudy is a pretty good little chef, isn't she, Roger?"

Roger came along the bar and joined them. "Yep, my Trude can cook up a fair storm. Like to see the menu?"

"Well, what a lovely idea. We haven't eaten a thing since breakfast, have we, Freddie? Perhaps we could join you both? And two double vodka and tonics, please."

Victoria's sinking feeling had now officially sunk and she was trying not to feel annoyed. It felt as though Caroline was invading her world and butting into a part of her life that wasn't meant to include bonkers ex-work colleagues from her former life.

"Not a problem!" beamed Roger. "I'm sure we can amalgamate your orders. My Trude can work miracles, but having said that, it might be best if you order quite quickly and that will make life easier for her."

"Oh well, that's simple then," said Caroline. "We'll just have whatever they ordered."

"Great," said Roger and disappeared.

Albert laughed. "Well here's hoping we haven't ordered anything you'll hate!"

Ignoring his comment, Caroline clutched Albert's arm like an old, close friend and said, "So, Albert, you've met Freddie, haven't you?" She gave a shrill little laugh and smiled widely. Victoria thought it was amazing that Caroline could gloss over the fact that the occasion that they'd met was when her murdered husband's body was lying nearby, shrouded in a tablecloth. But then maybe that's what you have to do to 'move on' or 'get closure', or whatever it was, thought Victoria. But no, she was kidding herself. No one normal would act like this.

Clapping his hands and rubbing them together enthusiastically, Freddie said, "So, Albert, busy time of year on the land then?" Victoria rolled her eyes and wondered what reaction this was going to provoke from a tired and as yet unfed Albert.

"Always busy, always summat to do, you know," said Albert, quite congenially, thought Victoria. It could have been worse.

"Gotta lot of acres then?" Freddie continued.

"More than enough to keep body and soul together, to be sure. Mainly beef cattle, a few sheep, not a lot of arable."

"Ah, lovely! I've always loved sheep," said Caroline wistfully as though she were a small child asking to visit a petting zoo. "Actually no, I love lambs, not sheep," she added as an afterthought.

"Wouldn't mind a show round if you ever have time," said Freddie. "Sounds quite a place from what we've heard, what with all the land, and cars, of course."

Trudy appeared at that moment with the cutlery, napkins and condiments and, keen as ever, launched herself into the thick of the group. "How lovely to meet old friends at a favourite watering hole," she said. "Such a joy! Your meals will be out in a moment. Right, so who's having the pheasant and which of you are having pizza?"

Caroline and Freddie flashed agonised looks at each other and Victoria found herself hoping they hated goat's cheese and pheasant, but then reprimanded herself for being uncharitable.

"Oh, Freddie will have the pizza," said Caroline sweetly., "Never can resist pizza, can you, Fred, night or day? And two more double vodka and tonics, please."

"Right-oh. Here are the steak knives for the pheasant then, not that you really need them. Long slow cooking, that's the secret. I think you're in for a treat!" Trudy laid everything in its place on the table and then swept off to continue the preparations.

A group of six had arrived and were laughing noisily at the bar. Leaning forward to make himself heard, Freddie said, "So, you into sport then, Albert?" He was clearly trying hard to make conversation.

"Me, nah, no time for games really, get enough exercise round the farm. Like a spot of shooting if it's on offer and always fancied myself as a rally driver, but that never happened. You into anything, football or rugby?"

"Not really a sportsman, me, but yeah, I reckon I could get into the hunting, shooting side of life in time. My main interest is diving. Ever done any scuba or snorkelling, that kind of thing?"

"Not much of a one for the sea. I'm a countryman and a

landlubber. You go to hot exotic places for your diving then?"

Suddenly Victoria realised just what Freddie's game was. Caroline was staying quiet and gazing sickeningly at her lover. It would be interesting to see how Albert handled things. He often surprised her with his ability to read people and situations. She'd filled him in on the Shetland thing only yesterday, so he had probably twigged what was afoot.

"Oh no, there's no need for that. Much more exciting projects right here in the British Isles, and I'm not one for long flights, me."

There was a lull as a few more people came into the pub and ordered their drinks before sitting down. Trudy brought the first two meals and Roger wasn't far behind with the second pair.

"Right, goat's cheese and red pepper for you, sir, I believe and yours, Victoria. And the pheasant breast for you, madam, and yours, Albert. Can I get anything for anyone?"

Freddie was chortling away and slapping his thigh, "The old ones are always the best. Can't beat a good pair of peasant's breasts."

There was an uncomfortable silence and then Caroline laughed dutifully. "Well, this looks delicious. Well chosen, you two, and Freddie, how lovely to have a totally vegetarian pizza for a change. And another round of drinks, please, my man." Victoria smiled as she cut into her pizza and watched as Freddie stared at his in disbelief.

The pizza was delicious and from the first mouthful she knew she had chosen well. Freddie however, was not so enthusiastic, looking as if he'd like to put a peg on his nose to escape the smell of the goat's cheese. He worked hard at looking busy eating the accompanying side salad and the crust of the pizza.

"So, as I was saying, no need to go on long hauls to find exciting dives these days. There's lots right here in the UK."

"Is that so?" said Albert, his brow furrowed with interest. He was behaving impeccably, Victoria thought, allowing Freddie to weave his clumsy web a little wider. "So, where do you usually dive then?"

"Simple answer to that: up in the Shetlands, I know it sounds a fair distance from this sunny county in the south, but well, it's worth it financially and that's apart from the dive experience. Huge treasure hauls to be had up there, huge."

Caroline was focussing on her pheasant, pulling off tiny shreds and mixing them into the rich sauce, but not actually eating anything, and Victoria thought she could detect a slight level of embarrassment.

"Financially?" said Albert in a vague voice and Victoria realised Albert was enjoying himself. "How do you mean?"

"Yeah, I've been investing up there for some time. You should remind me to explain it to you one day. Landed gentry like yourself, often on the lookout for somewhere to stash more cash, I bet."

Albert must have swallowed a piece of pheasant the wrong way as he coughed for quite a while and couldn't seem to meet Victoria's glances. "A glass of water?" she ventured, but he waved her away with tears in his eyes. She wasn't sure, but thought they may have been of mirth.

Caroline stepped into the lull. "That was marvellous, wasn't it, Freddie?" Spotting Trudy at the bar, she called loudly in her cut-glass tones, "Wonderful food, Trudy. Just fabulous!" The pub, now about half full, fell silent and everyone turned to look at them. Victoria wished the ground would open up and swallow their entire table, but Trudy, always a lover of limelight, smiled broadly and gave a small bow. As things settled back down to a general hum of conversation, Victoria overheard a few muttered "Bloody incomers!" comments and "Why don't they push off back to London, comin' in 'ere and shouting their mouths off?" type remarks, and felt profoundly embarrassed.

"Yes, as I was saying," continued Freddie, unfazed, "good financial gains to be made in sporting quests like treasure diving, you know."

"Really?" said Victoria, determined not to be completely silent.

"Phew, I should say." Caroline rubbed Freddie's arm. "He's a clever old entrepreneur, my Fred."

Victoria wasn't sure which she found more distasteful, the fact that Caroline was openly being affectionate to Freddie so soon after Giles had died or that she appeared to be stupid enough to believe him.

"Perhaps I could come up to Upper Swaddle Farm and chat about the possibilities with you some time, or even tonight maybe – us men adjourn for a snifter and the girls can come along later?"

Albert smiled slowly at Freddie. "Well now, I'm 'fraid Victoria is the designated driver tonight, so I assume she will be driving me home. I'm not too sure which of you has the task?"

Freddie had his second double vodka in front of him, half-finished, and Caroline was starting her third.

"Ahh, right, raincheck then! But can I get you another drink, Albert?"

Albert paused for thought and then nodded. "Yep. Don't see why not. Pint of Frog's Leap for me, thanks."

Freddie hesitated and Victoria could see he didn't know whether to clarify what that was or just trust in Roger. He chose the latter and went up to the bar.

"Such ingenious names these local breweries have," said Caroline with an overly enthusiastic look on her face. She swayed a little as she spoke. The vodka was kicking in – or perhaps mixing with whatever she had drunk or taken before leaving the house. Victoria tried hard to be charitable. Most people might take to the bottle for a bit of comfort after the sudden death of a loved one.

Freddie returned to the table empty-handed, "Roger said he has to go down to the cellar to change the barrel of Frog and only has Badger's Breath or Old Trout, or something. I take it he was joshing with me. Anyway, he will bring the drinks over in a second."

"Oh no," said Victoria, "those are indeed beers. It seems real ales taste better if they have an amusing name." Freddie looked bemused. Real ale was clearly never going to be his tipple.

Roger came over with a tray. "Here you go, folks. Apologies for the delay. I know you like Frog, Albert, but it'll take me a while to pull it through, so I thought you might like to try a half of the Badger's Breath in the meantime."

Freddie watched the two of them speak as though he was seeing a tennis match and the commentary was in a foreign language.

"That's fine, Mudger. I like most of 'em. Not so much a connoisseur as a keen amateur."

"Right-oh, I'll bring the pint of Frog over just as soon as it's through. Sir, here's the vodka for you and one for your friend, and Victoria, I assumed you might like another mineral water?"

Victoria smiled at him. "Aren't I the lucky one tonight? Thanks, Roger."

"So excuse my intrusion, it's Mrs Peacock, isn't it?" Roger clutched the tray in his hands and took on a Dickensian air of sympathy. "I do hope you are coping all right after all the, well, the happenings…?"

"Oh, Mr Mudge, how very kind of you. And my heart goes out, obviously, to that poor girl's family. Such a tragedy for that to happen to a complete innocent." Caroline had become embarrassingly queenly and Victoria had an urge to slap her, but kept her hands under the table.

Had it been physically possible, Roger's eyebrows would have scooted up higher than his hairline when Caroline mentioned Jessica. As it was, he coughed to disguise a laugh and then, in time-honoured gossip style, lowered his voice to impart his next piece of information, "It was indeed a great tragedy, but she was not the innocent that everyone is making out. I'll say no more." He finished by tapping the side of his nose and walking back to the bar.

"Coo, that was a bit of tasty local knowledge, if I am not mistaken," said a gleeful Freddie.

Victoria frowned. "Well, I think it's all rather ungallant when the poor girl isn't here to defend her honour. Maybe Trudy will tell us more." Trudy was just making her way across to their table to collect their plates.

"Trudy, Roger was just telling us a little about Jessica. Did you know her at all? You are always such a good judge of character," said Victoria, looking round at the others, daring them to contradict her.

"Well," came the instant reply, "all I will say, and I never like to speak ill of the dead, mind, but all I will say is that if she had been my daughter I would have been very disappointed indeed. She used to come in here with her college friends. I kept saying to Roger we need to ID them constantly. The last thing we need is to lose our licence. Anyway, she would come in with sometimes two, or even three boys and then leave with one of the male customers. An outrageous flirt, she was. It worries me when a young girl like that has no self-control or modesty." She shook her head as if she was personally affected by the failings of the youngsters in the country.

Caroline was fidgeting in her seat and Victoria realised the conversation was making her uncomfortable, so maybe something had been going on with Giles and it hadn't just been a flirtation at the party. Victoria pulled a 'Sshh, that's enough!' face at Trudy, but once Trudy was in full flow there was no pause or mute option.

"I did wonder if perhaps she and Giles Peacock were meeting in another pub. I can assure you she never met him in here. I mean…" She tailed off and went red The present company had just dawned on her. "Anyway, I hope you all enjoyed your meals," she said hurriedly, gathering up the two empty and the two barely touched plates and rushed off to the kitchen.

Caroline laughed shrilly. "What a charming place this is, isn't it, Freddie? I must come here more often!"

"God help us!" muttered someone from a corner by the inglenook and a more strident woman's voice said, "We'd rather you went back where you come from." It was a voice that Victoria recognised and, judging by Albert's change of expression, so did he. The woman's comment was followed by raucous laughter at her table and people mimicking Caroline's posh voice. Fortunately, Caroline seemed oblivious and drained her third large vodka and waved the glass at Roger behind the bar.

"Would you mind?" She smiled winningly and tried to catch Roger's eye. He, in turn, seemed unusually engrossed in polishing some glasses.

The front door opened and another flurry of leaves scattered across the flagstones as a new customer came in. "Oh, it's Edwin!" cried Victoria, the relief in her voice obvious to the man himself, who bustled over to their table. "Victoria, Albert, how marvellous." He shook hands, and then instantly adopted what Victoria always thought of as his parson's pose, podgy hands clasped and resting on his ample midriff. "My dear Mrs Peacock, how nice to see you again. So good so see you out and about and enjoying the company of my dear friends." He then looked at Freddie questioningly. "I'm sorry, have we met?"

Freddie hesitated, seemingly mesmerised by the reverend's dog collar and quizzical gaze. His mouth worked, but nothing came out.

"Yes, I think you met, briefly, at the er – party," Victoria muttered. "This is Freddie, Freddie Montague, a friend of Mrs, I mean, Caroline's. From London."

The two men shook hands. "Montague, you say?" Edwin was frowning and plucking at his lower lip. "From London?"

"Well, isn't this jolly!" said Caroline, now sounding distinctly slurred. "Fred, darling, can you get me another drinky-poos? I can't seem to catch that blasted man's eye behind the bar."

Freddie's smile was brief. "I rather think you've had enough drinky-poos, Caroline, and it is time we were off."

"Oh, I'm sorry, I didn't mean to break up the party," said Edwin, still looking slightly puzzled.

"No, no, Caroline is rather tired and emotional, as you can imagine after everything, you know." He laughed and hauled Caroline to her feet. "Come on, Caro, let's get you home. You know I've got an early start tomorrow and, as Albert pointed out earlier, I must be the one doing the driving, so I can't have any more to drink anyway."

"What?" Caroline looked befuddled. "Where are we going...? I mean, why..." But Freddie was a man on a mission and, saying goodbyes all round, he steered Caroline towards the rear door and the car park. To Victoria's amazement, he stopped at the bar and dug in his pockets. "Here, put that towards the bill, there's a good chap," and shoved a note into Roger's hand, and they were gone.

Roger gave a low whistle. "Phew, you don't see many of those around here!"

"What, drunk stuck-up cows from London?" sneered the loud female again. This time, Albert wheeled round and shot a warning glance over at the table of cackling women. At its centre sat Patricia Podger, as Victoria had already deduced. "What's the matter, Albie? Not another one of you exes, is she?" More screeching laughter and

Albert looked murderous, but did not rise to the bait.

Roger was now holding the note up to the light to inspect it more closely. "It's a fifty-pound note!" he said in awe-struck tones.

"You'd better check it's a real one before you get too excited," said Albert.

Roger blenched and went running into the kitchen, calling, "Trudy? Trudy? Where did you put that information from the bank about counterfeit notes?"

Edwin chuckled. "That's odd, Albert, that's just what I was about to say!"

"Never seen such a weasely, dishonest specimen in my life!" he snorted with derision. Edwin, who had poured himself a pint of beer in Roger's absence and left his money on the bar, came and sat down opposite them. Albert folded his arms and sat back. "Would I be right in thinking you recognise that toerag from somewhere?"

Edwin emerged from his first draft of beer, his upper lip moustached with froth. "Indeed you would be correct in your thinking, Albert. I had been racking my brains and then it came to me – Montague!" He sat back and sighed. "All rather sad really. I don't know why I didn't realise it before, it's not that common a name. His parents, thoroughly decent people, let me think – Matthew and Linda – that was it, regulars at my church in the London parish." He waved his hand airily as if the exact location was neither here nor there. "Well, obviously, I can't say too much, breach of confidentiality and all that… but let's just say that young man is a wrong 'un. His parents left my congregation. I believe they were forced to sell up and 'downsize' as they say, somewhere in the north in order to bail him out."

"Oh dear," said Victoria. "I can't understand why Caroline is so besotted with him. He seems so thoroughly oily and unpleasant and now it sounds as if he is as bad as he looks."

"Well, you know what they say about bad boys!" said Edwin mischievously, as he took another gulp of beer.

"Edwin!" Victoria laughed. "But yes, we ladies do seem to have a weakness for the bad ones sometimes." She fiddled with her glass of fizzy water. "I think this lady learnt her lesson a while ago, thank goodness!"

Albert smiled at her. "Likewise – but I mean with the ladies, of course!" As if on cue Patricia's dirty cackling laugh rang out again. "Oh Lord, but you can't always avoid running into them again, can you?" He sighed and looked apologetically at Victoria and Edwin.

Victoria was now itching to get back home so she could google Freddie Montague and see if there was any information on his devious dealings.

Roger reappeared and trotted over to them. "Looks like a genuine note to me!" He rubbed his hands with glee. "Now, Albert, can I get you your pint of Frog now then? The new barrel is all ready to go!"

Sensing Victoria's restlessness, he said, "No, you're all right, Roger. I reckon I've had sufficient tonight, and there's some elements in this bar that I don't particularly care to spend any more of my evening with."

Roger looked perplexed and then followed Albert's pointed glare. "Oh, right, gotcha. I'll sort out your bill then, but I reckon that fifty-pound note will pretty much cover most of it."

"I wouldn't be so sure. They were on double vodkas. But anyway, you do your maths while we keep the rev company and then I'll settle up with you."

Edwin was most of the way through his pint and hadn't even got round to taking his coat off. "Don't worry about me, I was only calling in for a quick one. I have some work to do before I can call it a day, so I'll be off as soon as I've drunk this."

"There's no rush, Edwin. But that bit of information about young Freddie was certainly interesting."

Edwin swilled the remaining beer around his glass. "Do you think it has a bearing on, um, recent events?" he asked.

Albert shrugged. "I don't know, but it makes you think, doesn't it? He's obviously a fellow with money issues and maybe he'd go a long way to get his hands on some, so who knows?"

"Well, I'll leave you two super sleuths with it. I need to come up with some words of wisdom about the wickedness of avarice." He gave his high-pitched giggle. "Well, perhaps I don't need to look too far for inspiration!"

As they drove home, Victoria shivered. "Brr, autumn suddenly seems to have arrived!" She fiddled with the heater controls in her car and they almost went into the hedge.

Albert tutted. "You stop fiddling with that, maid, and keep your eyes on the road. I'll sort it out." He pressed a few buttons and moved a lever of two in a desultory fashion. "We'll be home in a minute and the engine won't be warm yet anyway, waste of time." He sat back, beerily content.

Victoria gave a start. "Oh! What was that?" A pale ghostly form had drifted across the headlights' beam in front of them.

"Barn owl," said Albert casually.

"Really? Oh, how wonderful."

"Magnificent birds, one of my favourites," agreed Albert. "Often see them this time of year, not sure why. Maybe 'tis because the mice are easier to see with the fields all cut. Your aunt loved owls, you know," he said. "She'd have known why we see more of them in the autumn. Clever woman, your aunt."

Victoria nodded. "I know. I wish I'd paid more attention when I was here as a child. There was so much she could have taught me, but I was too bound up in school and clothes and my silly chattering friends. But then, it's easy to look back and be critical, but much harder to realise it at the time."

"True, very true." Albert sounded as if he would drop off to sleep at any moment.

After a predictably rapturous welcome from Moss, Albert put the kettle on, yawning extravagantly, while Victoria opened up her laptop and began ferreting about on the internet.

"Isn't it a bit late to start doing that now?" he asked, yawning again. "I'm proper bushed."

Victoria was frowning at the screen and typing furiously. "I'm sorry, Albert, but my journalist's nose is twitching and I can't resist having a quick search – and wow!" Moss jumped up at her exclamation and gave an excited bark.

"What is it?' Albert, rubbing his eyes, finished making their drinks and came across to the table.

"I'm amazed it didn't ring any bells before. I remember reading about this when it happened. Here, look." She pointed at the screen and Albert pulled up a chair to see what she was so excited about.

Albert read aloud: "'Frederick Montague, 35, of Silver Street SW1, was jailed earlier today for his part in an elaborate scam that saw thousands of people lose their savings after they invested in Montague's non-existent luxury goods company.' Well, I'll be jiggered, so he really is a sleazy so-and-so!" Albert sat back. "So what on earth is your friend Caroline up to? I thought she was meant to be a smart woman?"

Victoria sighed and clicked on some further links to the story. "Well, they say love is blind, don't they, and perhaps this is a classic example. I think perhaps we've all failed to recognise flaws in our loved ones at some time or another. I know I certainly have. I refused to believe that my ex, Nigel, was the rotter that he was and ended up making a complete fool of myself."

Albert snorted. "You can't blame yourself at all. He was obviously a nasty piece of work from what you've told me, going off with your best friend like that and lying to you so blatantly. You had the truth concealed from you. This is different. This is out there in the public domain for all to see. Your friend must be even more bonkers than I thought she was."

Victoria sighed. "Or maybe she is more vulnerable than we realise and she is terrified of being on her own. Perhaps that's what it is."

Albert gently tucked a strand of hair behind her ear. "Victoria, you are such a softie! You need to understand that there really are nasty people in this world. Not many, I agree, but they exist, and you can't make excuses for all of them, you know."

Victoria kissed his cheek. "You're right, of course. I don't seem to learn from my mistakes much, do I?"

Albert smiled. "Maybe that's one of the things I like about you, Miss West!"

"Oh, stop being so soppy and finish making the tea."

"Done that. It's been sitting on the side getting cold. You coming up to bed, or not? I could fall asleep on my feet at the moment."

"Look, you go up and I'll be there in five minutes." She turned back to her screen and heard him sigh. "No, really, I will."

Twenty minutes later, Victoria was still following links about Freddie Montague. He had managed to bring down several other people with him, old school friends, it seemed. How awful. She'd found photos of him, too, noticeably younger, fuller in the face, hair slicked back and looking every inch the arrogant city trader. She'd also found a photo of a tall, handsome couple in their sixties, his poor parents, Matthew and Linda. Their faces were haunted and stiff with apprehension and they stood close together behind the gates to their house as if poised to duck out of the way of hurled insults at any moment.

Moss started an energetic and vocal dream and his soft whimpers and twitching feet broke the spell. Victoria tore her tired eyes from the screen and glanced at the clock. Oh dear, she'd been much longer than her promised five minutes. Checking Moss was secure in his puppy crate, she tiptoed up the stairs. Albert was on his side, fast asleep. She looked at his face and smiled. Such a dear man, he looked very young in his sleep. She had struck lucky when she had found him, that was the truth. For the first time in her life, she felt secure in a relationship and it was a wonderful feeling.

"Are you going to stand there admirin' me all night or are you going to finally come to bed?" he muttered, without opening his eyes.

Chapter 9

Victoria gazed at the display and wondered what it was meant to represent. It was another of Lavender's displays with a colour theme, but what tied it together? A green wellington, green plastic bucket, green woollen glove and a pair of green china dogs. (Or were they bears?) Anyway, they were green bookends. Two cabbages, a tin of custard, the label mostly green, and three greenish coat hangers. She stared and thought hard – it was always nice to be able to guess what the display represented as Lavender put so much work into them, but no, inspiration was lacking and she hadn't a clue.

She pushed open the door of the shop and stopped in amazement – all three sisters were dressed in green from head to toe.

Victoria laughed and said, "OK, I give up! It's a green theme, but what is it for?"

Dahlia smiled broadly and explained. "You see, dear, we thought we should set an example as we are the only shop in the village, so we are going green. No more free carrier bags. We are recycling those we've been collecting until they run out. We are only selling green vegetables today, well, that's apart from the carrots as Colin Wimble had too many and they were going cheap, so we are selling them off. But yes, going green, that's us, setting an example to the community. I know it doesn't suit some folks' tastes, but we like it – as colours go."

Victoria wondered how to break it to the triplets that their concept of going green was wrong on so many levels, but decided she would focus on the positive. "What an excellent idea to recycle carrier bags. I always keep mine, so I could bring you a few in if that would help."

"Thank you, gratefully received," said Iris. "Now what can we do for you today, Victoria? What splendid meal are you going to cook up for lucky Albert tonight?"

"I'm not sure Albert is lucky whenever I'm cooking. I ought to go on a cookery course really, but it's finding the time."

"Seems you're busy half the time with sorting out other people's messes, I reckon," said Iris, folding her arms. "That woman from up London, that Peacock person, she was in here again yesterday, trying to buy cigarettes for that man of hers, and her husband not even cold in 'is grave! I've not taken to him, I've not." She shook her head and the other two green personages tutted in unified dislike. Freddie's goose was most definitely cooked as far as the triplets were concerned.

"Ah, you mean Caroline? Poor thing, she's had so much more than her fair share of hard times recently, you know." Dahlia harrumphed and Victoria realised defending 'that Peacock person' was going to be an uphill struggle.

Deciding to change tack, she said, "I was up at Burntwood yesterday talking to Martha about her chickens for a magazine article. Is it just me or is Morris a bit scary?"

Lavender spoke up and looked as though she were talking about a serial killer or mass murderer. "He's evil. The devil will have a place for him!" she said and she disappeared out to the back of the shop.

"Ah there, she tells it like it is as usual." Dahlia wiped her hands on her apron and rearranged some broccoli florets, sitting proudly in the centre of the green-themed veg.

"Morris has always been nasty. Even as a child he had a proper cruel streak," said Iris. "You could tell he was going to be a bad 'un from the beginning. There was that time the hamsters and guinea pigs in the school all suddenly died and when someone looked closely, it turned out the poor little things had all been stabbed with a school compass – you know those things we all used to use for drawing circles and such like, with the sharp point on one end – ugh! They found the bloodied thing hidden in the straw bedding. Of course, we all knew who dunnit, but he never owned up. Wouldn't, would he? To that sort honesty doesn't come natural."

"Did you have any proof it was Morris?" asked Victoria.

"Didn't need proof, we all knew," said Iris sagely. "I mean, who else would do such a cruel thing? Wasn't long after that someone posted chicken poo through the teacher's letterbox. Miss Baxter, wasn't it?" Dahlia nodded at her sister. "Miss Baxter had spoken to Morris and as good as accused him, so we reckoned this was his way of getting his own back. Very strange boy, that Morris."

Victoria kept pottering round the shop gathering the bits she needed as once you wound the triplets, or any one of them up; all you had to do was wait, and listen.

"Mind you, he's met his match with that Sylvia, hasn't he?" Cue more sage nodding from Dahlia. "That Sylvia – as maze as a handcart as we says round here and not nice with it."

"Sorry, I don't quite follow that, maze as a…?" Victoria loved all the local sayings and was keeping a little notebook with them in to amuse herself on a rainy day and perhaps get an article out of them.

"It means you're not quite right in the brains department. You'd have to be to hang around with that bully. It's like she needs to worship someone, to be told what to do and then do it without question, bit like those religious fanatics. If Morris Podger tells her to jump she doesn't even stop to ask 'how high', she jus' jumps right off the nearest cliff, daft maid. She makes me mad, but then I remember…" Dahlia trailed off and looked at Iris. They both knew something but whether they intended to share it, Victoria had to wait and see.

Lavender came through from the back room and with her usual candour said, "That Sylvia killed her dad."

Victoria gasped. She had been expecting malicious gossip as they didn't like the woman, but was this true or village folklore?

"There's no proof of that, Lavender. We shouldn't say things we can't prove, you know," said Iris, who had flushed pink and was wagging a finger at her wayward sister.

"Well, 'tis true, and we all know why, but that doesn't excuse killin." Lavender was relishing having the moral high ground.

Victoria had to ask. "Why would she kill her own father?"

"Get her own back, no doubt. Awful wicked man, no telling what he did to her 'part from knocking her about, which we all saw happen. Smacked her round the head in here once when she asked for sweets. Would have felt sorry for her, 'cept she stole some after he'd said no. We've read stories in the paper about what some fathers do to their children and we reckon he was up to no good with her in all sorts of ways. That Sylvia had a tough time, but she was a hard child to like. Got a sly eye."

"How did her father die?" Victoria felt like a rabbit caught in the headlights of a speeding car. She knew she ought to get out of the way of the oncoming horror, but felt unable to move – she had to know the details about Sylvia.

Iris took up the story. "He were an electrickity man, plus he did a bit of general building work and he took her with him on a job one day as she was home alone. He just had to check the electric wiring on a factory extension he was working on. They never did work out how, but though he was well experienced, he made a simple mistake and electrocuted himself. Sylvia never rang 999, just walked home, cool as a cucumber. Told the police later she couldn't remember what number to ring, so she'd just gone home. As if that fooled anyone!"

"My goodness! So then what happened?"

"Seems nobody cared enough to follow through properly. She was a minor at the time and the police declared it an accident and left it there. Think probably most people, including the police, thought the beastly man had gone to the right place."

"Of course, you go to hell if you are bad," Lavender said almost gleefully.

The shop bell rang and all four of them jumped slightly – guilty conscience or just co-incidence that they should be talking about hell, wondered Victoria as the reverend's voice boomed around the shop.

"Morning, ladies. A fine day, and may we have many more of them."

"Morning, Reverend," chorused the triplets, accompanied by curious half-hearted curtseys.

"Just popped in for milk, "said the reverend, "and, of course, to see your enchanting smiles."

"Ooh, Reverend, you are too charming for a man of the cloth. You're wasted without a wife," Dahlia simpered and Victoria could see that a position as vicar's wife in the village would seem like stardom to one of the triplets.

"What do I owe you?" Now Edwin had arrived, Victoria could see a chance to escape so she handed over a ten-pound note and waited as Dahlia carefully counted out her change.

"We loved your singing at the Curryoke night," pushed in Iris, obviously not to be outdone." You do have a lovely voice."

The reverend was now blushing a little –all this adulation just for a simple pint of milk. "Oh pish, it was nothing. I get plenty of practice on a Sunday. If I didn't sing the church would be silent sometimes! You ladies should come and join me more often." This bold reply left them all looking suitably chastened.

"All well then, Edwin?" said Victoria.

"Absolutely, and how are your fine chickens, my dear?"

"My fine chickens are just that, fine. They are blossoming wonderfully now they have settled down. We even got a double yolker the other day. Lovely birds."

"Well, that's good news. Off for an afternoon of heavy writing then, I assume?"

"No, actually, I am going to Martha Podger's place, talking of fine birds. I'm in the midst of an article on fancy breeds of chicken and she has some beauties. You should come with me and have a look."

"Much as I would love to have a gander... sorry, ladies, my little jest! As much as I would like to look at her hens, I have a diocesan meeting this afternoon, oh joy! Besides which, I have unpleasant memories of the last time I attempted a friendly visit to the Podger household. I think Morris threatened me with a shotgun and his lady friend hurled fishwife-style abuse at me – or was it the other way round?"

The triplets were nodding at each other. "Shameful! And him a man of the cloth, too," comments were murmured.

"Dear me, the more I hear about the Podgers, the worse it gets, I do agree, they are not my choice of dinner guests, but Martha doesn't seem a bad old stick and the fowl are beautiful so I think they will make an interesting article. Anyway, I'd best be on my way. Do pop in later if you want to see how my hens are coming on."

Victoria beat a hasty retreat, leaving a slightly panicked-looking reverend in her wake and at the mercy of the triplets.

* * * * *

Five minutes later, Victoria pulled onto the crumbling concrete yard at Burntwood Farm and hauled her camera gear out of the boot. She had parked where she hoped Caroline could not see her. She didn't feel up for yet more dramas from her friend. She had enough to cope with keeping out of mad Morris's way.

Rather than 'hallooing' her arrival, she decided to keep quiet and see if she could locate Martha without drawing attention to herself. She walked towards the farmhouse, but the place seemed deserted. A distant clucking indicated some activity in the chicken coops, so Victoria ambled towards them. A figure wearing what looked like a large lilac-coloured hat and a shiny frock was moving about among the coops, busily filling hoppers with feed. Victoria wondered who on earth it could be and prayed it wasn't mad Morris's nutty girlfriend, Sylvia.

"Hello?" she called tentatively.

"Ah, there you are!" said the purple-headed figure, and Victoria's jaw dropped as the strangely-dressed woman turned towards her. It was Martha. "Didn't recognise me in my best togs, eh?" She smiled a gap-toothed grin and Victoria shook her head in wonderment. She was dressed in what looked like a mother-of-the-bride two-piece, only slightly second-hand, accessorised by her customary wellingtons, covered in chicken droppings as usual. Her hair, normally a bird's nest of wispy chaos, had been given a lilac rinse and curled and set into a bouffant that Dame Edna Everage would have been proud of.

"Absolutely!" blustered Victoria, nodding to show her

appreciation. "You look, err, amazing!" Martha beamed again and stood, hands on hips, giving Victoria the chance to admire her outfit more fully. Lord, how on earth was she supposed to get any sensible photos of a farmer tending her hens when she looked like a deranged relative at a wedding? "My only concern, Mrs Podger, is that you will ruin your lovely outfit. Do you have an overall – " she saw the old woman's face fall. "– no, better still, an apron. You could put on over the top? That way, we'll get to see the lovely styling, but you'll also be protected from any muck." Martha was looking thoughtful. Victoria ploughed on desperately. "I think I spotted an apron in your kitchen last time, a nice striped one, hanging up by the door? That would look great!"

"You really think so?"

"Yes, I do. We don't want to give our readers a false picture, do we, and I would hate you to ruin your outfit."

Martha seemed mollified. "Well, it did cost a fair bit when I bought it fifteen years ago for our Patricia's wedding, and I wouldn't want to spoil it. I'm hoping I'll be able to wear it again if our Morris ever decides to settle down and…" she paused. "Mind you, not that I want him to settle down with that potty Sylvia." She sighed. "Hang on then, while I go and fetch the pinny." She stumped off back to the farmhouse and Victoria suppressed the urge to scream.

With the apron in place, Martha looked marginally more farmer-like and Victoria set about taking photos. The combination of Martha's insistence on grinning full face into the camera and the chickens refusing to keep still, or worse, run away completely, made the whole thing extremely long-winded and very stressful. Eventually Victoria realised that if she snapped Martha while she was fussing about and trying to arrange the birds, or gather the eggs, just before she gave her false grin, she could get some quite decent reportage shots. After two hours, she was shattered and longing for a large glass of wine!

As they wandered back towards the farmhouse, the sound of the phone ringing caused Martha to set off at a gallop to answer it. Victoria paused and tried to calm her jangled nerves. Her inclination to nosiness in the name of investigative reporting made her wander nonchalantly into the barn. The interior was a sight to behold, an untidy heap of old tractor tyres, bits of rusting farm machinery, piles and piles of old empty feed sacks – why on earth would someone keep such rubbish? As she peered into the gloom, she wondered if this was where Morris kept his array of poisons. She shivered involuntarily. She walked slowly, trying to look as if she was just marking time and glancing around as if with some casual sightseeing while waiting for Martha to return. In a gloomy corner she saw discarded tins, clearly marked 'Rat Poison'. She spotted what she assumed were rat or mole traps and there, on a ledge far more neatly arranged than anything else in the barn, was a line of small, new-looking plastic bottles. Victoria edged closer. They looked like veterinary drugs, but she had no idea. They could also be poisons. She heard the farmhouse door bang and quickly took out her camera and fired off a few shots, before hastily shoving it back in her camera bag and slinging it over her shoulder.

"'Oi!" snapped Martha, "what you doing in 'ere then? This is private, this is!"

Victoria turned, an expression of mild surprise on her face. "Oh. I'm sorry, I just assumed this was where you kept the chickens' feed and bedding. I wanted to get a few shots."

Martha's scowl was fierce and this, combined with the lilac hair, wellington boots and striped pinny, suddenly made Victoria think of a pantomime dame, and she had to bite her lip to stop herself from laughing.

"No, this is mostly Morris's junk. I keep all the chickens' stuff at the front of the barn, over there, see?" She jerked her head over her right shoulder, but her eyes were looking past Victoria and regarding the small bottles on the shelf with as much interest as Victoria herself had shown.

"Oh, that's fine. I'll just take a few shots, if that's OK?" So, she didn't know about the drugs either, Victoria thought, as she strolled over to the feed and bedding. She got out her camera again and took a few shots. In reality, they were of no use at all, but they'd been the basis of what she hoped was a plausible excuse. She turned to see Martha squinting up at the shelf, a pair of reading glasses perched on the end of her nose, trying desperately to read the small writing on the labels.

"Well, I think I've got all I need now," said Victoria casually and stowed her camera away again. Martha spun round, shoving her glasses in the apron pocket.

"What?"

"I said I've got all I need now, thanks, Mrs Podger."

"Oh, er, right you are then." The woman suddenly seemed ten years older and her face, normally pugnacious, looked tired and even a little frightened.

"I'll get this written up and it will be in the next edition of 'Country Days'. I'm sure you'll get plenty of interest from it. I've got all your contact details. I will, of course, drop you in a couple of complimentary copies. It will be online, too."

"Online, you say? Oh, right, that's good, good."

Victoria could sense her unease and knew that she hadn't really taken in anything she had just been saying. "Right, well, I'll be on my way then. Thank you so much for your time. I'll be in touch."

"Yes, that's fine. You get along now. I've got things to do." And with that, she bustled past Victoria, head down and set off towards the farmhouse, not saying another word.

Victoria had a final quick nose around the barn, and then headed off to her car. She looked around cautiously, anxious to avoid the dreaded Morris, and climbed in. As she reversed, she saw Martha in her mirror re-emerge from the farmhouse and scuttle across the yard carrying a pen and paper, obviously intending to make a note of what was on those suspicious-looking bottles.

Victoria selected first gear and set off as fast as she could, back up the narrow lane to the warmth and safety of Upper Swaddle Farm and Albert.

* * * * *

As she turned into the farm drive, she was delighted to see Albert's tractor kicking up dust as it trundled across the field toward the barn. She hooted and waved and parked up.

"Where's the fire?" he said as he climbed down from the high tractor cab.

"What do you mean? I was just keen to get back and put the kettle on. Anyway, you can't talk, you drive much faster than I do!"

"I'm allowed to, I'm a local." He grinned. "Come on then, maid, you look like you're bursting to tell me something you've ferreted out."

After Moss had charged around the garden and the tea had been poured, Victoria said, "Well, I think I may have discovered something rather interesting in the Podgers' barn."

Albert put down his mug of tea and put on his stern face. "You been snooping again, Victoria? You know you are a fine one for getting yourself into scrapes and you also know full well that that Morris is a nutcase." Victoria tried to speak, but he went on, "And that Sylvia is no better, so I don't like the idea of you nosing around Burntwood Farm, not at all. So, what have you been up to?"

"If you're going to be all huffy about it, I'm not sure I shall tell you!" Victoria put down her own mug with equal purpose and glared back.

"Now, now, don't you take on so. You know I am only worried about you. You must agree that you have had a few close calls." She shrugged and tried to look nonchalant. "That peculiar lot at the jam factory, just think how that could have ended! And then the violent violet growers – I mean, come on!"

Victoria sighed. "Oh, all right, you may have a point, but I do like a bit of very low-key investigative journalism every now and then. And I think it's important we, or the police, do pin this on someone. Two people lost their lives here and it is a real tragedy. That poor young girl… I keep seeing her in your arms when she collapsed. It was just so awful."

Albert patted her hand. "Yes, I know, it was truly dreadful. But the police are not complete fools. Well, not all of them, and I am sure they are making progress and – "

"So do I get to tell you what I found out?"

"OK, fire away."

She picked up her camera and sat forward. "Well, you see, I was in their barn. Martha had gone inside to answer the phone, so I thought I'd have a quick wander about, and – "

"Being nosey as usual."

"Yes, OK, if you like!" she said crossly. "Do you want to hear?"

Albert laughed. "Oh get on, then!"

"It was full of the most awful junk and rubbish, you can't imagine – "

"Think I can! Probably looks like most farmers' barns!" He saw her face and stopped. "Oops, sorry, you go on then."

"Anyway, away from all the junk at the back of the barn was a shelf with lots of plastic bottles all neatly lined up along it. Look, I took some shots, bit dark, but I think you can see."

Albert squinted into the camera's display as Victoria zoomed in. "That's veterinary stuff. What's wrong with that? You'll find wormer and penicillin and all sorts out in my barn, too."

"Ah yes, but why all so neatly arranged when everything else is in chaos? There were empty tins of rat poison scattered about all over the place on the floor and then this stuff all neatly lined up."

Albert shrugged. "Veterinary stuff is damned expensive. 'Spect they were just being careful."

"Maybe, but I'm not so sure. When Martha came in, she looked as surprised as I was – "

Albert gave a start. "You mean she caught you snooping?"

"Well, sort of, but I made an excuse and I think she bought it. She looked really worried when she saw the bottles and, as I drove off I spotted her in the rear-view mirror dashing back out to the barn with a paper and pen to make notes, so I am sure she didn't know what was in there either. So there!"

Albert sat and considered his half-empty mug of tea. "Here, let me have another look at those photos." He looked closely at the image. "Bit too dark to read 'em clearly. Does that say succinylcholine?"

Victoria peered at the screen. "I think so, yes. Why, what's that?"

"Well, I'm no expert, but I reckon that's what Wallace the vet uses when he has to put a large animal down, but I could be wrong. You'd need to ask him." Realising what he'd said he added, "No, no, Victoria, hold your horses, I didn't mean that! Don't you go quizzing the local vet. He might report you to the police for asking suspicious questions."

"Oh, don't be silly. Anyway, I thought you always said Mr Wallace was a great chap?"

"Well, he is, as vets go, but still…Seriously, I don't think you should go around asking things like that. People might get the wrong end of the stick."

Victoria held up her hands in mock surrender. "OK, OK, I give in. I'll have a good nose around on Google then. There are some other great long medical names in the pictures. I'll see what else I can find out."

"All right then, Sherlock Holmes, now you mention Google, it's my turn to tell you what I've been discovering today."

"You?"

"Yes, boring old Farmer Moreton. I've been doing me own homework in my lunchtime. But I could down another cup of tea before I start yarning on. I'm a bit parched."

"Oh, you are maddening! OK, I'll put the kettle on."

With drinks refreshed, Albert said, "Well, I thought I'd do a bit more ferreting around furtive Freddie. So I started by googling diving off Shetland. I thought it would be a complete non-starter, so ruddy chilly up there, but it seems not. It's a very good place to go scuba diving, lots of underwater wildlife and stuff, and also lots of wrecks."

"Oh, so maybe Freddie isn't such a con artist after all?" said Victoria, disappointed in the extreme.

Albert grinned. "Oh, I think he is. It's such a popular spot for diving that it's all been done. The wrecks have been thoroughly explored already, picked over by every treasure hunter and dive enthusiast there is! There are lots of dive schools and people with many years' experience operating up there, so it's not at all a good place for some daft London interloper like Freddie to come in and make any headway at all. And what's more, many of the shipwrecks are from recent times and the older ones are often under the 'Protection of Wrecks Act 1973', so the websites say. The chances of finding gold or buried treasure that no one else has managed to find are minimal, to say the least. And salvaging anything like that would cost an absolute fortune, never mind make you one." Albert laughed. "No, the man is either an idiot or a con artist, and I know which one I think he is.'

"So you won't be investing then?"

"No, I damned well won't! But I must say reading up on all that diving stuff, and about the islands was mighty interesting. I might decide to trek a long way north one of these days and go exploring."

"Ooh, how interesting. Could I come, too?"

Albert tapped his chin and considered for a moment. "Well, I suppose it could be arranged. Anyway, the upshot is I reckon that Freddie is a wrong 'un through and through. He's unscrupulous and would do anything for money, most of which I then suspect goes up his nose with whatever designer drug these daft people take these days." He paused. "I did a bit of research on that, too, and I'm sorry to say, Victoria, I reckon your friend Caroline is probably high as a kite half the time as well."

Victoria sighed. "Yes, I think you're right. She certainly behaves very oddly and erratically. It's no great surprise. I had thought that was probably the case."

"So… I wouldn't be too surprised to find out furtive Freddie was involved in polishing off Giles and, accidentally, that poor girl, too."

Victoria looked even more crestfallen. "Oh dear. I can't say I am too surprised by that either. How awful." She sat back. "But before we pin the 'murderer' badge on Freddie, I'm also a bit puzzled by Patricia and the way she's behaved."

"Patricia Podger? Why? What's she done?" Albert was immediately on the defensive, which irked Victoria considerably.

"Oh, come on, Albert! The woman is a lunatic! Apart from

massively overreacting – ”

"She's always been highly strung."

"– she also lied about being at the party in the first place. She must have scuttled off and hidden when you went to ask all the catering staff to come and assemble outside. Now that's a highly suspicious thing to do. You didn't see her, did you?"

Albert was frowning. "No, no I didn't, that's true. But she is a bit, well, highly strung, like I said, and she'd probably run away from anything she thought involved the police, or was a bit risky. It's sort of in her nature."

"Charming!" said Victoria loftily. "Not very honest or community-minded, is it?"

Albert looked sheepish. "That's the Podgers for you. But, seriously, I really don't think Patricia would ever do anyone harm. She's all bluff and bluster. Her bark's far worse than her bite."

"Not that you could say that about Morris, her very own brother," said Victoria, triumphantly. "The guinea pig-slayer of Swaddlecombe!"

Albert looked slightly surprised. "Well, no, that's also true. But I still don't think Patricia would cause actual harm." Albert didn't look all that convinced; in fact, Victoria thought he looked quite worried.

"What is it? Have you remembered something?"

"No, not exactly, not about Patricia. It's about Sylvia."

"Oh, you mean Sylvia of the patricide."

"What? You mean you know about that as well as the school guinea pigs?" Albert was aghast.

"Of course I do. Nothing is secret in this village, you know that. I heard it all from the triplets, all about her nasty father who worked with 'electrickerty', or however they say it. He sounded like a monster and, although I shouldn't say it, got what he deserved.

But I don't see why Sylvia should go around killing the next-door neighbours for the odd slight against her beloved."

Albert sighed. "I don't know, I don't like all this gossip and tittle-tattle about people, it's not nice."

"Murder isn't nice."

"You have a point," he agreed.

"And we haven't given that much thought to the Brocks, have we? I mean, of all the people we are gossiping about, they have plenty of motive and also plenty of opportunity."

"Do you think so? I just can't see a young couple like that doing such a thing. I mean, what are they going to achieve, other than some strange sort of perverted satisfaction? Their father is dead. They can't bring him back, and the farm is gone, too. What's the point? Why ruin their very promising careers as catering stars? No, I don't buy that." He sat back and folded his arms, his point firmly made and not about to be budged. Then he sat forward again. "However, someone we haven't given nearly enough thought to is your friend Caroline."

Victoria gasped. "Caroline! Don't be ridiculous! What could she gain…? I mean why would she want Giles…? And why the young and lovely Jessica and… oh dear."

Albert smiled smugly and refolded his arms. "Quite."

Chapter 10

Victoria slept badly, her night broken by a series of disturbing dreams. She kept finding herself in awful situations and had to jerk herself awake to stop the ridiculous storyline from reaching a grisly end. How ridiculous! Why hadn't she been able to get her brain to switch off, or at least have sensible thoughts that were constructive, rather than rampaging around like some B-movie horror flick and upsetting her thoroughly? She'd found herself diving off Scotland – she only knew it was Scotland as the others were wearing tartan diving suits – and someone had cut her air supply and she'd woken up gasping for air. Then she'd been shut in a chicken coop with Martha and lots of squawking hens with gunshots going off all around, just waiting for the maniac gunman to fire at the flimsy wooden chicken house and blow them to bits. Caroline had popped up, looking rather like Alice in Wonderland, and Freddie as a sort of Mad Hatter, and they'd both had these awful revolving cartoon eyes – ugh!

Now she sat slumped at the kitchen table, bags under her eyes, hair on end, a large mug of coffee clutched tightly between her hands. It was quite chilly; autumn was well and truly on its way. She shivered and tied her dressing gown more tightly. Of course, it was all Albert's fault. If he hadn't started talking about Caroline being a likely suspect, she would probably have slept soundly. Talking of Albert, she assumed he had come and taken Moss out for an

189

early walk as the puppy wasn't in his bed and she could hear her own hens clucking contentedly in the distance, so he must have let them out, too. Why was he so wonderful? She sighed again. Even his wonderfulness was annoying this morning.

Her mind drifted foggily back to Caroline. All right, the woman was a flake, but would she really have murdered her own husband? Had Giles been having an affair with Jessica? There was no real evidence. He was just a dirty old man and Jessica was a rather flirty young woman. It wasn't as if she came from a poor family and hoped to get some money from him, which was surely the only reason such an attractive girl would have tolerated someone as old and offensive as Giles. No, she didn't buy it.

Victoria realised she knew virtually nothing about the Peacocks' married life, but what little she did seemed normal enough, well for people like Caroline and Giles – combative, driven and almost alcoholic. But she knew lots of couples like that up in London. There were probably plenty like that down in Devon, too. She'd just managed to avoid them so far.

She'd always thought Caroline had enough money of her own. She was a successful career woman, but clearly Giles had contributed the lion's share as the Burntwood Barn project must have cost a very great deal of money and she couldn't imagine either of them skimping on life's little luxuries.

Glancing at her watch, she made a determined effort to rally and think about getting in the shower, but lacked any energy at all. It was all she could do to pour another cup of coffee. Was she really friends with a murderess? No, she just couldn't believe it. Caroline would want to be seen to be the architect of her own success and not just inherit her money,and certainly not by murdering her husband! She was also far too vain and selfish to risk being found out and ending up in jail. Plus, she was also too intelligent, underneath all the drugs and Freddie nonsense, not to realise the risk of being caught was far too great.

Victoria felt better after thinking this through and decided to brace up and get in the shower. But then she thought of Freddie and how even the most famous or brilliant or inspirational of people could make complete and utter fools of themselves all in the name of love or, as was more often the case, lust. She slumped again.

The kitchen door burst open and an annoyingly cheerful farmer and very bouncy dog shattered the peace of the kitchen. "Good morning, maid. Oh my, lord, look at the state of you!" Albert stopped and regarded her, a smile playing on his lips, which he fought to suppress.

"Don't," she said weakly, "just don't! I've hardly slept a wink and I feel awful. I had dreadful dreams about diving and guns and Caroline and Freddie and – ugh!"

"Victoria, you could worry for England, really you could. Why don't you trot upstairs and get in the shower? No, better still, have a soak in the bath. I'll feed this little chap. We've had a good long walk. And then you'd better get yourself decent by ten o'clock."

"I don't think I'll be going out anywhere today, thanks. I might even go back to bed at this rate."

Albert laughed. "I don't think so. You obviously haven't looked at the calendar. Today is the day that you booked in old Jolly to come and introduce you to the delights of this here Rayburn." He patted the dark and brooding beast of a range with obvious affection.

"What? Who?" Victoria looked around in a daze.

"Go and get in the bath and be ready for the Rayburn man at ten. You'll find some fresh cake, it's chocolate – a good choice of mine given the state of you this morning – as Jolly always likes a bit of my cake with his lunch."

Victoria was on her feet now. "His lunch? Good grief, how long is he going to be here? Is he moving in?"

Albert sighed. "Come on now, maid, buck up. Jolly will be here much of the day, I 'spect, so you get on and get yourself sorted." He patted Moss and went to get his feed bowl, the little dog following his every move with his eyes.

Victoria turned at the bottom of the stairs and glared. "Why does he have to be called 'Jolly'? How very annoying. Why can't he be 'Miserable' or 'Fed-up'? Why does he have to be Jolly when everything so obviously isn't today?"

Albert threw a dog biscuit at her and she staggered off up the stairs, grumbling.

* * * * *

At precisely ten o'clock there was a smart rap on the back door and Victoria opened it to be confronted by a man who looked like something out of a Dickens novel and anything but jolly. Immensely tall, thin and stooping, wearing half-moon glasses on the end of a long, straight nose, his dark grey hair flicked up over his big ears and Victoria decided he looked exactly like a heron.

In a lugubrious voice he said, "Good morning, Miss West. I am Ludo Pettifer-Jolly, but people call me Jolly. I am here to service your Rayburn. May I come in?"

"Oh yes, of course Mr Jolly, er Jolly, do please. Would you like a cup of tea? Or perhaps coffee? Or perhaps a cold drink?" Victoria was aware that she was twittering, always a sign of nerves. "And please call me Victoria."

"Most kind. A cup of black coffee would be just the ticket, thank you."

Victoria filled the kettle and watched as Jolly carefully put down his old, battered toolbox and slowly approached the Rayburn, rather tentatively, like a matador slowly stalking the bull. "Ah yes, I remember this one well! A bit of a beast, if you don't handle it properly." He patted the Rayburn rather as Albert had done earlier. He turned to face her suddenly, eyes wide and said, "Inclined to smoke."

Victoria jumped and almost dropped the mugs she was taking down from the dresser. "Really? Oh dear, I don't much like the sound of that. I did originally want to get rid of it and get an electric hob but…" She trailed off as Jolly fell back and spread himself across the front of the Rayburn as if shielding it from her harsh words.

"It won't run well for you if you approach it like that, you know!" he said seriously. "Terribly temperamental."

Victoria suddenly burst out laughing. "You must be pulling my leg, surely? Please say you are?"

Jolly smiled and took out a large white handkerchief and polished his glasses. "Well, perhaps a little. I am an old rogue. But you do need to get to know your Rayburn and build a relationship with it, really. It's a bit like a living thing."

Victoria sighed. "Oh dear, why is life so complicated? I just want it to heat the house and produce some hot water and I might occasionally shove a jacket potato in its oven if I think of it. I don't want to marry the thing!"

Now Jolly was smiling broadly, his big horsey teeth on full display. "Goodness, you do remind me of your aunt!" He gave a wheezing laugh and shook his head. "She did battle with it for years. They never got on. Ah well…" For a moment he seemed lost in memories, Victoria assumed, of her Aunt Edith. She busied herself making coffee while watching him out of the corner of her eye. He wore an old dark green boiler suit over his ordinary clothes. It looked as if he'd borrowed it from a shorter, fatter man as it finished about six inches from the end of both his arms and legs and was gathered in tightly at the knees and waist with the obligatory farmer's fashion accessory – baler twine. It gave him the appearance of a very badly-tied cracker.

"Your coffee?" Victoria held it out to him and this seemed to wake from his reverie.

"Thank you, Miss West." He seemed to have no intention of calling her Victoria. She had clearly made a social faux pas as far as Jolly was concerned by even suggesting it.

"I've nursed this beast for more than twenty years, you know, man and boy. Perhaps it will behave itself better now you are in charge. Your aunt used to shout at it, you see, and I think sometimes she even kicked it, so I'm not all that surprised that it took offence."

"I doubt it. I am not much of a cook, I'm afraid, Jolly. But I will endeavour to sweet-talk it." She smiled, enjoying this eccentric man's chatter. He didn't sound local. He was extremely well-spoken and she didn't think Pettifer-Jolly was a Devonshire name, but perhaps she was being too judgemental.

"Well, I'll have a furtle about and see the lie of the land, shall I?" He put down his mug and opened one of the monster's doors. He tutted. He opened another and tutted again.

"Not looking good?" she ventured.

"Oh, I wouldn't say that. It's just looking rather sad and neglected, but we can soon get that sorted out, I think. Built to last, you know, bit like me!" The wheezing laugh came again.

"Well, I work from home, Jolly, so I will be in and out a bit, but I generally sit and work here at the kitchen table, so if you need to show me how it works, or if you need anything, just give me a shout."

He nodded and muttered, 'Yes, yes, fine,' while stroking his chin in a contemplative way, his eyes narrowed as he surveyed the beast.

Victoria called Moss and they trotted outside to check on the hens that were scratching about happily, singing in their funny little high-pitched voices. She decided you could never be miserable around hens. They always sounded so optimistic and contented.

* * * * *

Later, as Victoria tapped at her keyboard and Moss slept, dreaming noisily with squeaks and grunts and twitches, Jolly clanked and furtled away at the Rayburn. Odd bits of black metal were carefully removed from the bowels of the beast and placed, with infinite care, on newspaper that he had brought with him and spread out on the kitchen floor. Occasionally there was the clang of a hammer on metal and the rasp of a wire brush. Far from being intrusive, Victoria found it quite soothing and managed quite a few hundred words on the joys of rare breed chickens.

She had downloaded the photos of Martha and was pleased to see there were plenty of useable ones. She enlarged and lightened the ones she had taken of the veterinary supplies and thought she'd google them, but realised it was probably lunchtime and she ought to offer tea and cake.

"Jolly, it's almost one o'clock. Would you like tea with your lunch? I believe there's some cake in the tin, too."

It took him a moment to free his mind from the intricacies of the Rayburn, but eventually he straightened up and said, "That would be splendid, thank you!"

They sat at the table and Jolly produced a much-battered tin from his toolbox and took out a pack of sandwiches, neatly wrapped in greaseproof paper. Victoria wanted to hug him. It was like having her grandfather back in the room. In a separate piece of greaseproof, he even had some salt, just as Grandpa Cecil had done, and into which Jolly dipped a hard-boiled egg.

"Would you care for a sandwich, Miss West? They are Cheddar and my own home-made pickle."

Victoria had been going to refuse, but the words 'home-made' had been said with such modesty that she felt she couldn't refuse. "Thank you, Jolly." She bit into it and it was, of course, delicious. "Mmmm! That's lovely, sweet and yet spicy."

"It's a no-cook recipe. Actually, I believe your aunt gave it to me a good few years ago."

"She did?" Victoria was amazed and then rearranged her expression. "Oh yes, of course, she was keen on preserves and cakes."

"Ah yes, her cakes…" He looked dreamy. "I can't imagine where you cook yours," he said, nodding to the tin. "You can't have been using the Rayburn."

Victoria, who was a very poor liar, looked down and took another bite of her sandwich to buy time before saying, "Luckily for me, Albert lets me use his kitchen. It's quite well equipped actually."

"I see. Now I understand!" The twinkle in his eye made her realise that he did indeed understand how the wonderful cakes came to pass.

She removed the lid of the cake tin and pushed it towards him. "Do help yourself. There's a knife here." They ate in companionable silence and only Victoria was aware of the puppy drool that was collecting on her left foot as Moss longed to share some of their lunch.

"So, Jolly," she said, "how long have you lived in this part of the world? You don't sound like a native."

"The old cultured tones blowing my cover again, eh? No, I moved here from Cambridge about twenty-five years ago."

"Really? I know Cambridge slightly. I had a friend who went to Peterhouse."

He smiled wistfully. "My old alma mater. What a coincidence. I was a Fellow there, blissful times. But then, well, I had a bit of a 'moment', and I felt it was probably time to move on." He stared into his mug of tea. Victoria kept quiet, not wanting to interrupt his train of thought. "It was for the best, I think. Mrs Jolly decided to move on, too, but sadly not in the same direction as myself. But there, we can't have everything, can we?" He looked up and smiled sadly and sipped his tea.

He went on, "I have always been practical with my hands, unusual for an old academic. Most of my colleagues couldn't change a light bulb, you know. Curious. So, when I moved to this glorious corner of England, I decided to use my hands, not my brains, and I found I rather liked Rayburns, Agas, log burners and others of their ilk. It has kept me pleasantly entertained ever since. And, as we freelance technicians are generally a dying breed, I do not find myself short of work and I lead a pleasant, if undemanding existence. I travel the county, I sometimes even venture into Cornwall, such is the excitement of my life, and I work in all sorts of places, from the smallest woodman's cottage to what we used to call stately homes." He gazed at the cake tin.

"Do help yourself to a second slice if you'd like," said Victoria gently. He carved off another piece and set it on his plate.

"I'm more interested in the work than the people, of course. I do find some people terribly difficult. No, Jolly, be honest – I find most people difficult. It is a failing of mine. You, Miss West, I find quite restful, as was your aunt, so I think we will get along well."

Victoria smiled at him over the edge of her mug, feeling as pleased as if she'd just been awarded a gold star.

"One often becomes invisible in this job, you know, just a

tradesman performing a job of work, so one does get to overhear some amusing things. Or, like yesterday, some quite frightful things."

Victoria perked up and put down her mug. "Really? Do tell!"

Jolly attempted to look reluctant, but then grinned and sat back in his chair. "They really were the most frightful people, frightful. At one point, I even wondered if it was all some ghastly practical joke, but I rather think it wasn't."

"Whatever did you hear?" Her newshound nose was twitching.

"These two women, I can't really call them ladies, I'm sorry, bit of an old snob, another failing of mine. I digress, these two women were arguing like fishwives and using the most filthy language. Nothing I hadn't heard before, you understand, but one doesn't expect it in such luxurious surroundings – a quite extraordinarily lavish barn conversion. Cost millions, I should think. One wall almost entirely made of glass, if you can imagine such a thing." Victoria could, and was positively straining at the leash now.

"The householder, for whom I was working, was being given what could best be described as a severe earwigging by what I deduced was her sister-in-law, a woman saddled with the dubious moniker of 'India'. My dear, are you all right? You look like you've had a shock."

Victoria tried to look relaxed. "No, no, do go on, it sounds fascinating! Whatever were they arguing about?"

"Well, this India person was haranguing the Peacock woman, I don't think I knew a first name for her, but she is the owner of the property and of the neglected Rayburn. Brand new really, hardly ever used. As I told her, it didn't need any attention at all, but she insisted." He sipped his tea, taking an inordinately long time over it, in Victoria's view. "It appears that India was in possession of secrets about Mrs Peacock of a somewhat compromising nature and was more than happy to divulge them if she wasn't given her fair share of the family booty, as she put it." He sat back, smiling broadly. "I'm glad you are finding this so fascinating. Are they people you know, by any chance?"

Victoria coloured slightly. "Um yes, actually, they are, but don't let that stop you."

"As you will. The Peacock woman did not take this at all well, as you can imagine, and retaliated with some quite extraordinary claims upon the character and appearance of dear India. At one point, I had to put my head in the main oven as I feared they might spot me smirking, but really, they were completely oblivious to me, so I needn't have worried."

"Well, how very interesting, Jolly. Is there more?"

"Oh yes, but I wonder if I could trouble you for a little more tea? I am doing more talking than I usually do in a week and it is quite tiring on the larynx." Desperate to know more, Victoria made a new pot of tea in record time and sat back down.

"Now where was I? Oh yes, my head was in the oven. Well, as I emerged, I heard a great chiming and wondered what on earth it was. It turned out to be a hideously pretentious door chime. Anyway, the next thing I hear are the excited shriekings of two rustics. I am ashamed to say I couldn't resist strolling casually across to the kitchen door as I polished a burner into shape, just to get a gander at them."

"A dark burly chap and a neurotic-looking woman with long dark hair?"

"You've hit the nail on the head there, Miss West, well done. Well, these two obviously did not gain admittance, but they must have managed to get a grubby wellington boot at least partly over the threshold as the door was not slammed in their faces." He poured himself more tea, maddeningly slowly, and Victoria thought she would explode if he didn't get on with it.

"An extraordinary shouting match followed with the rustics accusing the nouveau riches, for that is surely what they are, of the ludicrous charge of chicken rustling! Really, it was fascinating. In all honestly, I had finished the service on the Rayburn ten minutes previously, but I couldn't bear to miss the excitement, so I just kept cleaning and polishing.

"At this point, it all got slightly more alarming. The India woman, who is a forceful personage, as I expect you know, laughed at the rustic male and rather belittled him. The neurotic rustic female then flew at India in an absolute rage – quite spectacular really, I'd never seen such behaviour! She used her fingernails like a cat and even spat like a feline. I rather think I stood open-mouthed at this point. Anyway, the male of the party grabbed her and had to restrain her forcibly. She kept screeching, 'Don't you laugh at him! Don't you dare laugh at him!' and other far worse threats."

"Goodness!" was all Victoria could manage.

"Well quite, that's what I thought. The Peacock woman seemed quite upset by all this, but India is clearly a battler and she stood her ground and was really quite eloquent in the face of such hysteria. Mrs Peacock was all for pacifying everyone and did her best to calm the situation. Explaining that she would not know how to pluck, let alone kill a chicken if she had rustled one and that she bought hers ready prepared from Waitrose was, I thought, not quite what the situation needed, but still."

"Ah yes, that does sound like Caroline."

"Her final suggestion was not unreasonable. She suggested to the man that he purchase an electric fence to keep his hens safe. Unfortunately, it appears he already has not one, but several, and he and the hysterical woman sloped off still muttering darkly."

Victoria slumped back, exhausted by the excitement of it all.

"Well!"

Jolly was neatly folding away his greaseproof paper and putting it back inside the battered tin. "Indeed. I have probably said far too much, my dear. I am sorry. I am always an all or nothing sort of person. Sometimes, I don't speak for a week."

"Really?"

"Oh yes. I sometimes find I just have absolutely nothing to say, and I just think instead."

Victoria sighed. "Well, I think you should write a book. It sounds as if you are perfectly placed to hear all sorts of things. I am sure you have plenty of tales to tell." She was already wondering if she could sell a series of interviews with him, or perhaps ghost-write a book with him herself – not so much 'It Shouldn't Happen To A Vet' as 'Aga Sagas – The True Stories', or something...

He smiled. "I suppose I do, yes. One is invisible you see," he repeated as he had done at the start of his tale. "Perhaps they will put that as my epitaph?"

Victoria smiled at him. "Oh no, I am sure not. It will be something much more, err, jolly!"

"Perhaps so," he said and looked rather sad. What a lovely, interesting and ultimately very lonely man, Victoria thought.

After a pause, Jolly suddenly stood up straight, took a deep breath and rubbed his hands together vigorously, "And now, Miss West, for the main excitement of the day – I must introduce you to the delights of managing a wood-fired Rayburn!"

Victoria listened, took notes, nodded, frowned, asked the odd question and at one point put her own head into the main oven to see exactly what Jolly was talking about. Moss sat under the table, his head cocked to one side, as if wondering what on earth they could be doing.

"Do you think you've got it?" asked Jolly after about half an hour, gathering up his tools and brushes and newspaper.

"Yes, amazingly, I think I have. It's not as complicated as I thought, and it would really be one in the eye for Albert if I could actually manage the thing competently – he will be amazed!"

"I assume the good farmer will be providing you with seasoned wood? If so, I suggest you start firing it up in the next week or two. I am sure you will find it a wonderful addition to your house, if not your life."

"Sounds wonderful and yes, there is a huge stack of dry wood in the corner of the barn, and I think Albert plans to make me my own little wood store just outside the kitchen."

"I expect it will take you a week or two to completely get the feel of it, and you'll probably have the odd disaster, but really, they are the most wonderful pieces of apparatus, built to last and immensely simple and practical." He paused. "Oh, one piece of advice – you might not want to call it 'the thing'. It might take offence and smoke more."

"Oh, now you are teasing me again!"

He smiled. "Perhaps a little, but your aunt found that giving it a name made it easier to relate to and to cajole and flatter, as required."

"I need to flatter it?"

"It might not go amiss."

Victoria laughed. "How wonderfully dotty! What did Aunt Edith call it, do you know?"

"I do indeed. It was Joe Frazier."

She burst out laughing again. "Don't tell me, as in Smokin' Joe Frazier, the boxer?"

"That's the chap. She would often say she'd been having trouble with Joe, or that she'd been exchanging blows with him. A bit of a character was your aunt, as I am sure you know. And now, I must prepare to take my leave." He packed the final few items into his toolbox and extended his hand. "It's been a pleasure, Miss West. Do feel free to call me at any time for any help or advice."

Victoria shook his hand and thought she may well give him a call, just for a chat, if nothing else.

"And do please give my regards to Mr Moreton. I haven't seen him for a while. He was always a fan of the Rayburn, as are most farmers. I expect you'll be finding sickly lambs in the warming oven next spring unless I am very much mistaken."

Victoria shuddered. "Ugh, I always think that sounds as if you are preparing the poor things for Sunday roast."

Jolly smiled and picked up his toolbox: "Well, my dear, in a way, of course, you are!"

Just as they reached the back door, it flew open and Farmer Moreton himself stood there, looking flushed and agitated.

"Jolly! Thought you might still be here. How the hell are you?" There was much hand shaking and general bonhomie.

"Are you all right?" Victoria, watching Albert closely, thought he seemed rather upset underneath his customary joviality.

"Well, to be frank, Victoria, no, I am not. I've just been told some very rum news, very rum indeed."

"Oh dear, had we better all sit down again?"

Jolly scratched his head, "Perhaps I should be going and leave you to it?"

"As you like, Jolly – but it's about the folks up at Burntwood Barn. Is that somewhere you ever go and work?"

"Strange coincidence you should ask, Mr Moreton. I have been regaling Miss West with tales of my recent visit. I was there only yesterday."

"Ah, well then," said Albert, flopping into a chair. "As you probably know some of the characters involved, you might be interested to know there's been another tragedy."

"Oh no!" cried Victoria: "Is it Caroline? Is she all right?"

"Your slightly bonkers friend Caroline is fine, but her sister-in-law, India, is very definitely not." There was a tense silence. "She's dead, apparently electrocuted in some freak accident with one of the electric fences on the farm."

Chapter 11

"I just don't understand it," said Albert shaking his head. "Bleddy nonsense – you can't just accidentally electrocute yourself on an electric fence! Otherwise, the countryside would be full of dead livestock and a few dead farmers and all!"

Jolly tutted. "It is possible, of course, but well, not accidentally, as you say." The two men pondered in silence over their mugs of tea.

"How did you hear about it?" Victoria asked.

"I knows a woman who works at the ambulance call centre. Well, her sister goes with Paddy, the postman, and he was just passing the end of the drive as I was coming in and – well, you know how it is around here." Victoria smiled. She certainly did! The bush telegraph was alive and well, plus the fact that, somewhere along the line, almost everyone was related to everyone else.

"Well, I'm sorry to leave in the midst of such unpleasant news, but I must get back to my humble evening repast and take a turn around the old homestead." Jolly rose to his feet, shook Victoria's hand warmly and, patting it, said, "Remember, my dear, any problems with Joe, and you give me a call." Albert looked puzzled, but said nothing and they both stood and watched him drive off in his very old Volvo.

As the engine died away, Albert turned and gave Victoria a hug. "Sorry, maid, this is all pretty nasty."

She sighed, happy to rest her head on his chest and feel safe and warm in his embrace. "I know, it is all so bizarre. I can't believe it." She wiped away a stray tear. "Oh dear, I don't know why I'm crying, I had hardly met the woman. You spoke to her that evening in the pub and I think you rather liked her, didn't you?" She drew back and looked up at him. His eyes looked particularly blue against his tanned face, bronzed by all the hours he spent working outside, but she noticed a sadness and tiredness that disturbed her.

"That I did. She was a feisty old bird and I quite admired her pluck. But I reckon it was her pluck that did for her. I reckon she said a bit too much to the wrong sort of people." He frowned. "Bleddy shame, all of it. Such a waste."

Nestling her head back against his chest, Victoria said, "I so wish I hadn't made you stop in the lane when we saw Caroline that day. What an idiot! If we'd just driven past, perhaps none of this would have happened."

"I don't know how you make that out, and don't you go taking the blame for everything again. I'm sure this ruckus would have happened one way or t'other, regardless of our presence or otherwise." He patted her briskly on the back and Victoria felt like a baby being gently winded. "C'mon now, let's get some fresh air and give this here pup a walk and – "

The phone began to ring and Victoria went to answer it, but she hesitated, suddenly fearing it might be Caroline. She lifted the receiver and before she could get it to her ear heard: "Victoriaaaaa!!!!!!!!!!!" Albert, hearing the wail of anguish from the other side of the room, sighed.

"Caroline? It's OK, calm down!" The wailing and sobbing continued. "Caroline, I can't understand a word – can you take a deep breath?" But the distressing noises went on unabated. Victoria looked across at Albert and he shrugged.

"Shall I go and get my car keys?"

She nodded apologetically. "Caroline? Caroline! Try and calm yourself and listen. We will be with you in fifteen minutes, OK?" The tone of the wailing changed slightly in a way that could have been interpreted as agreement. Victoria put the phone down. "Oh, for goodness sake!" She took Moss outside and gave him a very quick circuit of the garden and then settled him in his bed. "I'm sorry, sweetie. If we aren't too late, I'll take you out as soon as we get back." She heard a toot from outside, grabbed her bag, locked the door and went out to meet Albert.

They bounced along in the old Land Rover on their way to Burntwood, with Albert scowling and not saying very much. "I'm so sorry, Albert. You really don't need to get involved in all this nonsense. Could you stop scowling, and perhaps slow down a bit? You are making me anxious."

"What? Oh, I'm sorry, maid." He seemed to snap out of a trance and grinned at her. "I wasn't cross or anything, I was just thinking about this electrocution business and, as Jolly said, there's no way 'tis an accident. I hope I can have a snoop round when we get there and – "

"Albert Moreton! I do not want you touching anything that might be even vaguely dangerous!" she cried.

"No, no, don't be daft. I know about electric fences and – "

"No! I really mean it!" She banged her hand on the dashboard. "I can't bear all these awful things happening! There are some very bad people around, really evil, and I think you know it, too"

Albert pulled into a gateway. "Hey now, come on, don't you start getting all het up as well. Be sensible, Victoria. Am I a risk-taking sort of chap?"

Victoria felt shaky. She suddenly realised that the thought of losing Albert was more than she could bear. "Well, no. But you do have your moments. All I'm saying is, well, don't do anything rash. We are only onlookers. I – I'd hate you to get hurt or involved in anything…"

He smiled and squeezed her hand. "All right, you daft woman, I promise to keep me nose out. I'll just keep me ears open and me hands in me pockets!"

Smiling at this ridiculous image, Victoria said, "Promise?"

"I promise. Scout's honour!" He engaged the clutch and they set off again along the narrow lane.

"You've never mentioned being a scout," she said, looking out, as she always did, for the tiny glimpse of sea that could be seen between a cleft in the hills just before the next turning.

"That's because I wasn't."

While Victoria was still trying to work this last statement out, they arrived at the entrance to Burntwood, and Albert had to drive tight into the hedge to let an ambulance pull out and head off in the direction of Westerley with neither its blue light nor siren in use. Clearly, there was no need to hurry. They exchanged resigned looks and Albert parked out of the way of the two police cars and another truck that looked familiar. "Here, that's young Tufty's!" said Albert. "Wonder what he's doing here."

They walked into the barn, half expecting to be challenged by the police, but they were not, and spotted Caroline draped in classic distraught woman pose on one of the huge leather sofas. Victoria went straight across to her and sat down next to her friend. "Caroline! Are you all right? Tell us what happened." She looked twenty years older than when they'd last met. Her face was tear-stained and her hair was a mess. It really looked as if this time her distress was genuine. She slumped into Victoria's arms making a sort of mewing noise and Victoria patted her back slightly distractedly while Albert shoved his hands in his pockets and wandered about looking uncomfortable. A policewoman seemed to be in charge of making tea while a male officer was tucked away in a corner talking into his radio with his back to them.

"Caroline, look at me." Victoria held her at arm's length and almost shook her. "Tell us what happened." Caroline snuffled and hiccupped and sat back, swaying. Albert offered her a snowy-white handkerchief, laundered and neatly ironed by his own fair hands.

Caroline took it gratefully and looked up at him through swollen eyes. "Thank you so much, that is kind," she said meekly. He smiled in return and her lower lip began to quiver.

"Now, now," he said, sitting the other side of her. "This won't get us anywhere, will it? You dry your eyes and let's hear what occurred." Victoria gazed at him like a love-sick teenager. How wonderful he was in a crisis.

The policewoman handed Caroline a mug of tea that she cradled in her trembling hands, but showed no inclination to drink.

"Well, it all started when that awful Morris person came round yesterday and he shouted and bawled at us. I couldn't really understand what he was saying, such a dreadful accent, and well, I think it was something about us 'rustling' his chickens? I don't think I even know what that is, do you?"

Albert smiled, and in his best broad Devonshire accent said, "Well 'tis stealing, basically."

"Oh, OK, I see. Obviously that's ridiculous! As if we would, I mean, chickens – yuk! Fluffy things and their poo smells so vile! I mean, I couldn't! Seriously, I mean, no!" She shuddered and the tea slopped on to her white jeans, but she didn't seem to notice. "He had that strange shrew-like creature with him and she was shrieking, a bit like an animal, actually, and really being terribly rude. And saying such odd things about 'her man'. Quite deranged, of course. And then India, well, you know what she's like." She stopped and looked up at Albert. "Oh dear! I mean what she was like, and she started arguing back. I think she was enjoying it really. She loved a good row." She put the untouched tea on to the coffee table and carefully wiped her eyes on Albert's handkerchief, leaving great black streaks across it. Victoria thought she saw him wince.

"India started really laying into Morris. She was actually terribly witty. She made him look really small, but then the female creature sort of lunged at her and I thought they were going to come to blows – awful, awful! I was trying to calm everyone down and I suggested to that hideous Podger being that he – " she stopped again and swallowed. "Oh I do feel so guilty. You see, I suggested he bought an electric fence to keep his foul fowl under control… and then look what happened!" She gave a great wracking sob and Albert patted her hand.

"Now then, come on, tell us what happened later on. I want to hear the details from you as I can't understand how it happened," he said quietly.

"No one can! That's the awful thing! It was all quiet last night and India went back to stay at the pub. Then she was back again this morning, still going on and on about the money and we were bickering again just like before, and then we heard all sorts of noises from the farm. I think he was putting wooden posts in the ground, or something. Lots of mechanical banging. Then, when we heard his frightful noisy tractor thing start up and drive off, we crept outside to see what he'd done, and there was a new wire fence thing along the boundary, so we thought 'good'. Anyway, I decided to give it a teeny tiny touch. God, I can't believe I did that!" She put her hands to her mouth and her eyes were huge. "I mean, I touched it! It gave me this funny little sort of jolt and I squealed. It wasn't very nice, but it wasn't awful. But India told me I was a wimp, of course, and she came marching over and grabbed the fence with both hands and, and…" She stopped and screwed up her face as if trying to erase the memory. Albert patted her hand again.

In a tiny voice, she went on, "It was as if she was stuck, stuck to the fence. It was horrible. Her face was all rigid and she bared her teeth and… I started screaming and screaming and I didn't know what to do. I thought if I touched her it would get me, too!" The sobs started again, and she began to rock back and forth.

"There, there," said Albert, administering more hand patting. Caroline slumped sideways on to him and snuggled into his shoulder like a child. He and Victoria exchanged stunned looks above her tousled head. "So then what happened?"

From the depths of his shirtfront, Caroline went on. "Suddenly a funny little man with red hair appeared. I hadn't even seen him arrive, and he was marvellous! He ran into the Podgers' farm and managed to turn off the electricity. When it stopped, India sort of deflated and sank to the ground. It was so horrible. She was obviously dead. Very dead. I mean, ugh! If that man hadn't come, I don't know what would have happened."

As if on cue a door opened on what looked to be a study, and Tufty walked out, followed by a burly man who Victoria vaguely thought she recognised. "Thank you, Mr Turner, you've been most helpful," he said and shook Tufty's hand. "I'll let you know when we'll want to see you down at the station." As he left, Tufty glanced across at them and pulled a grim face before scuttling out to his truck and driving off. The plain-clothes man stared hard at Victoria and glanced at Albert. "Jenkins?" he snapped. The man who'd been talking on the radio walked quickly over.

"Sir?"

The burly man cocked his head and the two of them went into the study and closed the door.

"I don't like him," said Caroline, still firmly attached to Albert's chest. "And he doesn't like me. He thinks I murdered Giles, you see."

"Oh surely not!" said Victoria, her voice sounding loud in the huge room.

A thump from upstairs made them all look up and Caroline gave a little gasp. "That will be Freddie. Freddie!" she wailed.

"So he's still here then. What's he doing? Why isn't he down here with you?" snapped Albert. A toilet flushed and there was another thump from above.

"I don't know, oh, I don't know." Caroline was crying again. "He's trying to leave, to – to pack up all his stuff. He wants to avoid the police, you see. They do pick on him so."

"I'm not surprised," said Victoria under her breath, but Caroline didn't seem to hear. The toilet had flushed again, helping to muffle her aside. Albert glanced up at the ceiling again.

"He, well, he's not awfully good in stressful situations," Caroline went on. "I think he's trying to get all his stuff together and get back to London, or perhaps go up to Scotland, I – I'm not too sure really…" She trailed off lamely. A car drew up outside and they could hear doors being opened and closed.

"What did Tufty say?" persisted Albert, steering Caroline back to the earlier fateful events.

"Who?" Caroline stared at him.

"Tufty, the chap with the red hair. Mr Turner, what did he say?"

"Oh, I'm not sure, something about it being wired up to the main something or other. I don't know anything about electricity. I just plug things in and they work, like magic. But I know they think I did it, even though I wouldn't know how!"

"I think that's a bit far-fetched, don't you?" Victoria said, although she wasn't entirely sure what she thought about any of it.

Caroline lowered her voice. "You see, India had been being

very difficult with me. She'd made threats, you know."

"Oh dear," said Victoria, pretending she hadn't already heard Jolly's version of events.

"Well, she knew a few things about me, I mean, nothing awful, but we all have a few teeny skeletons in our cupboards, don't we?" She looked imploringly at Albert and Victoria waiting for them to agree. When they didn't she went on. "She was saying that if I didn't give her some of Giles's money she would make life difficult for me. How ridiculous is that? I mean, it's my money, fair and square! She said some pretty vile things and we did both get a bit cross."

"I see," said Victoria, "but why do the police think…"

Caroline fidgeted like a naughty child. "I think I might have said a bit too much when they first arrived. I was still terribly, terribly upset, you see, and I was trying to say who India was and why she was here and, well…"

As Victoria and Albert exchanged looks of disbelief the door to the office was flung open again and the two policemen reappeared. "Call in the men," said the burly one and Jenkins went outside.

Just then, Victoria caught sight of the end of a piece of rope that was being lowered from the first floor and slowly inching its way down past a floor-length window at the back of the barn. She looked at Albert, who was equally aghast.

Jenkins returned with three uniformed men. Caroline gave a squeal and jumped up.

"You!" said the burly one, pointing at her, "Sit down and shut up! Anderson – sit with her." Albert and Victoria got to their feet as the policewoman came across and sat down next to Caroline.

"Sir!" shouted Jenkins and pointed to the rope that was now almost down to the ground.

"Christ!" snarled the burly man. "Come on!"

Then it all got very exciting and rather like an episode of

Chapter 11

The Sweeney, in Victoria's eyes, as the policemen rushed upstairs together. There was lots of crashing and banging and raised voices. They all looked up as they followed the thunder of footsteps as they travelled from one room to another before there was one extra loud thud, which they assumed was Freddie succumbing to the inevitable arrest.

"Freddie, Freddie!" shrieked Caroline, jumping up. The policewoman promptly pulled her back down and placed a restraining arm across her body.

"Try and stay calm, Caroline. It's much better if you can," said Victoria.

"But they think it's me, I know they do! And it's all so wrong! I haven't done anything!" she wailed. The policewoman was staring at her and holding her firmly by the shoulders.

"Caroline, be quiet! Do you have a solicitor?" said Victoria.

"Um, oh, I think so. Well, Giles had one that dealt with all the trusts and legal stuff, but – "

"Well, I expect he'll do as a start. Where is his number? I think you might want to call him."

"It's in my phone." Caroline went to stand up, but the policewoman pushed her down. "Take your hands off me! Who do you think you are, manhandling me in my own house, you ghastly officious oik!" She pushed the woman away, who instantly came back at her.

"Just stay calm,Caroline, and tell me where your phone is." Victoria knew they were running out of time.

"In my bloody jeans pocket, but this uniformed jobsworth won't let me stand up to get at it – oh!" she cried as the policewoman, finally losing patience, put Caroline into an effective, but relatively gentle-looking restraining hold.

The noise upstairs now consisted mostly of shuffling and

grunting and gradually the strange tableau of contorted bodies appeared, moving slowly down the stairs, with the three uniformed men holding Freddie in a much less gentle restraining hold. "Bloody idiot was just about to climb out the window on a rope!" sneered Jenkins.

Freddie was white-faced and furious. "You wait until my lawyer gets here! Just you wait!" he snarled as they bundled him out of the front door and shoved him firmly into a marked police car and roared off.

The burly man came back into the room and stood in the doorway, arms folded across his barrel chest. "Miss West, isn't it? I knew I'd seen you before," he said brusquely, glaring at Victoria through narrowed eyes.

"Correct," said Victoria, and was gratified to see Albert step forward and stand several inches taller than the policeman. "I think we did meet once before, but I'm afraid I can't remember your name," she said terribly politely.

"Amery, Detective Chief Inspector Amery, and, if I'm not mistaken, you had something to do with a previous murder case. That's a bit of a coincidence, isn't it? Sleepy old place like this, and you pop up twice? Should I be taking you down to the station, too?"

Victoria held up her hands in mock surrender. "If you like, but you already have my statement about Mr Peacock's death and no one has been in the least bit interested in me so far."

"Victoria – Miss West – has nothing to do with any of this latest dreadful happening," said Albert, folding his arms to match Amery's. "She's just a friend of Mrs Peacock, trying to be helpful in a nasty situation."

"And who the hell are you?" snarled Amery.

"Albert Moreton and you've already got my statement as well. I was at the party when the deaths occurred."

"I suggest the two of you clear off PDQ then before I decide to take a closer interest. I don't like coming across people 'accidentally'. Always makes me suspicious…"

Albert took Victoria's arm and steered her to the door.

"Tori!" squeaked Caroline. "Don't leave me!"

"I'm sorry, but there's nothing we can do, Caroline. Call your solicitor, that's the best thing to do," said Victoria. As they left, they could hear Amery reading Caroline her rights in a monotone and Caroline starting to wail like a siren. Outside, a marked police car stood ready to receive her, its back door open, with Jenkins waiting.

"Oh God," said Victoria. "How awful!"

"Let's just get in the car and get out of here," said Albert and he hustled her over to the old Land Rover.

"I need a drink," he said as they made their way back towards the village. "Pub?"

"Why not?" agreed Victoria. "I don't know about you, but I'm not sure why the police are arresting Caroline and Freddie now. Surely they can't think they had anything to do with poor India? And if it's about Giles, well, why now?"

Albert shrugged. "I don't know, maid. Perhaps they've uncovered things we don't know about. But if it 'twere me, I reckon I'd be looking on the other side of that electric fence."

"My thoughts exactly," said Victoria.

The Swaddle Arms was quiet. It was just gone six and the bar was almost empty, except for a small red-headed individual perched on a bar stool and nursing what looked like a whisky.

"Tufty, on the hard stuff?" Albert slid onto the stool next to the little car mechanic.

"Whachya, Albert. Yeah, I felt I needed something a bit stronger than usual."

Victoria climbed onto the stool on the other side of him and patted his arm. "Sorry, Tufty, it must have been awful."

He nodded and took a swig of his drink. "Yeah." They fell silent.

Roger appeared from the kitchen and beamed at them. "Albert, Victoria, good to see you! What will you have, the usual?"

Albert nodded. "Yep, a pint for me and a glass of white for Victoria – a large one, I think, nice and chilled, mind."

Roger busied himself with their order, and said, "You heard about Tufty's heroics?"

Tufty snorted. "Don't be daft, man., Nothing heroic. Didn't save no one, did I? Her was proper dead, poor maid."

"Well, yes, but…"

"Yes, sadly we know all about it," interrupted Albert. "We've just come from Burntwood ourselves."

Roger put down the drinks and scratched his chin. "I don't understand it. Always been such a quiet place, Swaddlecombe. Then all these incomers arrive and it's like an episode of Midsomer Murders or something. Oh, no offence, Victoria!" he added suddenly, realising what he'd said. He paused. "But you do always seem to be in the thick of it. What with those jam people and all that carry-on, and then the violet farm lot. Blimey, I mean, you'd think jam-making and flower-growing would be peaceful pastimes!"

Victoria felt a little uncomfortable. "Well, I don't seek it out, Roger, honestly. I just seem to be in the wrong place at the wrong time, or perhaps we incomers are cursed. Maybe it's all a plot by you Devonians to get us to go back where we came from," she said slightly irritably.

Completely missing the irony, Roger laughed uproariously. "Oh no, no, we wouldn't do that! We like you all coming down here and spending your money! Talking of which, does anyone want a coffee?"

They looked at him, bemused. "We've just got our drinks. Why would we want coffee?" asked Albert.

"Oh right, yes, 'course. But well, we need to sell more coffee, now that Trudy's gone and got this fancy machine. The coffee won't keep and I don't think it's good for the machine if it doesn't get used much." He glared at the huge silver coffee machine lurking at the end of the bar. "To tell the truth, I'd be glad to see the back of the blasted thing. Frightens the pants off me with all its steam and froth and slurping noises. Always sounds like it's about to blow up."

"Perhaps it is," said Albert. "Then we could have another drama and you could blame that on Victoria, too!" Roger went pink and they both grinned at him. "Oh, go and chat up your wife or something, and stop looking like such a dollop!" said Albert, not unkindly. He turned his attention to Tufty, who was swilling the amber liquid slowly around his glass and staring into the depths. "Tufty, old mate, shall we go and sit in the corner?"

"What? Oh, yeah, yeah, why not?"

They decamped to the cosy round table in the corner with high-backed settles, a popular spot, especially in winter when the huge inglenook was filled with a warming log fire.

"Are you all right, Tufty?" Victoria was concerned. The little man was usually so bright and sparky and the tragedy had obviously affected him deeply.

He took a deep breath. "Yeah, thanks, Victoria, I will be. It was a bit of a shock, mind. I'm just grateful I didn't have the boy Eddy with me. Wouldn't have wanted him to see that."

"No, absolutely. But why were you there anyway?" she asked, taking a large swig of her wine.

"I was on my way back from a job and wasn't in no great rush, so I thought I'd just swing by and tell Mrs Peacock about her husband's Range Rover, oh I mean ex-husband, no – deceased husband – I dunno what to call him! Anyway, I was just going to say what the insurers had said and basically, what did she want me to do with it. It's getting to be a bit in the way at the garage, truth be told, and I'd like it shifted."

"Lucky you turned up when you did," said Albert.

"Well, not really. Wasn't very lucky for me, was it, and it wasn't lucky for that poor woman, neither. That Mrs Peacock was hysterical, running about like something off a comedy show on the telly, wearing daft-looking pink and blue wellingtons and flapping her arms about like some mad bird. There was some bloke there when I pulled up, but he scarpered straight back indoors. Dunno who he was."

Victoria chipped in, "Was he skinny and dark and furtive-looking?"

"Yup, that sums him up proper. Tell the truth, I'd forgotten about him until now. Yeah, weasely git. Why didn't he come and do something useful instead of leaving her stranded like that?"

Victoria and Albert exchanged glances. "It's in his nature, I'm afraid, running away," said Albert darkly. "So what happened?"

"Well, I saw that poor woman, India – weird name, and she was obviously in trouble. I couldn't understand what was goin' on at first. I mean – 'twas an electric fence, that's all. I bloomin' nearly went over and told her to let go and then it sort of dawned on me that she couldn't and that there was something not at all right happening. That was when I ran round into the Podgers' place. I shouted and bawled, but there didn't seem to be no one there.

"Martha's old banger of a car wasn't there and neither was Morris's tractor, but there were a couple of other old heaps lying about so I don't know if they was there or not, but I was getting a bit frantic by then and I just ran into that tip of a barn and – well!" He paused and took a slug of whisky. "You've never seen nothing like it!"

"What? What?" Victoria was on the edge of her seat. Out of the corner of her eye, she saw Roger had stopped mid-glass polish, mouth open and as engrossed as she was and obviously earwigging the whole story, even though he must have already heard it when Tufty had first arrived.

"'Twas like Spaghetti Junction in there, so bloomin' dangerous! I dunno how the barn didn't catch fire." He took another gulp of whisky and emptied the glass.

"Someone had lashed up cables, one coming off the big electric main feed on the barn wall, and there were plugs and wires all over the place. It was fizzing and sparking and I was pretty bloody worried, I can tell you. I know about cars and a bit about electrics, but I don't know what the hell had been happening there." He picked up his glass, saw it was empty and put it down again. "Anyway, I just went for the fuse box that was near the barn door – that was standing open and looked messed around with, too – and I just hoped for the best and pulled the main fuse out."

There was a silence. Roger walked across to them, and put another whisky in front of Tufty and walked silently back behind the bar. "Cheers," said Tufty and took a swig. "I'll regret this tomorrow, I know it. I'm not a drinking man, but…" They waited while he collected his thoughts.

"I came back to the poor woman, and she was just lying on the ground. 'Twas obvious her was dead. Real horrible it was." He took a deep breath. "That Mrs Peacock, her was sort of gibbering and saying something about thank God she'd been wearing her Bodens, or something. I dunno what she meant. But she said if she hadn't been, it could have been her lying there all frizzled like."

Albert looked enquiringly at Victoria. "Her Boden wellies. Boden is a fashion label. She meant her rubber boots. How ironic that Caroline's undying sense of fashion might just have saved her life."

Albert shook his head. "Never heard such nonsense in me life! They're all bleddy bonkers!"

"Anyways, I asked if she'd phoned the police or the ambulance, and, of course, she hadn't, she was in such a state, so I went and did it. Lord knows how she is going to get on without her husband around!" he added rather perceptively.

"I expect she'll be heading back to London before long," said Victoria with a sigh. "Much safer up there!"

"What with all those muggings and shootings?" asked Tufty incredulously. "Cor, you wouldn't get me living up there, no fear!"

"So," said Albert, bringing Tufty back to the matter in hand, "was that complete incompetence in setting up that electric fence, or was someone trying to – you know..."

Tufty gave a contemptuous snort. "Come off it, Albert! What farmer doesn't know how to set up an electric fence, and usually with just a battery!" He tossed back the remains of his drink. "Sorry, but that's me done. I'm going home to have a bath and then get an early night. I just hope I can sleep…"

"But Tufty, did you tell the police all this?" asked Victoria as the little man got unsteadily to his feet.

"I did, but they didn't seem to take much notice, to be honest." He moved away from the table. "G'night." And with that, he walked slightly unevenly towards the door, half tripped up the step and disappeared outside.

Chapter 12

The following morning was distinctly autumnal and Victoria felt a mixture of excitement and apprehension as she realised it was nearly time for the inaugural lighting of the Rayburn. Albert had already brought a few barrowloads of logs round and had muttered something about building her a log store. He was so generous with his time that she didn't like to pester him, but she hoped the store would get built sooner rather than later as she was quite looking forward to getting Smokin' Joe to bend to her will.

She rummaged in one of the many cupboards and brought out her aunt's old battered kettle. She'd give it a good clean and polish ready to start using it on top of the Rayburn. How lovely it would be to hear a kettle whistle blowing as it came to the boil rather than the unromantic click of her electric model. Who needed modern clean efficiency when you could sit around for ages stoking a fire and waiting to get enough hot water to make your cup of tea?

While all these deeply meaningful thoughts were permeating her head, Victoria had used the scorned, yet effective electric kettle to make her much-needed morning coffee and now stood looking out of the kitchen window, frowning. She felt uneasy and she knew why. The police were on the wrong track.

The sound of a distant bark brought her to her senses and she realised that Albert and a very excited dog would soon be bursting into the kitchen after their early morning walk. She refilled the kettle, grabbed Moss's feed bowl and adopted a casual pose, trying to look more awake than she felt. Bang went the door, woof went the dog and Albert said cheerfully, "Hello, my lovely, you look like you've just woken up!"

Victoria smiled contentedly and, realising she'd fooled no one, said, "Tea?"

Albert, who looked as fresh as a daisy, said, "Proper job! I've let the hens out and fed 'em and Moss and I have had a good old rake around the farm. He's getting to be quite a grown-up little chap now, aren't you, boy?" He ruffled the dog's ears.

As they finished their toast, Victoria felt she couldn't put it off any longer. "Albert, we need to talk about India's death. Well, let's be honest, India's murder."

Albert finished his last mouthful of toast and washed it down with a swig of tea. He put down his mug carefully. "I can't say I don't think you're right, but I don't think it's our place to interfere. No!" He held up his hand as Victoria went to speak. "Victoria, you do like to meddle so and it gets you into some fearful scrapes. The police know their job and I'm sure they will realise soon enough that Freddie and Caroline had nothing to do with her murder. They might have arrested them for something else, for all we know."

Victoria's eyebrows had shot up. "Like what?"

"Well, hold on now, don't you go and get in a lather about it, I could be completely wrong, but we know Freddie is into drugs."

"True."

"And I regret to say it, but I think your friend Caroline might have more than a passing interest in the same."

"Also true, sadly," said Victoria with a sigh.

"So they might be acting on some information about that. And then, of course, there was all that toilet-flushing."

Victoria looked at him blankly. "Sorry, what?"

"When we were there with Caroline and the policewoman, and that idiot Freddie was upstairs rushing about and then started lowering a rope."

"You've lost me."

"I heard the toilet flush at least three times when he was up there. Now either our Freddie had an attack of the trots or he was busily trying to flush his drugs haul down the pan."

"Oh, I see! You clever old stick! I hadn't realised. Of course."

Albert scowled at her. "Less of the 'old', thank you, maid. And they will already have marked our Freddie's card for that embezzlement business a few years ago." He paused. "And of course, there's no reason to assume that whoever murdered Giles and that poor young maid Jessica was the same person who just fried India."

Victoria shuddered. "Ugh! Don't. Poor woman. I do hope Tufty is feeling better today. The poor chap was really shaken up yesterday."

Albert smiled wryly. "Well, I reckon he'll have a sore head this morning, if nothing else."

Victoria contemplated her empty coffee cup. She really shouldn't have a third cup, but she felt her brain needed an extra boost this morning, so she got up to make some more. "I assume you agree with me that the Podgers are behind this latest dreadful happening?"

"I'll lay you a pound to a penny that Martha Podger most certainly isn't involved. She may be a bit shabby around the edges, that one, but she's an honest woman deep down. Now as for Morris, well…"

Victoria turned to face him. "I reckon that Sylvia is as likely as anyone, what with her history. I mean, I wouldn't have a clue how to wire anything up. I'd probably give myself a shock putting a fuse in a plug, whereas someone must have known what to do and she clearly does."

Albert sighed. "You may have a point there, maid, I'm sorry to say."

Victoria made her coffee and refilled Albert's mug with tea from the pot. "So what about Giles and Jessica? Who have we got in the frame for that? Have the police confirmed what killed them yet?" She sat down and looked at him enquiringly.

"'Twas definitely poison, but I don't think they know exactly what."

"Or they aren't saying?'"

He shrugged. "Could be."

"Of course! There were all those drugs in the Podger's barn. I hadn't finished looking at those. I thought I might go and see that nice vet, Mr Wallace, and see what he has to say."

Albert rolled his eyes. "Oh now come on, I thought you'd given up on that idea? Don't you start nosing about. You might arouse suspicions where they shouldn't be any."

"No, you wanted me to give up that idea, I didn't. Don't worry, Albert, I plan to just casually pop in and have a chat with him when he's next holding a surgery. Unless you've got him coming out here to look at any of your cows or sheep, of course?"

"No I have not, and I'm not having you interfering with him here when he's working anyway. He charges quite enough as it is without you plying him with tea and cake and adding half an hour to the bill!"

"You old curmudgeon. Honestly, anyone would think you didn't want me to meet him." She paused and grinned as Albert glowered. "I heard Jean describe him as 'a bit of a dish'. She apparently gets all swoony over him when she takes her cat in to see him for its annual boosters."

Albert snorted. "That woman would swoon over anything with

a pulse. You can't put any store by that!" He rubbed his chin. "But it has to be said, he could be described as a fine figure of a man. Past his prime now, though, of course."

"Oh, of course," she teased. "Not like you!"

"I'll have you know Tar Wallace is a good three years older than me."

"Tar? Good lord, what's that short for?"

Albert looked puzzled. "I'm not sure I can remember. Tarquin, or something, dunno. Anyway, enough of your cheek! Leave the man alone. He's happily married!"

"Oh Albert, you are funny!" She kissed the top of his head as she got up to clear the table.

"Yes, well…" he said grumpily. "Just you behave!" Trying not to smile, he kissed her on the cheek and headed for the door. "I'm going to be out topping thistles most of the day, so I'll catch up with you a bit later."

"That sounds exciting. See you then."

As soon as the door closed, Victoria scuttled across to her laptop and started it up. She found the photo of the bottles from the barn and began googling the long medical names.

* * * * *

"Miss West, what can I do for you and, Moss, isn't it?" Tar Wallace, the vet, looked at her over his half-moon glasses, his eyes very dark and, she decided, quite definitely brooding. His thick dark hair was swept back and his sideburns, quite long sideburns, showed just enough grey to be classed as distinguished. A dark shadow of stubble on a strong chin added to the handsome effect quite pleasingly.

Victoria had waited about ten minutes in a quiet, neat waiting room before being ushered in to see the man himself. Moss had been unimpressed, clearly remembering his initial visits when people had jabbed things in him or, worse, squirted some horrible stuff up his nose, and he'd sneezed a lot. Victoria had only seen nurses or a young whey-faced vet on her previous visits and felt now that she had been rather cheated by not encountering Mr Wallace before.

She knew she was a useless liar, but hoped that by using Moss as part of her excuse to see the vet, she might seem a bit more convincing. She took a deep breath. "Well, you see, he's had a bit of a cough."

Mr Wallace looked at her steadily. "A cough?"

"Yes, a sort of barking cough – oh, sorry, no, that sounds stupid, he's a dog!" She laughed idiotically and felt herself going a little pink. "I'd say a dry cough, like a tickle in his throat." She cleared her own throat for added effect.

The vet stooped and picked Moss up in one smooth movement and placed him gently on the examination table. "Now then, young man, what seems to be the trouble?" He spoke quietly and earnestly to the little dog as if they were having a private conversation and gently stroked his head. "Your owner seems to think you're a bit under the weather." Moss's tail began to wag enthusiastically and Victoria was sure he was telepathically telling Mr Wallace that this was all a complete waste of time and he was sorry, and it wasn't his idea. The vet looked in his eyes and then used his stethoscope to listen to his chest. Next, he examined his mouth and looked at his gums. He stroked Moss slowly and deliberately. Victoria noticed how elegant the man's hands were and felt the very slight flutter of a butterfly in her stomach. As he stroked the dog, his hands seem to be feeling every bone and muscle and Moss stood still, entranced, seemingly as smitten as his owner.

"…I said, I can't find anything at all wrong with him, Miss West. Miss West?"

Victoria gave a start, not having heard half of what Mr Wallace had said. "Oh, I'm so sorry, I was miles away!"

"Clearly," he said with an arching of one strong dark eyebrow, a la Sean Connery, and Victoria felt her pinkness go up a shade. He took off his half glasses and slid them into his top pocket. "I said your dog is fine. He seems very well, a lovely, bright little chap."

"Oh, that is good news!" There was a silence as the vet continued to gently stroke Moss's back while the dog stood transfixed and gazed up at him in complete adoration. Victoria giggled. "Do you have that effect on all your patients?"

"Usually," said Mr Wallace with the faintest hint of a smile on his rather nice lips.

"Oh," said Victoria, even pinker now. "Err, actually, um, there was something else."

"I thought there might be," he said drily.

She laughed nervously. "Well, I er, I found some old bottles of drugs and things when I was clearing out my aunt's house and I wondered what they were. I mean, what they would be used for? She used to keep chickens and I think had other livestock sometimes, and…?

"I remember your aunt."

"Oh, do you? How amazing!"

"Not really, I was her vet," he said, then after a pause, "Interesting woman." He took the list of names that Victoria had printed out earlier and was now proffering half-heartedly in the vet's direction. He put his glasses back on. The eyebrow did its Sean Connery thing again. "You say these were at your aunt's house?" The glasses came off and she got the full-bore brown stare again.

Victoria felt her chest tighten. "Yes, well some of them were, the others I, er, found." The dark eyes were unblinking and she felt very silly. "…in a barn. At a farm. Nearby-ish."

The glasses went back on and he continued reading. Then he stopped and opened the consulting room door. "Cathy?" The plump veterinary nurse who had taken Victoria's details when she'd first arrived lumbered into the room. She had a somewhat bovine air, placid-faced and slightly slow, built more for comfort than speed.

"Yes, Mr Wallace?"

"Are Miss West's records accessible without too much difficulty?"

The girl's large brown eyes moved slowly from the vet's face to Victoria's and back again. This activity seemed to take up all her concentration and speech was clearly not possible at the same time.

Mr Wallace snatched his glasses off and said testily, "The original Miss West, Edith West, up at April Cottage… Well?"

"I'll have to have a look," said cow-like Cathy and ambled back to her desk. Mr Wallace followed and shoved Victoria's printed list under her nose.

"If you find them, have a quick check and see if any of these are on her records as having been supplied by this practice, although I think it's extremely unlikely."

"Oh, really?" asked Victoria, looking what she hoped was suitably puzzled.

"These are not the sort of things we would supply to the public. Some of them are drugs we would use ourselves, hefty anaesthetics and the like, but some of the others are drugs we wouldn't stock at all and are not common in this country." He was a tall man, standing over six feet and Victoria felt like a naughty child being lectured by one of her teachers. "Unless your aunt was a bit of a whizz ordering goods on the internet, which I doubt very much, I cannot imagine how she came by them." He hadn't raised his voice, but his tone made it perfectly clear that he didn't believe her story of how she'd come by the names of the drugs.

"Oh dear," said Victoria distractedly. "Well, I'd better come clean. You see, I'm writing a novel and I wanted to know how to kill someone quickly and using perhaps veterinary drugs off the internet, but I thought it would sound so silly if I came along here and said that …"

"So you managed to come up with something far sillier instead and used your very nice dog as an accomplice." Was there the slightest twinkle in his eye?

Victoria was by now past the pink stage and was positively red "Erm, yes."

"Excuse me, Mr Wallace," said Cathy slowly, "but no, we didn't give Miss West nothing like this. Her usually had wormer and anti-flea spray and something for a touch of red mite." She turned her moist eyes to Victoria, who suspected the girl had been eavesdropping on everything she and the vet had been saying. She just hoped she was as stupid as she looked.

"Well, there you are," said Mr Wallace and made as if to go on to his next patient.

"But, I still don't know the answer!" cried Victoria, now past the point of shame and desperate to get something of value out of this whole sorry tale. "Could I use them to kill someone quickly?"

Mr Wallace turned back. "If you had a very large syringe of succinylcholine and you had the opportunity to stand there and slowly inject it into your victim, that would do the trick – effective, but hardly subtle. But otherwise, no." He turned to go and then turned back and added, "But you could cure them of ringworm quite effectively. Good day." There had definitely been a twinkle that time! Mr Wallace called "Next!" and disappeared into the consulting room. A very small man with a very small dog that Victoria had not even noticed hidden away in the corner of the waiting room got up timidly and scurried in after the vet and closed the door softly, but not before turning horror-filled eyes in her direction.

Victoria sighed and gave Moss a pat. "Well, that was a bit of a mess!" she said to him. "Come on then, let's go home and get you some lunch."

"Excuse me!" called out Cathy, just as Victoria went to walk out of the entrance. "Your bill. We don't operate credit accounts here, I'm afraid." Victoria turned back, resisting, with difficulty, the desire to make a sarcastic response.

"Oh I'm sorry, I didn't realise!" She took the proffered A4 sheet from the veterinary nurse and saw the words. 'Consultancy fee £35' and sighed again. No wonder he'd had a twinkle in his eye. She took out her purse.

As she drove home, she felt she'd wasted her morning and made a fool of herself to boot. Then she remembered the brown eyes, and allowed herself a small smile. Just then, Gertude, the reverend's ancient Morris Traveller, appeared around a bend and came slowly towards her. There was just enough room for them to draw alongside each other and they each wound down their driver's windows.

"Victoria – fancy seeing you here!" beamed Edwin. "What news?"

"Well, the vet thinks I'm bonkers and a small man with a small dog probably thinks I am a murderer."

Edwin blinked. "Ah, an interesting morning then! Have you heard the latest from the police?"

"No! Do tell – have they made any more arrests?"

Edwin looked puzzled. "More arrests?"

"Albert and I were at Burntwood yesterday when they carted off both Caroline and Freddie, but I don't really know why."

"Oh, I see." The reverend took off his glasses, polished them on his jumper and put them back on. "Well, I don't know that's anything to do with the murders, is it? I rather thought it was that Montague's unhealthy lifestyle choices catching up with him at last."

Victoria smiled. "I think you are probably right. So what is the news from the police?"

"They have identified what killed Giles Peacock and that young girl."

"No!" Victoria almost leapt through the open window in her excitement.

Edwin looked superior. "I was right! It was Hemlock Water Dropwort!"

"Really?" Victoria said, stricken.

"Yes, really! I was rather hoping for a gold star or at least a pat on the back, Victoria, for my wonderful detecting skills."

"Oh yes, sorry, Edwin, well done." She frowned. "It's just that I had the mad Morris Podger and his equally flaky female firmly in the frame for the murder. That's why I'd been making an idiot of myself at the vet's this morning."

"What has the vet to do with it?"

She sighed. "Nothing, nothing, just me going off on a wild goose chase, I think."

"Geese? You're not considering keeping geese as well? Terribly noisy things, you know."

Victoria laughed. "Oh Edwin, you are funny! Look, why don't you come round for a drink this evening? I might even be able to rustle up something to eat."

"That would be delightful. About seven o'clock? I'll bring a bottle."

"Excellent. We will see you then." They waved and drove off in their opposite directions. So it was Hemlock Water Dropwort. She'd have to look it up again when she got home. She couldn't remember what its natural habitat was, but Edwin had implied it grew pretty widely when he'd first mentioned it. In a way, Victoria felt relieved as there was no way Caroline or even Freddie, come to that, would have a clue about such things or go rummaging around in hedges, or wherever it grew. She was even more sure now that they were not involved in either of the murders.

Another car had come into view and Victoria pulled into a dip in the hedge to let it pass. As the car drew alongside, her heart sank. Two furious-looking women were glaring at her from inside. Down went the driver's window.

"Oi you, you stuck-up cow!" Patricia Podger's opening salvo seemed destined to set the tone for the exchange that was bound to follow.

Victoria opened her window just an inch or two, enough to hear the invective, but not enough to allow any physical contact. She was relieved to note the lane was too narrow to allow either party to open their doors.

"Hello, it's Patricia, isn't it?" she said in what she hoped was an irritatingly polite manner.

"What? 'Course it is. You've seen me before, or are you stupid as well as stuck-up?"

"She ain't stupid, but she's interfering, I knows that!" piped up the passenger. Morris's love interest, Sylvia, leaned across the gear lever to make sure she made herself heard.

"Glad to see they've arrested that hoity-toity friend of yours and her boyfriend. About time, too!" sneered Patricia. "Going around killing people, it's not right."

"And stealing our chickens!" shrieked Sylvia.

"Don't be ridiculous! They aren't murderers and they aren't chicken rustlers," said Victoria with as much scorn as she could muster.

"Oh yeah? Says who?" Patricia pushed her face towards Victoria's window aggressively.

"They haven't been arrested for murder. Why don't you check your facts before spouting your mouths off," she bluffed. "And as for your chickens, she would prefer them ready plucked!"

"I bet you've got some in your boot now, haven't you, eh?" Sylvia shouted. Victoria rolled her eyes, but said nothing. Sylvia was twitching with anger, and Victoria was pleased there was no way the woman could get at her. "I bet you have! You're lousy thieves, all of you!"

"Leave it out. What you going on about chickens for?" asked Patricia, pushing the other woman back into her seat.

Sylvia lunged forward again, her voice shrill. "You wanna keep away from my Morris and the farm, you do!" Victoria smiled again with an expression of patient tolerance, which seemed to be having the desired effect of making Sylvia increasingly angry. "I dunno what you're smiling at, you posh bitch! You keep away from our farm! Don't you come around no more pretending to interview Martha, and all that nonsense you been telling her. You just been snooping all the time!"

"Come on, Sylv, let's get on to Westerley. No point wasting time here," said Patricia, who seemed as concerned by her companion's rantings as Victoria was. She put the car in gear and Sylvia made to grab the steering wheel.

"No! She needs to know to keep away! You keep out of it or you might just find yourself on the wrong end of the electric fence and all!" she yelled.

Patricia pushed her aside. "Oi, pack it in, Sylv!" Sylvia had twisted round in her seat and was trying to open the passenger door. "Don't be stupid. You can't get out here, there's no room!"

Victoria seized the moment and drove quickly off, just managing to squeeze past the rear end of Patricia's car. She found she was shaking. Sylvia was clearly very unbalanced and she hoped she hadn't pushed her too far. It now seemed absolutely clear that she was behind India's murder. But what about Giles and Jessica? She needed to get home and find that old book of her aunt's and check what it said. She glanced nervously in the rear-view mirror, but the road was clear and all she could see was Moss's dear little head looking out of the back window. It seemed Patricia had been as unimpressed by Sylvia's rantings as she herself had been and had obviously kept driving, thank goodness.

Back at April Cottage, there was no sign of Albert. He was obviously still off somewhere on the farm. She rummaged around on the bookshelves and found her aunt's book, Britain's Wild Plants and Their Dangers. She searched the index and then flicked through the pages under 'H' for Hemlock Water Dropwort, her urgency making her clumsy. There it was: "The water dropworts are a genus of plants in the family Apiaceae... The most notable of these is O. crocata, which lives in damp, marshy ground, and resembles celery. It has been referred to as the most poisonous of all British plants and is considered particularly dangerous because of its similarity to several edible plants."

She still couldn't quite believe it. Hemlock was so Agatha Christie! She had been sure it was one of the bottles of drugs she'd found in the barn. So was there marshy ground at Burntwood? She had no idea and she didn't think nipping out there for a quick nose around was going to be a very sensible option. How could she find out?

Having no natural sense of direction, Victoria had always been rather keen on maps. She could study them for hours, tracing contours and following river courses… and identifying marshy ground – of course! She scooted back to the bookshelves. There was a tatty collection of maps of various vintages and among them was an OS map for the local area. She unfolded it carefully. The paper was well worn on the creases and one corner seemed to have been torn off completely. She prayed it wasn't the vital section. It wasn't.

She pored over the map, found Swaddlecombe and, with her finger, traced the road to Burntwood. Of course! She kicked herself. There was a stream at the bottom of Caroline's garden and, looking at the map, no surprise there then, the little blue tufty grass symbol for marshy ground across several fields in what was now, years later, Caroline's garden and part of Burntwood Farm's land. So it was a distinct possibility that Hemlock Water Dropwort was growing there. Had the police been and checked, she wondered.

She heard the sound of a tractor pulling into the yard and Moss went from sound asleep to totally alert in less than a second and trotted over to the back door, ready to greet Farmer Moreton.

"Albert!" She rushed up to him before he'd even had a chance to get in the door. "It was the hemlock – Edwin was right! I reckon it grows at Burntwood Farm. There's marshy ground there, you know… so if Sylvia was there at the party she could have slipped the stuff in somehow."

"Woah there! Hold your horses, maid – can we rewind a bit? Let a man get his breath!" He flopped down into a kitchen chair and, as he petted the dog, Victoria made tea and went over it all again, more slowly, both for his benefit and her own as something was tugging at the corner of her memory, but she couldn't quite grasp it.

"So you see, it has to be Sylvia!"

"Well, I agree it looks pretty damned likely, but I 'spect the police will want a bit more evidence than that."

"What do you mean? Of course it's her! She as good as said so when she threatened to give me the same treatment with the electric fence when we met in the lane!"

Albert opened the cake tin and cut a slice of cake. "It may well be her, but it could be other people, too. It could be your friend Caroline, or – "

"She wouldn't know any form of vegetable unless it was washed, trimmed and pre-packed, so I can guarantee you she would not have gone wading around in marshy ground looking for hemlock!"

"Yes, you may be right. But it could have been one of the Brocks."

Victoria considered. "I suppose so, but they were busy running everything at the party, not handing round plates and substituting bits of hemlock for celery. It was a very targeted attack. Surely it had to be a waitress, someone right there dealing with the food and the guests face to face?"

He sighed. "I see your point. Not targeted enough, though, sadly. That dreadful Giles person feeding his food to that young maid in that lecherous way – made my flesh crawl at the time, and look how it turned out for the poor girl. 'Tis a cruel thing, fate."

"Yes, yes, but don't you agree then, it must be Sylvia…?" She stopped. A sudden flash or recognition cut across her thought processes. At last the nagging memory had come sharply into focus. "It was! Why on earth didn't I realise before? Sylvia was working as a waitress! She was very shirty with me when I asked her for a drink – and she was carrying what I thought was a plate of celery and was obviously on her way to serve it to Giles!" Victoria said, shocked. "My God, I was that close to helping myself to a piece of it, too!"

"What, she was a waitress? But I didn't recognise her..." Albert looked flummoxed.

"Well no, but she had her hair all scraped back and you weren't expecting to see her in that situation so she didn't register, but I am absolutely sure she was a waitress! She was rude to me, which drew my attention and she had a hole in her tights and looked a mess compared to the other young waitresses. I just can't believe I didn't work it out before."

He put down his mug of tea. "So what now?"

"I need to call the police!" Victoria jumped up to fetch the phone. She thought she heard a distant engine and car doors slamming. Surely that couldn't be Edwin already. It was far too early. "Oh! That's odd .The police seem to be here already..." She trailed off, the phone in her hand, as Inspector Amery and Sergeant Jenkins walked past the kitchen window and knocked on the door.

Albert looked at her. "Victoria... is there something you want to tell me?"

The policemen walked into the kitchen. "We meet again," said Amery, his voice heavy with sarcasm.

"We do indeed. Would you like a cup of tea?" Victoria asked calmly, although she felt anything but.

"No, thank you, Miss West and Mr Moreton, too, I see. Do you operate as a detective duo?"

Albert frowned. "I have no idea what you are talking about."

"No matter." Amery addressed himself to Victoria. "Do you know why I am here?"

"I assume it is to do with the events at Burntwood."

Amery did a peculiar thing with his mouth, as if he was rolling a large gobstopper around inside his cheeks, then he paused and said, "Well, I suppose it might be, who knows? What I do know is that I have had a report that you have been heard enquiring about the best ways to kill someone quickly and efficiently. Is this true?"

Albert gave a groan. "Oh, Victoria!"

Hands on hips, Victoria said, "Well, yes, but it's not what it seems. I'm writing a novel, you see, and I went to see the vet, Mr Wallace, and – "

"I put it to you, Miss West, that you are not writing a novel and that you are in fact just an interfering woman with too much time on her hands."

Victoria coloured. "Charming! Well someone has to make enquiries. What are you doing about arresting those lunatics, the Podgers?"

"I beg your pardon?" Amery stuck his head forward aggressively and Victoria felt her temper rising.

She took a deep breath. "You've arrested my friend, Caroline Peacock, who couldn't swat a fly, let alone kill anyone, and those peculiar Podgers are still careering about the lanes harassing innocent people like myself while they have a barn full of drugs, enough electric fencing to encircle the entire village and may well have hemlock growing on their land which, I believe, you have managed to find out was responsible for killing my friend's husband as well as an innocent woman!" she finished loudly and in a rush. She was now standing toe-to-toe with Amery.

Albert stood up and gently took Victoria's arm and pulled her back a little. "Chief Inspector, she may go about things in a slightly odd manner, but all that Miss West just said is true," he said in a reasonable tone.

Amery was looking at her through narrowed eyes. "I expect it is. What I'd like, Mr Moreton, is for you to keep Miss West on a shorter leash and out of my way."

"Me?" Albert laughed. "What makes you think I have any hold over her!"

"I was being optimistic," said Amery. "You may think we aren't doing anything, Miss West, or it maybe that we already know quite a lot and are perhaps biding our time, letting them have enough rope to metaphorically hang themselves…"

Victoria narrowed her eyes in return. "Really? I find that hard to believe."

"Ahem," said Albert, trying to defuse the situation again.

"Have you searched the marshy ground at Burntwood Farm? That's the ideal habitat for hemlock. Do you know that?"

"Yes, but no, not yet, but…" he spluttered,

"… but you're going to? I would go myself but I think Sylvia Black might actually do me physical harm, so I'd better leave it to you. You do realise how unbalanced she is?"

Amery nodded. "Indeed. If you could leave it to us, Miss West, I think we might make a slightly more comprehensive job of gathering that bit of evidence than you might yourself manage."

"And what about the electric fence business?"

"What indeed," he said, smiling patronisingly. "I am not at liberty to discuss the details of the case with you at this time."

Victoria shrugged. "OK, but have you looked into Miss Black's background?"

Amery's face lost its smug smile. "What? Jenkins, did you find anything?"

Jenkins took on a rabbit in the headlights expression. "Err, I'm not sure we've looked into a Sylvia Black. The Brocks, the Peacocks, Montague and Podger, but –"

Amery shot him a glance that would fell a horse at thirty paces and Jenkins closed his mouth and seemed to shrink inside his suit.

"I really think you should. Her family background is very interesting. Have you also worked out yet that she was one of the waitresses at the party actually serving food to people?" Amery started to go a funny colour and was staring hard at Jenkins again. The latter was furiously scribbling some notes as Victoria spoke. "As I said, I really think you should look into Sylvia Black's background and her recent movements, Inspector," said Victoria, pleased with how calm she was sounding.

"It's Chief Inspector, Miss West, and we will do so. Can you please ensure you keep out of our way? I expect we will be making arrests in the next twenty-four hours and I don't want to come across you again in connection with this case. Is that clear?"

"Perfectly," said Victoria, and watched as the two policemen turned to leave. "Oh, just one thing, Chief Inspector, was it Mr Wallace that told you about my visit to the vet's?"

Amery scowled. "What's that got to do with anything?"

"Oh nothing really, just idle curiosity," she said.

Amery, puzzled, nodded at Jenkins, who consulted his notebook again. "Er, no it was a Miss Cathy Cooper that rung us, and then we had a slightly confused report from a Mr Harold Sloper, too," he said, looking up expectantly.

Victoria smiled. "Oh that's fine, thank you. You can find your own way out, I assume?"

Amery glared at her and they left.

"Victoria!" Albert burst out. "What do you think you're doing? You can't go framing up to the police like that. What's got into you, maid?"

"Oh, it's all nonsense! Yes, OK, I went and saw Mr Wallace who, as you say, is a fine figure of a man! I asked him about the drugs I'd seen in Morris's barn and that great lump of a veterinary nurse, Cathy something-or-other, was obviously eavesdropping and there was a funny little man waiting to see the vet after me, one Mr Sloper, and they must have told the police. Anyway, at least it wasn't Mr Wallace that called them. He is indeed a decent chap."

"I think you're getting a bit loopy yourself, you know, Victoria," said Albert, sounding tired "You must stop meddling."

"But the police are idiots! Sylvia and Morris are unhinged. They should be under arrest. I'm not saying Caroline and Freddie are without fault, but still…"

Albert sighed. "Perhaps you are right, I don't know, maid. I'm a bit whacked and I think I'll just nip over to my place and have a bath, if you don't mind."

"That's fine. I bumped into Edwin this afternoon and invited him round at seven o'clock for a drink and perhaps something to eat – but I don't know what we can give him. That was shortly before the lovely Patricia and the insane Sylvia harangued me in the road."

"Patricia? Oh dear, was she getting involved again?"

"Half-heartedly, but even she seemed surprised by Sylvia's antics. She had moved on from accusing Caroline of stealing Morris's chickens and was now claiming I had some stashed in the boot!"

"She does sound a bit of a mess."

"That is an understatement. I was just glad the lane was so narrow she couldn't get out of the car or I think she'd have attacked me."

Albert took her hand. "Victoria, for God's sake, have a care! Don't get so involved in things. You'll get out of your depth."

Victoria nodded. "You're right, and I was scared this afternoon, seeing how Sylvia behaved. She really hasn't got much grip on reality. She almost makes Morris look normal."

Albert sighed again and wearily got to his feet. "Let me have a bath and gather me wits, and then maybe we can just take Edwin to the pub. I'm too bushed to cook and I don't suppose you have anything in the fridge."

"Sad but true! You go and have a relaxing soak. I'll take Moss for a quick walk before Edwin arrives."

Chapter 13

Moss barked once and then, realising who it was, rushed to the back door with much wagging and bouncing.

"Hello, little fellow, how are you?" Edwin bent down to fuss the dog, who then got even more excited.

"Moss, down. We all know you love Edwin, but do calm down." Victoria put on her best stern voice and pointed to the dog's bed. Moss slowly slunk towards it, head hanging in despair, his attempts at adoration yet again thwarted. With a sigh, he flopped down in his bed and was soon asleep.

"So how has your day developed, Victoria? You seemed to be at a bit of a low ebb over the vet incident when we met in the lane earlier."

"Well, in all honesty," said Victoria, sitting down at the kitchen table, "I would have to say I have had better days. I was harangued in my car by two mad women shortly after I saw you, and then that nasty police inspector and his dim sidekick came calling and said they'd had information from two people who thought I was a possible murderer. Me – I ask you! They left telling me very firmly to keep my nose out of their business as they know what they are doing and I don't, a statement I seriously doubt. And then, to cap it all, Albert is cross with me for my meddling ways as well." There was a loud sigh from the dog basket. "And now Moss is fed up with me, too, as I stopped him from showing you his undying love!"

"So, an excellent day all round really then?" Edwin smiled and shook his head. "You can't take all the cares of the whole world on your shoulders. I am sure the police will find the true murderer in due course. It may just take them a little longer than such a super sleuth as yourself!"

Victoria snorted. "Well, I jolly well hope so. They need to get on with investigating the Podgers – urgently. Never mind Caroline and her ridiculous carrying on. I just have a bad feeling about it all, as if time is against us somehow..."

A cheery whistling could be heard from the farmyard and Moss sat bolt upright in his bed.

"Well, Albert sounds fairly happy now if that racket is anything to go by," said Edwin, turning in his chair to see the freshly scrubbed, pink-cheeked Farmer Moreton barrel his way into the kitchen.

"Evening, Reverend! Apologies for the slightly late entry, but I have had a long day in a dusty tractor and a good soak in the bath seemed just the ticket."

"Don't give it a second thought, dear boy. I was just talking to Victoria about what a difficult day it has been for both of you, by the sounds of it. Are you sure you want a boring old vicar like me intruding on your evening meal? Perhaps you'd rather just have a quiet evening together?"

"Don't be silly, and you are never boring or old! We were looking forward to seeing you, but you will have to forgive me for being my usual useless self when it comes to food planning and cookery, so we thought we'd take you to the pub instead." Victoria smiled across at Edwin and he gave an exaggerated appearance of being perplexed.

"Oh, all right then, twist my arm! It will be very pleasant."

"How has your day been anyway, Edwin?" she asked, getting up to locate her handbag and a jacket. The night was definitely chilly.

He stroked his chin. "I defused a potential mutiny over the church flower rota. I avoided a meeting with the bishop, always so very, very dull, I'm afraid, and I had a very good idea for a sermon, so not a bad day in the House of Ruminant!"

Albert rubbed his hands together and got to his feet. "That's grand. Glad to see you have everything under control, Vicar, especially those ladies on the flower rota. You need to rule them with a rod of iron, or so I am told. Let's get down to the pub. I could murder a drink." He looked somewhat contrite when he realised he had used an unfortunate turn of phrase.

"You be a good boy, Moss, and we'll be back soon." Victoria stroked Moss, half wondering whether to take him to the pub but, as Edwin would be in the back of the car and Moss was so deeply in love with him, she thought the vicar might get licked to death on the drive there, so decided to leave him in his puppy crate.

They climbed in the Land Rover and set off towards the village. After a mile or so Albert said, "Can I smell smoke? Funny time of day for a bonfire and no one should be stubble-burning just now."

Victoria suddenly pointed to the right. "Look, over there! My goodness, look at all that black smoke! What on earth is it?" A column of thick black smoke and sparks was rising into the evening sky.

Albert narrowed his eyes and leant nearer to the windscreen. "That's mighty strange. Looks to me like it's over near Burntwood, but they wouldn't be burning anything off yet." Albert stopped the vehicle and they all stared. The smoke seemed to be coming from one concentrated spot rather than from a wider area, like a field. Albert rammed the vehicle into first gear and they shot forward. "I don't like the look of that!"

Edwin leant forward and peered at the smoke: "I think you're right. Victoria, have you got any mobile signal?"

Chapter 13

She struggled to get her phone out of her bag as they careered along the twisting lanes, narrowly avoiding a rabbit and two pheasants. She looked at the screen on her phone. "Damn, no I haven't, but I think it will work as we get nearer to the farm. Oh, this is terrible! I wonder what's on fire. I do hope it's not one of the houses."

As they tore around the last few bends, with Victoria praying they didn't meet anyone coming the other way, the smell of the smoke was very strong, with the acrid reek of burning rubber adding to the stench.

"It's Burntwood! It's got to be!" said Edwin and they lurched around the final corner and saw ahead of them the barn at Burntwood Farm engulfed in flame. The noise was tremendous, cracking and roaring like a wild beast.

Albert parked in a passing place in the road and all three leaped out of the Land Rover and ran into the main farmyard. Martha Podger stood in the middle of the yard, staring at the burning building, her face set, tears running down her cheeks, her hands clenched by her sides. "Martha!" yelled Albert, "for God's sake, what's happened?" But she didn't seem to hear him.

"Help me! Help me!" cried a voice and they spun around to see Patricia crossing the yard, her face twisted in anguish, sobbing loudly, a bucket of water in each hand slopping the contents as she tried to run towards the barn.

"Oh God!" said Victoria, her hands over her mouth. Edwin had pulled out his own mobile phone and was pointing it this way and that, unable to get a signal. "Here! Try mine." Victoria handed him her own phone and soon she could hear him shouting directions into it and asking the fire brigade to hurry.

"Mother, for God's sake, help me!" screamed Patricia. Albert grabbed her and made her stop. Martha remained where she was.

"Pat, stop it. You can't do anything. Can't you see? Let it burn. It's just a barn." He shook her shoulders, water slopping all over his shoes.

"Get off me, get off!" she screamed at him.

"Patricia!" Albert fairly bellowed into her face. "Stop!"

"But they are in there! They're inside!" She shook herself free from his grasp and staggered forward, still pathetically clutching the half-empty buckets.

"Victoria – talk to Martha," barked Albert and he lunged after Patricia, catching her arm and spinning her round. The buckets and their contents went flying.

"Let me go, let me go, please!" She was sobbing hysterically and Victoria watched in amazement as Albert, after a moment's hesitation, slapped her face to bring her to her senses.

"How bloody dare you!" said Patricia, regaining her usual feistiness and for a moment Victoria wondered if she was going to hit Albert back, but she gasped and seemed to slump. "Oh, Mother..." she said weakly and walked across to Martha.

Victoria took the old woman's arm and said gently, "Mrs Podger – who is in there?" although she thought she already knew.

"My son and that madwoman," she said quite calmly. "It's too late now. It's all over."

Edwin came across to them. "The fire brigade is on the way."

"Did you ask for an ambulance as well?" asked Albert.

"No, I, didn't think." He looked questioning at Albert and then Victoria. He hadn't heard Martha's words.

"My brother and that stupid, mad bitch are inside that barn," said Patricia in a low, shaking voice. "I always knew she was bad news. I always said she'd be the death of him, didn't I, Mother?" Her voice was menacing now. "Didn't I, Mother?" she yelled at the old woman. Martha kept staring straight ahead as if mesmerised by the flames.

They all stared at the inferno. The heat was terrific and Albert shepherded the small group back further away from the fire. Sparks were shooting into the air and ominous cracks and bangs could be heard. Now Victoria realised the source of the nauseating burnt rubber smell must be all the tractor tyres that had been stacked up inside the barn. Then, to everyone's relief, they could hear sirens in the distance.

"Come on," said Albert. "There's nothing we can do here and it could all get a lot more dangerous if the roof goes, or if there's anything in there that might explode. Let's get right back to the log store over the far side of the yard."

In the eerie light from the blaze, Victoria could see other vehicles and figures arriving. She thought she saw the bulk of Bill Bramley and another farmer she knew. Albert walked over to them. A few moments later the two men got in their vehicles again and drove off.

Albert jogged back to the small pathetic group. "They've gone up the lane to stop anyone but the emergency services getting down here," he said into Victoria's ear. The noise from the fire was terrific and she realised she was shaking. "You all right?" He gave her a squeeze and she nodded, although she felt very far from all right. Ludicrously, given the awfulness of the situation, she found herself wondering about the poor hens. Had they all been incinerated along with Morris and Sylvia?"

She tore her eyes away from the blaze and it took a while for her eyes to adjust, but then, to her relief, she saw the motley collection of coops and sheds, like some Lilliputian village, arranged neatly at the far end of the field, well away from the fire.

She turned to Martha. "Thank goodness all your hens are safe."

"Yes, I moved them yesterday." She spoke without expression.

"Seemed to me it was high time they had some fresh grass."

Patricia gave a low moan and cried, "Why isn't anyone doing anything? My brother is in there! I can't bear just standing here!" She made as if to dart forward, but Martha stunned them all by suddenly reaching forward and slapping Patricia herself. "Now you stop that, girl. There's nothing to be done. He's gone – you get a grip of yourself if you know what's good for you." Patricia, now with both cheeks stinging, stared at her mother open-mouthed. Edwin took Patricia's arm and said, "Now come along…" and walked her slowly off toward the farmhouse, talking softly to her.

Suddenly, the yard was filled with flashing blue lights as one, and then another massive fire engine roared into the yard. Firemen starting jumping down from the engines, moving quickly and efficiently, uncoiling hoses and shouting instructions. Albert went forward and spoke to them, Bramley reappeared and there was much gesticulating and then one of the firemen went back to one of the fire engine cabs and began speaking on his radio. Victoria assumed he was summoning an ambulance.

Albert returned to stand with her and Martha. "Well, Martha," he said, "what do you think happened?" He held her gaze steadily, but the old woman blinked and looked away.

Then she spoke. "Well, I reckon something must have gone wrong with that electricity supply, don't you? Look what happened to the fence the other day when that poor woman was killed." She paused and wiped her eyes with a grubby handkerchief. "I told that Morris, I told him it was an accident waiting to happen. All those cables and the like, right next to all that hay and everything. But would he listen?" She shook her head and sighed.

"I saw him and that trollop go into the barn a few hours ago. He always loved a tumble in the hay, did Morris. Always put lust before everything, that boy. Lord knows where he got it from. 'Twasn't his father, nor me." She sniffed and after a pause added, "There was some home-made beer in the barn. I expect they drank that and fell asleep." She licked her lips, showing only the slightest trace of anxiety. "You can't have two people like them being together, can you? A dangerous combination, I always knew that. Brady and Hindley, Fred and Rosemary West, and then Morris and Sylvia. It was always going to end in disaster, wasn't it?" She met Albert's eyes and now it was his turn to look away, unable to bear the pain and the resignation in the old woman's face.

"Come on." Albert put one arm around Martha's shoulders and the other around Victoria's waist, and walked them both slowly towards the farmhouse. Just then a terrific roar, almost like an anguished scream, made them turn and they were just in time to see the barn roof collapse and a huge shower of sparks light up the sky and the faces of the sweating firemen.

"Oh dear," said Victoria, as several cars sped into the yard and screeched dramatically to a stop. Doors flew open and people jumped out. Among them she recognised the hapless Amery and his sidekick, Jenkins. "Now I'm for it!" she said. Next an ambulance arrived and there was a brief skirmish as police, firemen and the ambulance crew all jockeyed for space.

Like a ham actor, Amery made a despairing gesture, as if he was throwing an imaginary hat to the ground and then, to confirm his frustration, he clutched his head. Jenkins stood, mouth agape and seemingly hypnotised by the blaze. People pushed around them, intent on their various roles in the drama. Amery, now hands on hips, surveyed the terrible scene and turned to look slowly around him until eventually his gaze fell on Victoria, Albert and Martha. He walked slowly and purposefully across the yard towards them, stopping barely a foot in front of Victoria.

"Miss West. Perhaps I didn't make myself clear earlier?" he

said, his voice low and menacing.

Victoria, never much of a rebel, did a reasonable job of looking insolent. "Is it my fault we were driving past? It was one of our party that called the emergency services. You should be glad I was here." Amery stared at her, glanced at Albert and then looked at Martha.

"Mrs Podger? Please come with me and tell me exactly what has happened here," he said, and with a parting glare at Victoria, he escorted Martha to a police car.

A wailing began and Patricia tottered into view, the reverend in her wake. "Mother!" she cried plaintively and caught up with Amery. He took her firmly by the arm and bundled both women into the car.

Edwin walked across to them and all three stood in silence, watching the fireman as they pumped gallon after gallon of water onto the blackened and still burning barn. Victoria realised they were pumping water up from the stream and remembered the marshy ground where she was sure the hemlock grew. The ambulance crew got back into their vehicle and drove away. It would obviously be some time until any human remains would be recovered from the barn and then they'd have no place in a hospital and would be in the care of a pathologist, Victoria guessed.

"Well," said Albert, his arm still protectively around Victoria, "I suppose we may as well head back to the Swaddle Arms. Nothing else we can do here. That OK with you, Reverend?"

The vicar nodded. "To be frank, I feel somewhat in need of a drink."

Their arrival in the pub was met with a hushed reverence by the few people in the bar. "Are we too late for something to eat, Trudy?" Albert slumped on to a barstool.

"No, no, my dears. Of course not." She patted Victoria's hand.

"What a terrible sight you must have witnessed, you poor lamb." Victoria felt this was somewhat over the top as she wasn't the one who had just watched a relative go up in flames, but she smiled gratefully anyway, knowing that Trudy was itching to know all the gossip.

"Am I bein' presumptuous if I just order three steaks and a bottle of red wine?" asked Albert, glancing at Victoria and Edwin. They both nodded and murmured their agreement. "There you are then, Trudy. I reckon you know by now how we like 'em cooked. Roger, a bottle of the Merlot and three large glasses, please." Roger nodded and went to fetch the wine.

They made their way to their favourite table, the one with the curved, high-backed settle that gave a comforting feeling of privacy and cosiness. Roger brought the wine, and they all sat and sipped silently.

The door opened, and Tufty walked up to the bar and ordered his customary pint of cider. "Mind if I join you? I just heard about Burntwood." He pulled up a chair and sat opposite them, and sniffed the air, looking even more like a small rodent than ever, Victoria thought. "Blimey, you can tell you were there. You lot smell like a bonfire!"

Albert nodded. "Hell of a blaze, Tufty. All that old junk Morris had in the barn, plus the hay, of course. Martha reckons it was the electrics that started it." The two men exchanged glances and Tufty made a face that said, 'Well, if that's what she wants to believe...'

Edwin spoke up. "By the way, I meant to say I popped round to Burntwood earlier today, you know. By lucky chance, there was no one around. I took a stroll along by the stream, down in that marshy area. Plenty of water dropwort growing there, I noticed." He sipped his wine. More knowing glances were exchanged.

"You obviously heard that the police identified the poison?"

Victoria said to Tufty. He nodded.

"Yeah, I reckon it's common knowledge now. What a thing to do. You'd have to be mad as a hatter to risk something like that. Could have killed more than just those two."

"Good job I can't stand celery," muttered Albert.

"And the electric fence?" Victoria looked at the three men.

"Has to be the same person, surely?" Albert swirled the wine in his glass. "I reckon Martha was right. She said to me that those two together were lining up to be the next Fred and Rosemary West. That Sylvia would do whatever he said and Morris was just getting into his stride. I think we should all be glad that they've been stopped in their tracks."

"What an awful thought!" Victoria shuddered. "But was their home-made beer that potent do you think?" Victoria asked, still rather puzzled by how the two lovers had perished.

"Well, what I think – " But before Albert could say any more, Trudy appeared with their meals.

"Oh, don't mind me!" she trilled. "You carry on with your conversation." They all remained silent. "Tufty, do you want something? Seems a bit rotten you being the only one not eating."

"Well, I've already had me tea, but if you don't mind cooking me a few chips, that would be proper."

"Of course. Anything for one of our regulars." Trudy beamed and trotted back to the kitchen. "Back in two ticks!"

"Albert, you were saying?" said Edwin. They were all speaking quietly, even though there was no one else within earshot. It just seemed the right thing to do.

"I reckon those drugs that Victoria spotted – several of them were tranquillisers – well, I reckon that might just have had something to do with them not escaping." He paused and added so quietly that they could barely hear him, "I just hope she gave 'em enough and they didn't know what was going on."

"But why did they have those drugs anyway?" asked Victoria, still unsure about everything.

"I reckon it was Morris being an idiot as usual. I reckon he ordered stuff off the internet – or perhaps she ordered it, I don't know. I think it started as a cheap way to bypass Tar Wallace and his legitimate vet's practice charges. Like Monty said, Morris had stuff for ringworm and tick fever, the normal sort of things us farmers have lying about in our barns, but he also had the serious stuff that would put down a horse. My theory, for what it's worth, is that Morris started thinking about what he could do with such things. He was power-mad, of course. Ego the size of a planet." He poured more wine for them all.

"I think, given time, they would have progressed from hemlock and electricity to more insidious things with the drugs. I mean, this is all just my theory, mind. But Sylvia was proper unbalanced. I think we all knew that. You'd certainly seen it, Victoria, hadn't you?"

She nodded. "If anyone so much as criticised Morris she would fly at them. If he showed any interest in another woman, she would become completely irrational. With hindsight, I realise I had quite a lucky escape really." She shuddered and took a gulp of her wine. Their food sat untouched.

Albert continued. "It would have been her idea to use the hemlock as it's fast acting and she would be daft enough not to care if other people died. The electrocution – she'd have no trouble organising that. Your friend Caroline had a very, very lucky escape!"

"So do we think she was there, waiting for India to touch the fence, and then just turned up the current?" asked Edwin, incredulous.

"I reckon," said Tufty. "Mad as a box of badgers. Got no social conscience, no inhibitions and the like – that's a psychopath, isn't it?"

Trudy appeared with a generous bowl of chips for Tufty. "Oh my! Is there something wrong? You've not touched your food! It'll be cold."

"Sorry, Trudy," said Albert, hurriedly picking up his knife and fork. "Too much yapping going on. Let's all tuck in." Silence fell again as they all began to eat and Trudy was left, yet again, shut out of the conversation and all the lovely gossip she so desperately wanted to glean and then share with all her cronies.

They were all ravenous after the dramas of the evening and the plates were soon spotless. Trudy reappeared instantly and began gathering plates and cutlery. "That was lovely, Trudy, thank you," said Victoria.

"So," said the landlady in a stage whisper, "is it true that Morris and Sylvia are dead?"

Albert leant forward and also in a stage whisper said, "We don't know. We will have to wait for the police to confirm it, won't we?"

Trudy looked at him suspiciously, trying to decide if he was making fun of her or not. "Right, I see. Well, I'll get back to the kitchen then." She turned away dejectedly.

"Oh Albert, you are rotten!" Victoria dug him in the ribs.

"Well, I can't stand all the tittle-tattle that goes on. It's like those blasted women in the shop. Add two and two together and they get 104."

They all seemed lost in their thoughts as they sipped their drinks. "Well, I wonder what will happen now," ventured Victoria.

Edwin shrugged. "It is difficult to know. Do the police have enough proof of anything? The two main suspects are no longer around, so…"

"I don't know how these things work," said Albert slowly, "and of course, I was only hypothesising earlier. It will be up to Martha to let that obnoxious character Amery know what she does, or doesn't know about the whole sorry state of affairs." He finished his glass of wine. "I really couldn't hear what she was saying earlier, that fire was so noisy. Did you hear anything from Patricia, Edwin?"

The reverend shook his head and studied his empty glass. "No, sadly, I fear she was quite incoherent."

Tufty finished his cider. "Well, there you are then. I reckon we can all go home and sleep sound tonight." He got up, nodded and left the pub.

"I don't know about that," said Victoria. "I think tonight's events will stay with me for a long time."

Albert squeezed her hand. "Edwin, let us give you a lift back to the vicarage."

Chapter 14

"Please, Albert, could you wash the plate once you've finished? I've only just polished the sink."

Albert looked down at the plate covered with crumbs, "I fancied another slice, but that was the last of the banana loaf – tell you what, shall I make another one for later when these friends of yours come over?"

"Oh no, I never thought about cake! Well, I did, but Gray is gluten-free so he can't eat anything we make with normal flour. But we must have something to offer." She slumped down at the kitchen table and absentmindedly tidied up some small crumbs that were scattered on the table.

Albert laughed and then turned it into a cough. "Well, it shouldn't be beyond the wit of man to whip up something before three o'clock this afternoon. I think I may have some gluten-free flour lurking in a cupboard. I'll have a look in a bit. Anyway, you were going to the shop. Perhaps they'll sell some."

"But what if they don't? In fact, I'm sure they won't! If they can't get my skimmed milk in stock, what hope is there for gluten-free flour? No, I'll just have to go straight into Westerley and buy things ready-made." She jumped up and looked around for her handbag.

Albert stood holding out her bag while she turned in circles looking under cushions, under the table and even in the dog's bed. "This what you're looking for?"

"Oh Albert, you could have said!"

Albert gave her a hug. "Yes I know it's important to you, maid, but the sky won't fall in if we don't have a selection of gluten-free home baking to welcome your friends. I'll rustle something up. Don't panic."

"Sorry, I know I'm getting all het up, but I want them to love my new home and love Swaddlecombe and love –" she stopped as she was going to say 'you', but thought that might not go down too well, so opted for "everything!"

"OK, so what else do you want to get sorted before they arrive?"

Victoria consulted a large notepad on the dresser that was covered in scrawled notes.

"The chicken coop, the spare bedroom – in case they change their minds and want to stay – empty the rubbish, dust the mantelpiece and all the ornaments on it, clean the silver bits in the sitting room, vacuum everywhere, oh, and should I bath Moss?"

"No, Victoria, the pup is perfectly acceptable as he is."

"Right, well, what else is there? Um, sweep the front path and weed that little bed just outside the window. I keep meaning to plant herbs in it and never get round to it. But I suppose the flowers look OK."

"Should I polish the front step and trim the hedge?" said Albert with a wry smile on his face.

"Well, you could – " She stopped as she spotted his expression. "Oh, do stop it! I know I'm flapping, but this matters to me. Right, I'm off to the supermarket. Now where's the shopping list? I'll add some gluten-free bits to it."

"Please – don't buy too much so that we're eating the leftovers for weeks afterwards. You know I'm not a fan of shop-bought stuff."

"See you later then, and you're still happy to give the chicken coop a wash and brush-up?"

"Go on – get off with you. Yes, I'll sort your damned chicken coop out." With that he wandered out of the back door and Victoria grabbed her jacket and raced off towards her car.

Once on her way to Westerley, she consulted the shopping list again and wondered if she'd forgotten anything. Flowers! That was a good idea. No, on second thoughts she ought to create something wonderful and artistic from bits growing in the garden. She pondered how much gardening she had managed lately and agreed with herself, flowers from the supermarket would be a good idea.

As she wasn't really concentrating on the road ahead it came as a shock when she had to slam on the brakes to avoid a car speeding towards her, travelling far too fast for the narrow road.

More by luck than judgement, both vehicles came to a halt at a point where the road widened into a passing place. Victoria had half a mind to wind her window down and offer some gentle chastisement to the other driver but decided that, in her current frazzled state, it would probably come out as a complete rant. As the cars edged past each other, she glanced at the driver – and gave a start. "Caroline!"

Caroline wound down her window and said breezily, as if the past few traumatic weeks had never happened, "Tori, how are you? And how handy to catch you like this just as I head off."

"Head off? Where are you going?" Victoria glanced round and saw that the rear of Caroline's car was absolutely crammed, piled to the roof with all sorts of paraphernalia. Thank goodness she hadn't needed to reverse as she had no rear view at all and Victoria couldn't believe Caroline could use her mirrors for anything other than fixing her lipstick.

"Why, London, of course. I've had more than I can take of this godforsaken dump, I can tell you. Rude and terrifying people, appallingly crass policemen, absolutely hopeless mobile reception.

I mean, for goodness sake, how much does one have to put up with just for the so-called pleasure of living in the country? On a good day I can hardly understand a word the yokels are saying and you have to drive miles to get anything essential like decent champagne or fresh mint to put in the Pimms. I mean – there are limits!"

"But..." Victoria paused. Was there any point in telling her that most people grew mint in their back gardens and there were such things as supermarkets just along the coast near Westerley, and then decided not to waste her breath.

"The last few weeks has been a living nightmare for me, frankly," said Caroline. "The police, well! The incompetence! If I had enough time I would regale you with some of the idiotic things they have done and said. The whole force in this area needs a damn good shake-up. I might speak to a friend of my late uncle's who works for the Met. He may be able to do something. But for now I need a complete rest, a prolonged shopping trip in Bond Street and a hairdo at Giovanni's."

"So you're off for a few days, are you?"

"A few days?" Caroline almost shrieked. "Darling, I don't think so! I am moving out lock, stock and barrel and never coming back!"

"Oh." Victoria didn't quite know what to say. Hearing what she regarded as a rural idyll smashed and trampled on and treated with contempt was rather hard to swallow. "You mean you're going for good? Have you sold the house? Don't the police need you anymore?" She realised there were too many questions and she was being far from polite, but they just tumbled out.

"Left the keys with the agents in Westerley. Just been there now. I told them any interested parties can have the furniture, everything, the whole caboodle. There is nothing in that place that means anything to me and I'll be glad to see the back of it. The police have my London number and address. I have to say that policeman, what was his name, Amery? He was very rude, suggesting I might have had a hand in these dreadful goings-on, it's just ridiculous. Anyway, understandably they have said they will not be pressing any charges. And I should bloody well think not." She snorted with indignation.

"Is Freddie leaving, too, then? I thought he would be with you," asked Victoria.

"Oh, don't talk to me about poor Freddie! The wretched police have already dragged him up to London. They want to talk to him about some other business. I really think they've got it in for him. They're as good as suggesting he's a common fraudster and a drug dealer, which my Freddie most certainly is not, so I fear it may take his lawyer a while to sort it all out. Poor Freddie. Anyway, he knows where I am so he'll join me there tomorrow, I'm sure."

Victoria decided to say nothing about Freddie, but surely it was obvious to Caroline that the man was an out-and-out bad lot? Now the police had him in custody she doubted whether he would see the light of day for quite a few years.

"Right, well thanks for bringing me up to date, Caroline, after everything we've gone through of late. I hope everything goes well for you." Victoria felt extremely put out that Caroline hadn't even planned to tell her she was leaving. A short thank you and a 'talk soon' would have been enough, but no. There had been many moments over the past few weeks when she felt she had gone above and beyond anything a close friend should have to do and they had barely been friends to begin with. That had been the story of her life in London, all give on her part and everyone else being all take. Apart from Gray and Sebastian, of course. They were the exception. It was only now she had settled in Devon and found new friends in this funny little community that she felt at home and comfortable and could face the future with a smile.

Chapter 14

"Have fun with your farmer friend, Tori. This is all so much more your kind of thing than mine. Come back Harvey Nicks, all is forgiven. See you!" With that Caroline drove off without a backward glance, but with the back of the car so crammed she wouldn't have seen anything anyway.

Victoria sat still for a moment, trying to sort out in her mind why she felt so hurt and, come to that, why she was surprised she felt hurt. Caroline had always been supremely selfish and Victoria was always far too loyal and supportive. Albert had warned her against getting too involved. She smiled to herself. He was a much better judge of character than she was. Then she thought of Patricia Podger and frowned. Well, most of the time, anyway.

Taking a deep breath, she continued on to Westerley and focused on her mission for gluten-free goodies.

* * * * *

When Victoria reached the till, she already had an inkling she may have over-bought, but the total demanded by cashier was still a shock. Oh well, it was important that the boys liked her home, and hospitality must always involve food. She straightened up, her back aching from loading all the carrier bags into the boot. Goodness… there was a lot of stuff!

She turned into the driveway and parked carefully, making sure the best place to park and the nearest to her cottage remained free. She didn't want Gray and Sebastian being panicked by Albert's tractor filling the yard. She began lugging the bags into the kitchen, hoping Albert might be around to bring in some of the heavier things. All the mineral water she'd bought was in glass bottles as that particular brand was all Sebastian used to drink. She could remember embarrassing scenes in restaurants when he had been forced to accept 'second-rate' sparkling water.

The sound of voices came through the open back door. Albert was sitting with his feet up on a second chair chatting merrily to Edwin.

"Aha, just the lady I was hoping would join us." Edwin stood and held the chair out for Victoria.

"Hello, Edwin, how lovely to see you. Apologies if I don't sit and join you. I'm happy to chat, but must just get this shopping put away and a few other things sorted. Albert, would you mind grabbing a couple of the heavy carrier bags from the car?"

Albert gave the vicar a knowing wink as he went out to collect the shopping.

"So how are things with you, Edwin?" said Victoria as she began cramming things into the fridge. Gluten-free scones, clotted cream – she must show the boys how yummy this local speciality was, with soya milk and coconut water in case Sebastian was still on his non-dairy phase – but then that would mean no clotted cream! She sighed. Oh whatever, she was feeling a bit irritated and flustered by the whole thing.

"Not too bad, thank you. I came to talk to you both and to offer some sort of 'closure', to use modern parlance, about the whole Burntwood Barn debacle."

"Oh, right. Well, I'm all ears, and Albert will be back in just a second."

Albert carried in the two heavy carrier bags with the bottled water, some beers and a bottle of wine. "What are you stocking up for, maid? There's no drought or a blizzard forecast, and it isn't a bank holiday. Shops will be open again tomorrow, you know!"

"I just wanted to make sure I'd covered all options, that's all. I didn't know what they might want to drink."

"Just don't give them a damned choice, if you ask me," grumbled

Albert and resumed his position next to Edwin. "So, Reverend, you were waiting to tell all."

Edwin took off his glasses and polished them with his handkerchief, a sparkling white number that he produced out of his pocket. "Well, some of the information I must keep to myself as I cannot divulge things said in confidence."

Albert looked at Victoria and they both nodded their understanding.

"You see, I had a call on my mobile, from Exeter Prison. I was out and about having just seen Mrs Armitage. Poor dear is a martyr to her lumbago." Edwin replaced his glasses and, as Victoria seemed poised to interrupt, looked at her over the top of them and gave her a look that said 'patience'!

"So, I got a call on the mobile saying there had been a request for me to visit someone being held on remand. Obviously I could never refuse a mercy mission like that."

"Did they say who it was?" asked Albert.

"Not initially, no, but I toddled along, expecting to have to talk to some rough cove who had committed some heinous crime and had suddenly thought God might be of some help, or at least delay the inevitable."

"And?" pushed Victoria.

"It turns out it was Martha Podger."

"Martha!" Albert and Victoria spoke in unison.

"Well, you may not know, but Martha is no stranger to the church. Until about ten years ago she was a stalwart worshipper. She would be there come rain or shine on a Sunday morning, not just a feasts and fancy days worshipper like most of this village."

"Well, I certainly didn't see Martha as the regular church-going type or helping out with the church fete or the Mothers' Union," said Victoria.

"Things were very different back then," said Albert.

"Indeed," continued Edwin. "Sadly, as Morris developed into a rough and unruly adult, the less she attended services. I now know from our chat that she had come to realise that deep down Morris was fundamentally flawed and the poor woman was wracked with guilt about the monster she had produced."

"But surely," said Victoria, "it wasn't her fault that he turned out to be so wicked?"

"I agree with you, my dear. I think some people are born and not made evil, but she obviously felt responsible. Then Sylvia appeared on the scene and things became more complex. She was like the final piece in the puzzle and she and Morris became one rather terrifying whole. Martha realised things were starting to get out of control. She didn't like or trust Sylvia and she stopped coming to church as she felt she couldn't, shouldn't be there when there were so many bad things going on in her own family. Poor Martha, all these latest events have greatly distressed her."

"So what's happening to the poor old girl? Is she going to be charged?" Albert leant forward, intent on the subject in hand.

Victoria had been putting the shopping away, but had stopped to give Edwin her full attention. She had just unpacked some macaroons for tea to go with whatever Albert made, if indeed he had time to make anything at this rate. And there were jams in pretty jars with gingham lids and a new stash of bone-shaped dog biscuits for Moss – she tore her mind away from the shopping and concentrated on this far more important conversation.

"Martha has made a full confession and yes, she is being charged with two counts of murder, that of Morris and Sylvia. When she realised that the pair of them were in one way or another responsible for multiple deaths, the guilt overtook her. Afraid that the police wouldn't reach the right conclusions, or if they did they might take too long about it, she decided to take matters into her own hands and felt God would agree that she had made the right choice – the sacrifice of her own flesh and blood."

"Poor Martha," said Albert sadly. "I remember her as such a proud woman doing her best to bring up Morris and Patricia with no damned help from that drunkard husband of hers. I thought things might improve for her when he drank himself into an early grave, but no. It's a sorry end to her story."

Victoria stood up to continue with her unpacking. "So Martha drugged Morris and Sylvia before setting light to the barn?"

Edwin sighed and shook his head. "It's not for me to reveal such detail, I'm afraid."

"Hell of a way to go, being burnt alive," said Albert.

"Yes, but what about poor India, Giles and young Jessica? Their deaths were just as horrible," said Victoria, somewhat amazed that Albert seemed to be showing sympathy for Morris.

"Now, now, Victoria, that's not what I meant, and you know it. Any violent and untimely death is a terrible thing but, well, burning…" He shuddered.

Edwin spread his hands palms down on the kitchen table top and said slowly, "Let's just say Albert's hypothesis expounded in the pub was pretty much spot on. That's really all I can say."

Albert let out a long slow breath. "Right, I see. So the home-made beer had been drugged!" Edwin made a little moue with his mouth and studied his hands some more. "Well, that's something of a comfort," said Albert, "and would explain why Morris and Sylvia didn't escape. That Martha Podger, she always was a clever old stick."

"Well, I'm just glad it's all over. It has been awful, just awful!" Victoria continued her unpacking and ignored the look of amazement on Albert's face as she produced more and more packets and jars. "As you two seem to be fairly settled, shall I put the kettle on and make us all a pot of coffee?"

"That sounds like a splendid idea," said Edwin, relaxing back into his chair, seemingly relieved that they hadn't pressed him for more information.

"And then, it will be all hands on deck, Albert, as there are quite a few things you were supposed to be sorting out for me this morning, and not just sitting here chatting!" she said pointedly.

"Hang on there, maid. I've been working my way through the list, don't you worry! Some London friends of Victoria's are visiting this afternoon – you'd think it was royalty, given all the fuss," he said to Edwin.

The two men renewed their conversation and Victoria put away the last jar in the dresser and made the coffee. As casually as she could, she moved over to the Rayburn and opened the main door. She had already set the fire with newspaper and kindling and merely had to strike a match and hold it to the dry wood. Her actions were hidden behind the vicar's broad back, and she closed the metal door quietly, opened a vent and turned a dial and got on with pouring the coffee. She had decided a nonchalant approach and a 'Well, I don't care if you burn properly or not' attitude was the best one to take with Smokin' Joe. She felt that, rather like a naughty child, it was more likely to behave if she ignored it.

Victoria began rummaging under the sink and pulled out a duster and some spray polish. "I thought Jean came in and cleaned for you every week?" asked Albert, looking puzzled.

"She does, but it's five days since she was here and I don't want any of the plates on the dresser to look dusty. Sebastian will be sure to notice." She began carefully removing each plate and wiping it with the duster, and putting it back.

Albert rolled his eyes. "Honest, Edwin, I've never seen anything like it! There'll be a delivery of red carpet arriving in a minute."

Victoria ignored him, but was pleased to notice a distinct warming of the kitchen.

"Well," said Edwin, looking a little pink. "I'd better be off, get out of your way before the VIPs arrive. Goodness, it's warm in here!"

Albert peered at Edwin and then switched his gaze to the Rayburn. "Victoria West! You've lit it!"

Victoria turned to face him, arms folded triumphantly. "Yes, Albert, I have, and Smokin' Joe seems to be running quite nicely, thank you!"

"Well, I'll be –" said Albert, laughing and shaking his head.

"I wish someone would tell me what's going on?" Edwin looked lost.

"Ah, 'tis a bit of an in-joke, Vicar. It's that old Rayburn over there. Poor Edith could never get the blighter to run decent, and now Victoria has had it serviced and had a lesson in how to manage it from old Jolly, and it looks like she's got the knack!"

Edwin beamed. "Lovely! Nothing like the cosy fug of a Rayburn once autumn arrives. I look forward to taking tea in front of it. But for now, I must wend my way. I am on Shanks's pony today as poor Gertrude has a puncture, so I must get on and get her reshod!"

"Do you need a lift?" offered Albert and Victoria glowered. He seemed to have no concept of time.

"No, no, dear boy, but thank you all the same. The walk will do me good. Chin chin!"

"Right, all hands on deck then!" said Victoria briskly as Edwin trotted off across the yard.

"I just don't know what you're making such a fuss about. This is the country, take us as you find us – we aren't all neat and tidy, for heaven's sake!"

"I know that, Albert, but I still want my little cottage to look its best. And the chickens of course – have you?"

"Yes, of course. I said I would. It's all spick and span. Brushed down outside and clean bedding and everything. You want me to go and fluff up their feathers a bit?"

"There's no need to be sarcastic!" Victoria was getting increasingly hot and flustered.

"Look, maid, I know it's wonderful that you've got the Rayburn going, but do you reckon you could shut it down a bit? It's like a furnace in here!"

"You're right. Sorry. Now, I've just got to remember what to do… it's this vent here and – ow!"

"You see that big pair of oven gloves hanging up there, all singed at the edges? Well, that's what they're for! You be careful. The thing gets red hot." Albert handed the gloves to her, while Victoria inspected her fingers for any serious damage. Then she gently adjusted the vent and hoped the temperature would drop back a little. My goodness, the thing really pumped out heat!

"Well, if I've done all me chores, I reckon I'll clear off. I've got a few jobs of my own to do and I need to check on the sheep. I feel all out of place and untidy in the midst of all this perfection."

"Oh, but I want them to meet you. Please don't disappear!" Victoria was appalled.

Albert paused. "Well, I don't know, maid. They're your friends and I'm not too sure your London pals are my sort of people, judging by what I've seen of late."

Victoria felt tears welling. She had so wanted Gray and Sebastian to meet Albert and to like him. It seemed terribly important somehow.

"Now then, don't you take on," he said, his voice softening. "I'll go and check on the stock and then I'll come back around and say

271

hello after they've arrived. You'll have got all your frantic nattering out of the way by then, I 'spect." He gave her a peck on the cheek and headed off as the reverend had done a few minutes before.

She took a deep breath and gave herself a quick pep talk. She was a mature woman, not a teenager, and she must pull herself together and get everything sorted out. Albert was right. It would be good to have a natter and a catch-up with the boys and Albert would have felt out of place. She consulted her list and threw herself into the final preparations. She had a couple of hours, she could do it.

At three o'clock, there was a 'beep beep' from the farmyard and the sound of a big, throaty engine. Gray and Sebastian had arrived. Victoria rushed out to greet them.

"Darling!" Gray was out of the car, arms held wide, "Come here, you luscious thing!" He enfolded her in a luxuriously scented baby blue cashmere embrace. "God, how we've missed you!" Victoria wiped away tears of happiness, and also sadness, as she really had missed them, too.

"Tori, come here," Sebastian, always the more reserved of the couple, had climbed out of the driver's seat and was walking towards her. "You look wonderful, disgustingly healthy and – dare I say it – happy." He embraced her in his more musky scent and her face nestled against the rough tweed of his jacket.

"How wonderful to see you both – at last! You got here without any mishaps?"

They exchanged glances. "Well, not exactly, no. We had quite a few incidents at crossroads – why do the signposts down here lie? And we overshot the turn into your drive, but we spotted this gorgeously tanned farmer chap over the hedge and he directed us here."

Victoria had gone slightly pink. And Gray pounced. "Aha! You see, I told you, Seb, that was the handsome Albert! I knew it! Oh, very much your type, sweetie, too old for me, sadly. What do you think then, Seb, as the senior member of the party?"

Seb smiled patiently, used to being constantly teased by flirtatious Gray, who was at least ten years his junior. "He looked charming. He also looked very interested in my car!" He smiled and patted the huge gleaming black, well-muscled vehicle that looked as if it was crouched and ready to spring.

"Wow!" Victoria hadn't really paid it any attention. "What is it? Albert is car mad."

Gray flapped his hand at her. "Oh poo, it's just a Porsche, a 4x4 thing. We thought if we brought the Ferrari down, we'd never fit between the hedges or get over the bumps in the road and, having been down your drive, we were right!"

Sebastian smiled. "It actually has more to do with helping Gray's mother to move various bits of furniture across half of Cornwall. The Ferrari is not much use as a van. This manages rather better."

Victoria ushered them both through the barn and round to April Cottage. "How sweet!" Gray stood, palms to cheeks and surveyed the cottage surrounded by its small cottage garden and neatly trimmed lawn.

"Kind of you to say, but it's just a little farm cottage. It's no chocolate box thatched effort, but it's home and I am very, very fond of it." As if on cue, one of the hens decided to lay an egg and a great cacophony of jubilant crowing burst forth.

"My God! The noise! Is it in pain?" Gray cried, rushing over to the hen coop.

"No, silly, she is just telling you she has laid an egg and is very happy about it."

"Can you imagine laying an egg, oh Lord!" Gray grimaced. "Ah, my girls, look! Aren't they sweet, oh, and such gorgeous colours. I knew we'd co-ordinated them well."

"There seem to be a few more than we sent you," said Sebastian, peering at the birds through the wire mesh.

With her fingers crossed firmly behind her back, Victoria said, "Well, I so fell in love with the ones you sent me – such a lovely house-warming present, thank you – that I decided to add a few more. In fact my latest blog is all about chickens and breeding fancy hens." Victoria paused, and thought of Martha sitting in Exeter Prison. "Well, I think it is. There has been a bit of a complication, though, but still…"

They watched the chickens as they pecked and scratched contentedly and made their sweet gossipy 'pock pock' noises. Gray was entranced. "I never realised how soothing a chicken could be. I could sit here with a G&T and listen to them chattering all day – enchanting!"

"It takes all sorts," said Sebastian dryly. "I prefer mine with bread sauce and a bit of sage and onion. I find that quite soothing." Gray slapped his arm and they followed Victoria into the cottage.

They met Moss, or rather fended him off as he bounced and rolled and played the fool, and then had a complete tour of the house. They made appropriate sounds of appreciation at Victoria's swish new bathroom and admired the thundering Rayburn with due reverence. Victoria was pleased to see it was still going and was now merely glowing gently, with no sign of smoke.

There was a loud rap on the back door and they all turned to see Albert in the doorway. "Albert!" Victoria beamed and rushed over to him. "Come and meet Gray and Sebastian!"

Albert strode forward and there was much handshaking. "We've already met, actually," said Albert. "That's a proper beast of a vehicle you've got there," he said to Seb. "The Cayenne Turbo S, if I'm not mistaken?"

"Spot on," said Sebastian with a smile. "I'll give you a tour later, if you're interested?"

"That would be good," said Albert. "You can have a go on my tractor, if you like!"

They all burst out laughing and then Sebastian said, "Do you know, that is actually something I've always wanted to do, drive a tractor!"

"It could be arranged!"

Victoria fussed and made tea. It seemed that neither Seb or Gray were on any kind of diet and, as they were running late, they had skipped lunch and confessed to being ravenous.

"That's handy," said Albert, "as I did a bit of baking earlier and you'll find some fresh fruit scones in that tin on the dresser, Victoria, and in here," he paused for dramatic effect before whipping off the lid: " – is my award-winning chocolate and beetroot cake! Both gluten-free, and still warm."

Victoria, Gray and Sebastian all gaped at him. Victoria gaped as she wondered what on earth she was going to do with all the stuff she'd bought in the supermarket and when had Albert had time to bake these wonderful cakes? Gray and Sebastian gaped at the gorgeous baking and the imagined vision of a tall, tanned farmer toiling over a hot oven.

After a delicious tea and lots and lots of laughter, and after Albert had drooled over the Porsche and Seb had pottered up the lane and back in the tractor, the boys said they had to be on their way. "Well, now you know where I am, will you come and visit again – and stay over next time?" pleaded Victoria.

"We promise," said Sebastian. "I can see this really is your rural idyll, and I am so happy for you, dear girl." He hugged her, and Victoria was wiping away tears again.

"Darling! We mustn't leave it so long." Gray enveloped her in cashmere again and she cried some more. "It is simply divine here, but honestly, I couldn't bear it for any length of time. Don't you just die of boredom? I mean, nothing ever happens in the country!"

Victoria and Albert exchanged glances and thought of the events of the past few weeks. Albert slipped his arm around her and gave her a squeeze. "Oh, I don't know," said Albert, "we have our moments!"

The boys climbed into the Porsche and just then the distant sound of wailing sirens could be heard. "Oh, I take it all back!" laughed Gray. "Must be a fire in a haystack! Don't get too over-excited by the vision of hunky firemen, Victoria!" He waved, blew her a kiss and Sebastian turned the black beast round in the yard, and with a throaty roar, they disappeared up the drive in a cloud of dust.

After they'd gone, there was a pleasant lull, the twittering of birds only slightly disturbed by the distant wailing sirens. Albert and Victoria stood together. "Nice chaps," said Albert eventually. "Knows a lot about cars, that Seb does."

"They are both lovely and they were the most wonderful friends to me in my hours, no weeks, of need and I am very fond of them."

"Well, I'm pleased to have met them. Long as they don't ask me to go and visit them in London, we'll be fine!" Victoria wasn't quite what to make of that statement, but let it pass unremarked.

"Come on then, let's nip to the pub and catch up on all the gossip. I don't think I will ever want to eat again after all that cake and scones, but we could go and have a drink."

Victoria went and checked on Moss – fast asleep after all the excitement of the visitors, and climbed into the Land Rover next to Albert. "I want to know about those cakes, Albert. When on earth did you bake them? I bought all that food and – "

"I wasn't having no visitors to Upper Swaddle Farm served

with shop-bought – no, worse – supermarket-bought cake and jam and scones, my girl. We have standards!" He selected first gear and they set off down the lane.

"But I don't see how –"

"You shush. I can knock up a batch of scones in ten minutes and I've made that beetroot cake so many times I could bake it in me sleep. I already had some gluten-free flour, so it was a doddle. I only spent ten minutes checking the sheep – just happened to be when those chaps were dithering about at the end of the lane, so quite good timing really." He smiled. "Anyway, I managed it and although I don't reckon the results were as good as normal flour, it wasn't too bad, was it?"

She leant across and kissed his cheek. "You're a genius!"

"Steady on, I'm trying to drive here!" They bowled along and were soon entering the village. "What the hell…?" Albert pulled up and they both surveyed the chaos before them. Two fire engines were parked in front of the Swaddle Arms, villagers milled about and a couple of policemen directed traffic and generally caused more of a hold-up than if they'd let everyone sort it out for themselves.

"Look!" cried Victoria. "There's a hole in the end of the pub – look, there! A hole in the wall! Whatever has happened? Is it a bomb?"

"Nah, don't be daft! Who'd plant a bomb in the Swaddle Arms? Trudy might want to put one under Roger, but I don't think she'd risk damaging the pub." Albert pulled the Land Rover onto the verge and the two of them climbed out. One of the policemen glared at Albert, but he simply waved at him and strolled across to the pub.

Everyone seemed very relaxed and, whatever crisis had happened, it was clearly all over now. Victoria recognised a local builder who was peering at the hole in the wall, scratching his head as he contemplated how best to patch it up. A heavily tanned man, dressed entirely in brown, was walking slowly towards them. "Albert, Victoria!' he called. They both stared in amazement. It was Roger Mudge, the landlord.

"What on earth – " Victoria peered at him closely and had to try very hard not to laugh. "Roger, you appear to be covered in coffee."

Roger shook his head and wiped at his face with an already brown-stained tea towel. "That I am," he said, sounding slightly stunned.

"Let me guess," said Albert, not doing such a good job of keeping a straight face. "That fancy bleddy coffee machine of Trudy's finally got the better of you?"

Roger nodded sadly. "I left it switched on and hadn't done something or other with one of the valves. I mean, I don't know, I never wanted the damned thing anyway! Well, it got itself in such a lather, it blew up, went straight through the bar wall! Luckily no one was passing."

Victoria was now laughing openly. "They could have been laid out by a latte, or mugged by a mocha, or –"

Roger looked quite put out. "Well, I know it seems funny to you now, but I can tell you, it didn't half go with a bang!" Victoria and Albert were now roaring with laughter. Through their tears of mirth, they spotted Trudy trotting around with a huge platter of sandwiches that she was offering to all the firemen. She was chatting and giggling and not looking at all concerned.

"Best you go and have a bath, Roger," said Albert. "You've got coffee grounds in your hair and you don't smell too aromatic either!"

Roger sighed. "Well, we haven't got any water at the moment as the fire brigade have turned everything off."

"So you closed for business then?" asked Albert, not looking so amused now.

"Well, yes, gotta be. A whole evening's takings gone, just like that! I 'spect Trudy will kill me!"

"Oh, poor Roger," said Victoria. "I'm sure one of your near neighbours will offer you a bath. And as for Trudy... I think you'll find it's a case there's no such thing as bad publicity, so you might just have hit the jackpot there!"

They watched as a large white van emblazoned with 'BBC TV South West' drew up next to one of the fire engines and two men got out. Victoria recognised one of them as a reporter from the local news programme.

"Blimey!" said Roger, "My big moment, and here's me covered in coffee!" He trotted towards Trudy, who was waving at him furiously and making all sorts of faces.

"Poor Roger," said Victoria again. "I do feel for him!"

A cheery 'toot toot' made them turn, and there was the reverend in Gertrude, the old Morris sporting a clean and shiny new front tyre. "My dears! Hop in! Come back to the old hallowed portals for an early evening sniffter and tell me about your visitors and – good grief – whatever drama has been going on here!" Edwin peered at the scene before him, bemused. "I was just on my way home from the garage when I came upon all this!"

Victoria and Albert smiled happily and climbed into the back of the old car, both breathing in the smell of leather and polish and, sitting back contentedly, Albert took her hand.

"Well," said Victoria, looking at the writhing mass of fire hoses, the TV crew and the flustered policemen before them, "I don't know that we have anything much to report really, Edwin. You see, nothing ever happens in the country!"